Journey to America

Journey to America

BY SONIA LEVITIN

ILLUSTRATED BY CHARLES ROBINSON

SCHOLASTIC INC.
New York Toronto London Auckland Sydney

Copyright © 1970 by Sonia Levitin.
Cover illustration copyright © 1987 by Deborah Chabrian.
All rights reserved. Published by Scholastic Inc., 730 Broadway, New York, NY 10003, by arrangement with Aladdin Books, an imprint of Macmillan Publishing Company.
Originally published by Atheneum Publishers in 1970.
Cover design by Lisa Hollander.
Printed in the U.S.A.
ISBN 0-590-46728-X

4 5 6 7 8 9 10   40   99 98 97 96 95 94

TO MY MOTHER AND FATHER
AND TO MY SISTERS,
EVA AND VERA

Contents

Journey to America

Good-bye to Papa

THAT WINTER had been the coldest and the longest I had ever known. It was a deep, chilling cold, the fog turning to rain, and rain turning to sleet and snow, until the streets of Berlin were white and silent. It was a strange silence, with people hurrying into their homes before late afternoon, as if the darkness itself might bring danger.

I sat in the window seat, my favorite place, for it was warm and cozy there, and I could see everything, both outside and in. Beside me lay my lesson book, with the arithmetic problems still unsolved. I had written only the heading, *Lisa Platt, February 7, 1938*.

"Are you doing your lessons, Lisa?" Mother came to ask, glancing anxiously down to the street.

"Yes, Mother."

We looked down together, neither of us speaking, watching the two uniformed men who strolled back and forth as if they were trying to reach a decision.

"If the doorbell rings," Mother began uneasily, then she said, "Never mind, Lisa. Just do your lessons. Everything will be all right."

How could I do my lessons, and how could everything be all right when Papa was leaving tonight? And what if the doorbell did ring, and those men asked for Papa?

I could hear my parents talking from the other room.

"I've packed six new handkerchiefs for you, Arthur," Mother said. "They're folded inside your shoes." Since early morning she had been packing and repacking the two suitcases. Papa would take no more than he could carry, as if he planned to return.

Papa chuckled. "Now, Margo, don't you think they sell handkerchiefs in America? You mustn't worry about such little things."

"I worry about little things," Mother replied, "to keep from thinking about the others."

"I know. Where's Ruth?"

"At her violin lesson—don't you remember?"

"I don't like her out so late."

"It's just past four, Arthur."

"I want her home!" Papa said sternly.

"I can't keep a fourteen-year-old girl in the house like a baby!" Mother cried.

There was silence, and I knew they had drawn close together, regretting the least little argument that they might remember after tonight.

"Are you meeting Benjamin at the station?" Mother asked, her voice gentle again.

"Yes. There's no reason for him to come here."

Annie burst in. "I want to see Uncle Benjamin!"

"Not tonight, dear. Papa's leaving."

Papa had left us before, two years ago, to get Ruth from boarding school in Marienbad. We had planned to move to Brazil. That was the year the Nazis made the law that Jewish children could not go to public schools anymore. It was, Papa said, a sign of worse things to come.

Mother, Annie and I had met Papa and Ruth in Italy; then we took a ship to Brazil. The heat in Brazil was unbearable. I was sick nearly all the time, and Mother, too, was miserable. Papa could find no work, for who wanted to buy coats in that tropical climate? So we returned to Berlin, and for a time it seemed that things might get back to normal, and that perhaps we had been foolish and hasty, as my uncles said, for leaving Germany in the first place.

But Papa had been right. Now the only way to escape was in secret, and the only place Papa wanted to go was to America. Who could picture America? I only knew that it was far, far away, and that I wouldn't see Papa for a long time.

I heard his footsteps and tried to smile.

"Ah, there you are, Lisa." He sat down on the cushioned seat. "I always know where to find you. While I'm away I'll think of you sitting here in your special place. But you haven't even started your lessons! What are you doing?"

"I've just been looking out," I said. He drew me close, and I shut my eyes for a moment, to remember this feeling.

"You must not neglect your schoolwork," he said seriously. Then he smiled and his dark eyes twinkled. "Numbers are the same, you know, even in America, so don't think your learning will be lost."

"I can't seem to concentrate."

"Sometimes we have to pretend, Lisa, that we don't see things."

"Like those two men? Why do they keep walking back and forth here?" I asked angrily. "Why don't they go away?"

"They're going now," Papa said. "See? There was nothing to worry about at all."

"Maybe that's what the Mullers thought," I said, immediately wishing I had not spoken.

"What do you know about them?" Papa asked, startled. "You hear everything, don't you?" He sighed, but in an instant his eyes were gay again. "Sometimes I forget that you're not a little girl anymore. When did that happen?" he teased. "Wasn't it just a few days ago that I came home from work and Frau Leuffelbein met me at the door and said, 'Dear me, another girl. Oh, I *am* sorry!' "

I laughed in spite of myself. "That was when Annie was born."

"Oh, yes," he said. "Now I remember. Poor Frau Leuffelbein—she had promised me a boy that time. She was quite shocked, I recall," he laughed.

Papa was always teasing about Frau Leuffelbein and about having all girls. "If I had ten children," he would say, "you can bet they'd all be girls." But he always carried our pictures with him in his wallet and showed them around to everyone.

Now he spoke seriously, "I'm depending on you to

help Mother while I'm away. You're so good with Annie, and I know you can take responsibility. And please, Lisa, don't worry Mother by talking about things like—like the Mullers."

"I won't, Papa. I'll be cheerful."

"Good! You're rather pretty when you smile, you know."

Annie came running in. "Am I pretty too?"

"You—you're a little clown!" Papa scooped her up in his arms and tickled her until she squealed, then he put Annie on his shoulders the way he used to do with me. Just then Ruth came in, with her cheeks red from the outside, and Mother tried to get us all settled down for supper.

"Stop playing, Arthur," Mother said, concealing a smile. "You're worse than the children. Go wash your hands, Annie. Ruth, you're dripping water on the rug. Lisa, ask Clara if dinner's ready."

"An organizer, that's what your mother is," said Papa. "Look at her, children! A fabulous woman—beautiful . . ."

"Oh, hush, Arthur. Come to dinner."

Clara had been cooking furiously all day, and scrubbing and cleaning in between. It was her way, when she was troubled, to keep her hands busy.

For dessert Clara had made Papa's favorite, plum cake.

"Clara, you're a genius!" Papa exclaimed. "How did you find plums in winter?"

"You can get anything for a price," Clara said, then she quickly excused herself, and I saw that there were tears in her eyes.

Clara was like a second mother to us. She had been with us ever since Ruth was little, and when we returned from Brazil she was waiting at the station. "Frau Platt, you are like my own family," she always said.

Even when the Nazis made the law that Christians could not work for Jews, and the penalty was imprisonment, Clara refused to leave.

"I'm not afraid of them and their laws," she said, and her voice bristled with defiance.

"But I'm worried about you, Clara," Mother said. "You should find yourself another place."

"You think I'm like that Marie, to run off like a scared rooster?" Clara said. Marie had been hired to do the housework, while Clara looked after Annie and did the cooking. Now that Marie was gone, Clara's work was doubled, but still she remained firm.

"Oh, Clara, what's to become of you?" Mother sighed. "I think you'd thumb your nose at the devil!"

"Perhaps not at the devil," Clara laughed, "but at Herr Hitler, you can be sure!"

I tried to forget that Papa was leaving tonight, to pretend that it was an ordinary evening. But all through the meal I felt that I was just listening and watching, that I wasn't really a part of it.

"Lisa, you're dreaming," Mother said. "You haven't even touched your cake."

"I'll have it later. I'll go help Clara with the dishes." I purposely pushed aside the thought of my arithmetic homework. I wanted to be with Clara, watching as she washed the dishes in a large pan filled with suds. She worked vigorously, but she talked in a gentle, easy way.

"Ah, Lischen, you've come to help me," she said. "I was wishing for company. Tell me, did you have dancing at school today?"

"No. Tuesdays and Thursdays. I don't want to talk about school."

"So. Are you going to cry?" Her look was direct and challenging.

"If it weren't for Uncle Benjamin," I said, "Papa wouldn't be leaving."

"That's nonsense," Clara retorted. "Who told you that?"

"It was Uncle Benjamin's idea for him and Papa to go to America together."

"Your father didn't need anyone to tell him. It's the only wise thing to do."

"Then why aren't the others leaving?" I demanded. My grandparents, uncles, aunts and cousins—all were staying in Germany. "Rosemarie says that her parents say there's nothing to get upset about," I went on heatedly. "They say that nobody should take Hitler seriously, and it's silly for people to move away, because it will all blow over."

"It's far more silly for people to ignore what's going on right under their noses!" Clara exclaimed. "Your father is just smarter than the others," she continued, "and he has courage. Don't you think it takes courage to give up everything, his home, his business, and to start all over again in a strange country? You," she said sternly, "should be proud of your father."

"I am!" I cried. Already I felt empty inside, as if Papa

had left. "I'll miss him," I whispered. "And what if they stop him at the border?"

"Now, now," Clara soothed. "I know you're thinking about the Mullers. *I* know you listen to everything. But think, Lisa. The Mullers were arrested because they were trying to smuggle out money."

"It was *their* money! It doesn't make sense . . ."

"They broke the law."

"What kind of law is that?" I demanded.

Clara sighed deeply, then she wiped her hands on her apron and turned to me.

"How can I explain it? I don't even understand it myself. What kind of law? you ask me—an evil law, that's all I can tell you. Laws should be for the good of people, not against them. But these are terrible times."

I knew that the Nazis hated us, and only because we were Jews. But why? What had we done? One of the laws was that Jews could not take money out of the country. The Gestapo, the secret police, saw to it that Hitler's laws were enforced.

The Gestapo had searched the Mullers at the border, even taking the baby from Frau Muller's arms to look through its clothing. Under the little vest they found a bundle of bills, and the Mullers were taken off to jail. What became of the baby, I didn't know.

"Your father won't take any chances," Clara said. "He is a clever man. And soon you'll be going. Think of it!" Her eyes shone. "Oh, what I wouldn't give to go to America!"

"Come with us then," I begged, flinging my arms around her. "Oh, please, Clara."

"No, Lischen, I can't. My mother is too old to travel, and I'm the only one she has. Go now. Your father wants to talk to you. And don't show such a long face!"

I went into my parents' bedroom. Papa's suitcases stood by the door; his overcoat and briefcase were laid out on the chair. I watched while Papa combed his hair, then patted his cheeks with shaving lotion and fastened his cuff links. I always liked watching him. When I was little he used to dab my cheeks with the foamy soap from his shaving brush. Then he would laugh. "Oh, pardon me. I forgot you're too young to shave."

When Mother and Ruth came in, Papa said, "Time now for talk, then for presents."

We sat on the bed, Mother and Ruth and I, and Papa pulled over a chair.

"Ruth," he said, frowning, "I'm going to have to ask you to make a sacrifice."

Ruth flushed slightly and stared at Papa.

"I'm afraid that you are going to have to interrupt your violin lessons for a while."

"But Papa!" Ruth began to twist the dark lock of hair on her forehead.

"I know how much it means to you, but you cannot be out alone so late in the afternoons," he said. "And I don't want your mother to be worrying about you."

"All right," Ruth whispered, and then she glanced at me as if to say, "Now, what will *you* sacrifice?"

There was nothing for me to give up. I had stopped taking ballet lessons from Frau Zimmerman more than half a year ago. "She cannot teach you anymore," Mother had told me, and I didn't ask why.

Papa leaned forward in his seat. "I want you to listen closely now. Listen well, and remember. I am going to send for you. As soon as possible, we will be together in America."

"When?" I whispered, almost frightened by the look in Papa's eyes.

"Soon," Papa said. "Don't ask me more. Ruth and Lisa, I am going to ask you for the most important promise you have ever made. You must not tell anybody about our plans, not even your closest friends. Promise me."

Together we promised, Ruth and I, and my heart was thumping as if, in some strange ritual, I had sworn a sacred oath in blood.

"It will take time," Papa continued, "for me to get settled in America and to make the arrangements. When it is time for you to leave, you will tell nobody where you are going. It will be as if you were only going on a short vacation, to Switzerland or to France."

"But how can people think that," Ruth asked, "when we'll be moving out?"

"You won't move out," Papa said, his hand uplifted for attention. "Everything will be left here."

"Everything?" I echoed.

"Yes," said Papa, "except for your clothes and personal things. But listen! The most important thing is that you must obey your mother, immediately and without question. Your lives," he said, "could depend on it."

"You are frightening them, Arthur," Mother said in a low tone.

"Better to frighten them," said Papa sternly, "than to take chances." He reached into his pocket, and in that

instant his eyes were gay again. Papa loved giving presents, I think, as much as we loved receiving them.

We knew that he had no patience with wrappings and
strings. "Close your eyes," he said, "and hold out your
hands."

When I opened my eyes, there was a ring on my finger
so deeply red and glowing that it seemed to warm my

whole hand. I couldn't even think to say thank you—I only gasped, while Ruth exclaimed,

"Oh, thank you, Papa. Thank you!"

I saw that on her hand was a ring like mine, except that the stone was bright green.

"I'm glad you like them," Papa said, chuckling. "You have good taste. These are real," he added, taking each of our hands into his own. "Your stone is an emerald, Ruth, and yours, Lisa, is a ruby. But we'll pretend that they are only glass. That is another secret we'll keep between us." He turned to Mother. "You could sell these anywhere, if necessary, and get a fair price."

"You mean we won't keep them?" Ruth asked, and I could see that she was close to tears, for she pulled at the curl on her forehead.

"You'll keep them," Papa replied, "unless your mother needs them. Then, of course, you must give them to her. You are to wear these always," he said, "from the time you leave Germany until we are together again. That way you won't lose them."

Papa looked at his watch. "It's time to say goodnight."

It was the moment I had dreaded all day, and I saw Ruth go calmly to kiss Papa, as if tonight were like any other. I wondered why Ruth didn't feel as I did that terrible tightness inside. Or did she? Did she, too, hold back a cry? "Don't leave me, Papa. Don't go!"

I kissed Papa's cheek, and he put his hand on my hair for a moment, holding me close. "Goodnight, Lisa," he said, and then he whispered close to my ear, "God keep you."

For a long time after Ruth's breathing had grown deep

and even, I lay awake listening to the sounds in the
house. Finally I heard the front door close. Papa was
gone.

Promises to Keep

THROUGH THE LONG DAYS of waiting to hear from Papa, Mother was calm. But when we received the telegram, "Arrived safely, all is well," tears rolled down Mother's cheeks.

Since Papa had left, relatives came to visit every night, hoping for news, giving advice.

"Now that Arthur's gone, they might suspect something," my grandmother said. "Maybe you should send the children ahead to England, Margo. At least they would be safe. Many people are doing it."

"I won't do anything without consulting Arthur," Mother always said firmly. "The children and I will stay together."

"I'll be glad to keep Annie with me when you leave," Grandmother Platt offered. "Don't you think she's too young for such a trip?"

"No," Mother said. "I couldn't leave her."

Always their conversations turned, finally, to "the question." Then their voices were hushed and they glanced about as if the very walls had ears. How much longer should they wait? How much longer would it be safe for them to walk the streets of Berlin? Wouldn't someone, somehow, bring this madness to an end?

I tried not to listen. I wished I could be like Ruth, always in the midst of a good book or off on some project. Instead, I found myself hearing and knowing more than I wanted to. Every day brought new incidents.

"Isaac Cohn's store windows were smashed today. He's talking about leaving for China."

"Helen Kraus told me they came for her husband early this morning. They took him for 'questioning.' You know what that means."

"People won't come to my store, since the Nazis painted that sign on the wall. 'I can't buy from Jews,' one man told me. 'Nothing personal, you understand.' "

Despite everything, Mother said we were to act natural. We told Annie nothing of our plans. She was too young to be trusted, and too much of a chatterbox. We didn't even tell her that Papa would send for us. She believed that he was coming back.

Late in March Papa wrote that we must prepare to leave Germany as soon as possible. Hitler's armies had marched into Austria. We sat huddled by our radio listening to that thundering voice. "My German comrades, Austria is ours! It is only the beginning. It will come to pass, my comrades, as I have promised. Germany will rule the world!"

Even in his letter, Papa was careful to reveal nothing,

for nobody questioned the actions of the Gestapo anymore. They could and did barge into homes and restaurants, hauling people away without explanation. They could and did inspect the mail to learn the names and intentions of those who were "unfriendly" to their cause.

"I think it would be a good idea," Papa wrote guardedly, "for you to take the girls to Switzerland for a short vacation. Make all the arrangements, Margo, and write me of your plans."

"When are we leaving?" I asked Mother again and again, and she always shook her head. "I'm not sure. There is so much to do."

"May I tell Rosemarie that we're planning a vacation?"

Mother hesitated, then nodded. "I suppose we might as well tell our friends, but only that we're going on a vacation. It would be the natural thing to do."

I had not shown Rosemarie my ring, afraid that I might reveal something. We had never had any secrets before.

I told her at school one day, while we were sitting on the bench waiting for Frau Meyers, the ballet teacher. "I think we'll be going on a vacation soon, Rosemarie."

"That will be nice," she said, smiling. "Where?"

"To Switzerland, I think."

Just then Hanna Hendel came up, smiling in her mysterious way and shaking her head to make her curls bob. "Have you heard?" she said breathlessly. "Have you heard about Eleanor?"

"No," I said, tired of Hanna's endless gossip.

"Nobody's supposed to know," Hanna said, "but

Eleanor and her family have left for good. Don't you want to know how I found out?" She looked at Rosemarie and me, wanting us to coax her to tell, but we kept our faces blank.

"I know you're dying to tell us," Rosemarie said.

"Well, our Lucy knows the woman who worked for Eleanor's parents," Hanna said, flushed with eagerness, "and she told Lucy that they are going to America."

I looked down at the floor, so that Hanna would not guess how I felt at hearing the word "America."

"I wouldn't want to go to America," Hanna went on. "They speak French there, you know, and who wants to have to learn French? I'd hate it."

We didn't even correct her. I was too disgusted by her gossip and her hating things. She hated school; she hated Frau Meyers and the ballet lessons, and I think she hated me. Maybe it was because Frau Meyers said I was the best dancer in the class, and Hanna couldn't stand to take second place. She had a way of finding people's weaknesses and picking on them. Even on my first day at school, she had noticed the scar on my leg and asked rudely,

"Where did you get that scar? Were you in an accident?"

"I had an infection there," I told her. "It happened when we were in Brazil." I really didn't feel like talking about it.

"How awful!" she gasped. "You'll always have to wear thick stockings. I hate thick stockings, don't you?"

It was then that Rosemarie came up to me and, smiling, introduced herself, and warned me about how unpleasant Hanna could be. It was the day that Rosemarie and I became best friends.

Now I told Rosemarie, "We might be leaving even before school is out. Mother is going to see about our passports today. I just want to tell you . . ."

"Don't tell me anything," Rosemarie said quickly, taking my hand. "Just give me a picture of yourself that I can keep while you're in Switzerland. Look, here's Frau Meyers. Let's get in line."

There is something about dancing that makes me forget everything else. I feel free then, as if I am flying. How I love the feel of ballet slippers on my feet!

But it was to be the last dance lesson. Frau Meyers was leaving. One by one the teachers were leaving, without explanation. We had learned to ask no questions, knowing that answers were impossible to give.

"Don't ask any questions," Mother told me again that afternoon when we were on our way to the passport office. "Don't talk, unless you are spoken to."

Ruth had decided to stay home and practice her violin, and Annie was napping. I had begged Mother to let me come with her.

"I'm glad you're with me," Mother admitted as we stood before the large office building. "Are you afraid?" she asked.

"No. I am *not*." But my heart was pounding when we walked through the door.

The man behind the desk had a square, strong face. He breathed heavily, through his mouth, and his thick fingers were busy among the papers on his desk. "Well?" he said, without looking up. "What do you want?"

"I have come to pick up my passports," Mother said, and I marveled that her tone was so calm and even. "Here is the receipt showing that we have paid all our taxes."

"Why do you want to leave Germany?" he demanded.

"My children and I have planned to take a short vacation in Switzerland. You will see that all my papers are in order."

Mother handed him the tax receipt, and as I glanced at it I saw a word printed across the top in bold red letters, *Jude,* Jew.

The man glanced at the papers, then looked fully at Mother. "Your papers are definitely *not* in order," he said, breathing deeply. His face was red from some great effort. "I cannot give you a passport." He waved his hand and called loudly, "Next!"

"But I have everything ready," Mother said patiently. She pressed my hand tightly, warning me to be still.

"You had a passport before," he declared. "What happened to it?"

"It was taken from me two years ago," Mother answered, "when I returned to Germany from Brazil."

"So!" His breath was a hiss, and his eyes seemed to bulge from his face. "People have been known to sell their passports. We have strict rules . . ."

"Oh, Karl," came a loud voice from the back of the room, and I jumped, not having noticed that anyone else was with us. Now a tall young man came forward. "Why are you making such a fuss about this?" he asked, grinning and shaking his head. "Can't you see this woman just wants to take her children on a little holiday? I can't blame her—it is a superb time to go."

He smiled at me, and I struggled to return his smile.

"But you know the rules, Fritz," the other man objected.

"Her passport was taken by our own officers," the young man said impatiently. "Don't you see the notation here?" He pointed to one of the papers. "Come on now, and don't take all day about it. We'll miss our afternoon coffee."

"Then you must take the responsibility," said the other stiffly. "I refuse to be responsible." But as he spoke he took a slim green book from his desk drawer, stamped it several times and handed it to Mother. "The children," he said gruffly, "can go on your passport."

"Thank you," Mother said briskly, and I kept my face rigid, as if I didn't really care.

"You are allowed to take out ten marks for each person," the man said.

"Ten marks!" Mother's eyes were plainly troubled. "I thought it was more."

"Ten marks," he snapped. "The rules change, you know."

"Have a pleasant holiday!" the young man called after us. And as we left I heard him say, "Oh, Karl, you are getting so suspicious," to which the other replied, "But Fritz, they are Jews."

Ruth and Annie were sitting on the front step waiting for us when we got home. "There's a man in the living room!" Annie cried happily.

"Did you get it?" Ruth asked. Her tone was low and urgent.

"Yes, dear. But who is here?"

"Herr Mendel," Ruth replied. "We didn't know whether to let him in."

"He insisted on seeing you," said Clara softly, "and Ruth told me you know him, so I thought it was all right."

"Yes, I know him," Mother said. "My husband did business with him. But what could he want?"

I followed Mother into the living room. I had left a book on the window seat, and now I went there, as if to read. The drape was half closed, and I sat very quietly with the open book on my lap.

Herr Mendel did not even seem to notice me, although he had been very nice the day Papa took me to his shop. Herr Mendel made the patterns for the coats that Papa designed. I remembered seeing the stacks of bright cloth that were cut into peculiar shapes, bits of wool and silk that were left over. Herr Mendel gave me a sack full of the scraps to take home to use for making doll clothes.

He had smiled at me then, and I had thought how much his little mouth resembled a prune, for he barely moved his lips, and I had very nearly laughed aloud.

Now he spoke in a different voice as he faced Mother. "I have come for the money your husband owes me."

Mother walked toward him slowly, then she stood beside the easy chair, as if to steady herself. "My husband," she said firmly, "owes you nothing."

For a moment they only looked at each other, Herr Mendel with his eyes narrowed, as if he were judging Mother's strength.

"I know that my husband paid all his accounts before he left," Mother continued, holding her ground.

"He never paid me for the last delivery," Mendel insisted. He took a yellow piece of paper from his vest pocket. "You see? Here is the order form. Check it for yourself."

"The order is right," Mother said, "but apparently you forgot to mark that it was paid. My husband always pays his bills on the first of the month. In all the years he has worked with you," she said heatedly, "you have never had to come and ask for your money. Isn't it true?"

"My dear Frau Platt," said Mendel smoothly, "I have no doubt that it was an honest mistake. Probably in the excitement over his trip, your husband simply forgot to pay me. His plans were rather sudden, weren't they? It's not as if I am desperate for the money. I have, in fact, a large contract from the government to make uniforms. So you see, I am on good terms with the Nazis."

"I see," Mother whispered, blinking rapidly.

"Everyone knows your husband has left," he continued. "It might be difficult for you, unpleasant indeed, if I had to go to the police about this. It's only a small matter—two hundred marks. I'm sure your husband would want you to pay it—under the circumstances."

"Wait here," Mother said. All the color had gone from her face, and I could see her anger in the way she walked.

When Mother was out of the room, Herr Mendel moved toward me. He smiled with his thin lips pursed and held out his hand, but I could not make myself go toward him. "How are you, my dear? I suppose you miss your Papa. He and I have always been good friends. Are you going to see him soon?"

My throat was so dry I couldn't have spoken had I

wanted to. I wondered whether he could see in my face how I hated him, and I wished desperately that I had never taken his gift, that bag of brightly colored scraps.

"Here you are, Herr Mendel," Mother said stiffly, and she watched him as he counted the money. "You may give me that order form as a receipt."

"Gladly," Mendel replied, smiling. "I want everything to be done properly. Everybody knows how I do business."

"I'm sure," Mother said, taking him to the door and closing it swiftly behind him.

Mother sank into a chair, breathing heavily. "Call Clara," she told me, and when Clara stood before her she said, "From now on, Clara, don't let anyone into the house when I am gone."

"What is it, Frau Platt?" Clara asked, wringing her hands.

"He said my husband owed him money, and I had to give it to him. He would have gone to the police."

Clara shook her head. "He told me he was your friend! How sorry I am, how sorry!"

"You couldn't have known," Mother sighed. "It's times like these that prove what people really are. Well, let's have supper. I feel exhausted." She coughed, pressing a handkerchief to her lips. "It's this cold," she murmured, "that's making me tired. I should see Dr. Michels. Ah, there is so much to do. At least we have our passports. That's the main thing."

"Oh, there's a letter," Clara said, "from Herr Platt. It came while you were gone."

Instantly Mother's face brightened, and Annie cried,

"Read it! What does he tell me? Read it!"

Annie climbed up into Mother's lap, and Ruth and I stood close beside her to see Papa's handwriting while she read.

My dear Wife and Daughters,

My thoughts are with you constantly, and I hope you have made plans for your holiday in Switzerland. Annie, be a good girl and stay very close to your mother on the trip.

I have found a place in a rooming house where the landlady speaks German. The woman is a good soul, and reminds me somewhat of our Clara, although, of course, her cooking cannot compare.

We all looked at Clara, and she smiled self-consciously.

At night I go to school to learn English. My girls, you would laugh to see me sitting behind a desk like a young schoolboy!

My very dear friend has a job selling neckties. He also works in the mornings, sweeping and dusting in one of the large office buildings. In the afternoons he goes to the garment district to sell his neckties and to talk with men in the clothing business. He is hoping to go into the coat business here some day.

All my love,

Papa

"What does he mean?" I whispered. "His very dear friend?"

Mother shook her head slightly, then glanced at Clara.

"Come on, Annie," Clara said. "Help me take those cookies off the pans."

When the kitchen door had closed behind them, Mother said, "Do be careful what you say around Annie, Lisa. Papa means, of course, that *he* has a job selling neckties—and sweeping. He's just being cautious. If people should find out he is working in America, they would know he doesn't intend to come back, and it could be—well—awkward for us. Now, we don't have to tell Grandmother Platt what sort of work Papa is doing. You know how she is."

"He's a janitor," Ruth said, wide-eyed.

"Yes," Mother replied sternly, "and probably the best janitor they ever had."

I kept silent, but somehow I, too, had imagined that in America Papa would be making and selling coats, as he had always done. I had heard that in America everybody was rich. I could not picture my father, whose shirts were always spotlessly white and whose shoes were polished until they gleamed, being a janitor, perhaps in overalls. It was too absurd, my Papa! He's doing it for us, I thought, overcome with love and longing to see him.

The Sacrifice

O N THE LAST DAY we would be in school, I gave
Rosemarie a snapshot of myself. The day after next we
were leaving.

"It's a good picture of you, Lisa," Rosemarie said.

"It shows all my freckles," I objected.

"I think freckles are interesting," Rosemarie said seriously. "Really, I think they add character to a face. Your
hair is really nice here, too. You know," she said, looking
at me closely, "I think it is getting a little more red in
it."

I laughed. "Remember the time I put lemon juice on it?
Then vinegar? I smelled like a tossed salad."

"Yes. Remember that book we read? What did it say?
'Her hair was like sparks'?"

I quoted, having memorized the passage. " 'In the sunlight her hair shone with dazzling red lights, like sparks
from a firecracker.' " We had read the book together in

Rosemarie's room, until her sister caught us and took it away.

"Remember the afternoon we went ice skating, and your beads broke and spilled all over the ice?"

"Remember the day we took Annie to the park, and we couldn't get her down out of that tree?"

We spent the afternoon together, remembering, and I am sure that Rosemarie knew I wasn't coming back.

"Write to me, Lisa," she begged, and I promised I would. Then she unfastened her silver bracelet with the cloverleaf charm on which her name was engraved. "I want you to take this," she said, "to remember me by."

"But it has your name on it," I objected, "and you've always loved it."

"That's why I want you to wear it," Rosemarie insisted.

"Is it all right with your mother?"

"Of course," Rosemarie said firmly. "Please take it. Look, you can give it back if you want to—when I see you again."

"But Rosemarie . . ." I stammered. I had never kept any secrets from her before. "Are you planning," I hesitated, "to take a—a vacation, too?"

Rosemarie shook her head. "I don't think so. My father doesn't want to leave his patients. You know how it is."

I knew how many people needed Rosemarie's father, Dr. Michels. He was our family doctor, too. Now, more than ever, his office would be filled with patients; for Jewish people could go only to Jewish doctors. And Dr. Michels was staying here, facing whatever dangers would come, for his first duty was always to the sick. My thoughts were jumbled, and I felt a heaviness in my chest. I couldn't help thinking of what Clara had said about Papa, that it took courage for him to leave Germany. For Dr. Michels, the courageous thing was to remain. How strange it was, how difficult to understand, that Rosemarie's father and mine must do exactly the opposite, and that in each case it was right.

"All this will blow over," Rosemarie said with a smile and a wave of her hand. "You'll be back sooner than you think."

She gave me a quick kiss. "Have a good trip, Lisa."

The next afternoon we said good-bye to the family. They came, one after the other, uncles, aunts, cousins, grandparents, all saying, "What a commotion! We ought to leave you alone so you can pack." They spoke only of pleasant things, as if we were truly going on a pleasure trip.

Tante Helga, my beautiful young aunt, held me tight, then said with a faint smile, "Just don't forget your native language, darling. Someday I will come to America to see you, and oh, what grand times we will have. You'll teach me to speak English then, won't you? And you'll show me the sights. But remember your German, too. It will always help you to know another language."

I loved Tante Helga more than any of the other aunts. Perhaps it was because she had no children of her own that we were so close. For some reason, of all her nieces and nephews, Tante Helga had always chosen me when it came to going places like the Children's Ballet or to puppet shows. At Christmas time she always took me to the big department stores to see the decorations, and she and I selected gifts for the whole family together.

"I'll miss you, Tante Helga," I said softly, kissing her cheek.

"Oh no," she said. "Not you. You'll be so busy storing up new information. You always collect new ideas," she said, laughing, "like a squirrel gathering nuts for winter."

We said good-bye to one after the other of our relatives. They left hastily, so that there would be no time for tears. But even so my grandmother cried terribly. She clung to Mother's hands, and the lines in her face were deep and pitiful. "Margo, my child," she wept, "when in this life will we ever meet again?"

"I'll send for you, Mama," my mother told her again and again. "I'll send for you, I promise."

At last our suitcases were packed and stood by the front door, ready for the morning. There was only one for each of us.

"Can't we take just one more suitcase?" I begged Mother.

"No," she answered. "We're taking only what we would need on a short vacation."

There were so many things I couldn't bear to leave— ballet costumes, books, school albums.

"You'll each wear a sweater and carry a coat," Mother said. "We have to save room in the suitcases."

"I would be taking my violin on a vacation trip," Ruth said.

Mother paused for a moment, then nodded. "Very well, Ruth, you may carry your violin."

"Frau Platt, what about the silver?" Clara asked, carrying a tray of silverware. "Couldn't you put some of this in among your clothes?"

"Of course not," Mother replied. "They will be inspecting our luggage at the border." She chuckled. "Do people bring their own silverware on a vacation?"

"But all these things!" Clara exclaimed. "Your books, the paintings, the linens . . ."

"Take whatever you can carry, Clara," Mother said. "Take it home with you after we are gone, and use it."

"I couldn't!"

"I want you to have it," Mother told her. "The Nazis will take what is left. You know that."

"I won't use it," Clara said, wringing her hands. "I'll take home what I can and keep it for you."

"Let's talk downstairs, Clara," Mother said. "Lisa, Ruth, it's time for bed. We're leaving very early in the morning."

"Try to leave Germany," I heard Mother tell Clara.

"I can't, Frau Platt. My mother . . ." Clara replied.

"Take your mother and leave as soon as you can. Go to England or France. There's going to be a war."

The door closed and I could hear no more. I began to walk through the rooms, looking at everything we would leave behind the next morning, but still I could not actually believe that war was coming. War was something distant and strange that happened to other people in other times. I had read of wars, of wounded men, of fleeing women and children and of death. I had heard of women ripping up sheets into bandages, of people searching for coal and for food, and even of people eating their pets in times of great hunger.

Mauschen! My mouth went dry with terror. My beautiful cat! What would become of him? Who would remember to feed him and call him in at night? Who would protect him if there were great hunger?

I ran into the kitchen. "Clara! Clara!" I burst out. "Will you take Mauschen home with you? He'll cry so when we leave. Please, don't let a stranger get him. They might—sometimes in a war . . ." I couldn't say it or even think of it, my little Mauschen, a little brown fuzzy kitten when I first got him.

"Lischen! Be calm. Of course I will take him," Clara said, coming to put her arms around me. "I won't let him go to any stranger."

I rushed to the back porch where Mauschen slept in his little basket. I had named him that because he looked so like a little mouse at first, but now he was sleek and beautiful. I picked him up and held him close, and he gave a soft, sleepy meow.

Clara took him from my arms. "He's a beautiful cat," she murmured, "a sweet cat. I'll take care of him always, I promise."

"And take his basket too," I said. "He's used to it."

"I will," Clara said, kissing me. "Now go to bed, and don't worry. Sleep well, Lischen."

"Goodnight, Clara." I turned back, for I had seen a long salami, still in its wrapper, lying on the counter. "Can I have that?" I asked.

"The salami?" Clara asked, bewildered. "You don't even like salami."

Still, I wanted it.

"Well, all right, take it," Clara said, shaking her head

in confusion. Then her expression changed to one of deep tenderness. "Of course. I understand. Take it with you, my child."

In my room I put the salami in the bottom of my suitcase, concealing it from Ruth, who would have laughed at me and called me a silly goose. "One salami won't keep you from starving," she would have taunted, but somehow it made me feel better to have it.

I lay down on my bed, feeling too tired to move a muscle. All day I had packed, choosing the few things I could take with me. Then I had cleaned and dusted everything, books, ice skates, games, my doll collection, taking each thing into my hands. Ruth couldn't understand why I was cleaning everything when it had to be left behind anyway, and I couldn't explain it. I just needed to have everything in order.

Ruth was still rummaging through her things. "Aren't you finished yet?" I yawned deeply. "Let's go to bed."

"I'm almost ready," she mumbled, bending over her violin case.

I sat up suddenly, realizing that Ruth was slipping something under the lining of her violin case.

"What are you doing?" I cried.

"Never mind," Ruth said.

"Ruth!" It was money that she was hiding so carefully. "You can't do that!" I exclaimed.

"Nobody will look here," Ruth said, still working. "You heard Mother say that we can only take ten marks apiece. Anybody can see that won't be enough to last until we get to America."

"That's smuggling," I gasped. "Don't you know what

happened to the Mullers?"

"Shut up," Ruth said fiercely. "Stop yelling. You don't
have to know anything about this. It's my money, my
birthday money."

I watched as she laid the bills flat against the side of the
case, took a tube of glue and applied it to the loose mate-

rial of the lining, then pressed it down firmly against the case.

"Look now," she said. "Nothing shows."

I went over to see. "Don't do it," I begged. "It isn't right."

"Don't be so stupid," she retorted. "We have to help ourselves any way we can. I've been planning this all along."

"I'll tell Mother," I threatened.

"If you dare!" Ruth stepped toward me, clenching her fist. "If you dare!" Then her tone changed. "Look," she coaxed, "Mother will be so happy when I give her this money in Switzerland. She'll need it for food. Can you imagine what it's like to be hungry? I mean really hungry, with nothing at all to eat. Think of Annie, crying for food. Mother's got enough to worry about. Papa even said we have to take responsibility."

"Look at this," I said, pointing to a damp spot on the lining.

"It will be dry by morning," Ruth said confidently. "You'll be glad I did this. You'll see. Look, it's good as new. Nothing shows."

I yawned again. It was impossible to win an argument with Ruth, and I was very tired. "It's all right," I sighed. "Just come to bed."

I must have fallen asleep in a moment. Suddenly I sat up with a start. Under the door I saw a faint light, and then I heard a thump and a soft cry. I slipped out of bed and tiptoed across the hall to Annie's room.

She was standing over a large carton holding several dolls in her arms. I heard a sniff and then I saw that she was crying, and she mumbled to herself, "I won't leave you. I'll take you all with me."

"Annie! What in the world are you doing?" I whispered. "You're supposed to be asleep."

"I'm packing," Annie answered without looking at me.

"But Mother's already packed your things. You can't take all those dolls."

"I'm not leaving them," Annie said with a stubborn nod.

"Now, Annie, listen to me. Please stop a minute and listen." I knelt down beside her, and Annie clung to me. Her face was hot and damp, and the short dark curls stood out all over her head. I kissed her cheeks and held her. "Don't cry, Baby, don't cry. Sit down here." I pulled her up on the bed beside me. "Let's talk about it."

"I don't want to talk," Annie mumbled. "I'm not going to leave my Susans here alone."

All of Annie's dolls were named Susan. We teased her about it, but she was determined to give all of them her favorite name.

"They won't be alone," I whispered. "They'll have each other, and when we come back . . ."

"You know we're not coming back!" she said in a voice filled with reproach.

"Annie!"

"I've heard you all talking. We're never coming back. We're going to America."

"Hush!" I said. "You mustn't say that, not to anybody. You're not supposed to know. Do you understand?" I had grasped Annie's arm too tightly, and she began to cry.

"Shh," I tried to silence her. "Mother will hear you. Now look at me and listen, because this is very important." Her large, dark eyes were frightened. "If anybody asks you where we are going, you must say that we're going to Switzerland for a vacation. Now say that."

"Switzerland," Annie mumbled.

"For a vacation," I added, still holding her beneath the chin, firmly.

"For a vacation," Annie repeated, struggling slightly, "and I'm taking all my dolls with me."

"You are *not*. We don't have room."

Annie's lip began to quiver again.

"Don't cry!" I warned her. "Now, Mother said you can take two dolls, and that's all." I took a deep breath, struggling for patience. "Let's decide which ones."

We took the dolls out of the carton and laid them on the bed.

"Which one first?" I asked Annie, knowing what she would say.

"The baby doll," Annie replied, clutching the torn stuffed doll to her chest. "She needs a Mommy the most, because she's always coming apart."

"All right, then you'll take her. Now one more."

Annie walked back and forth, biting her lip in concentration. She touched each doll, fingered their dresses and finally sighed. "I can't decide. I'll have to take them all."

I shook my head, knowing there was only one thing to do. It had been in my mind from the beginning. "You like my bride doll, don't you?" I asked her.

Annie's eyes were wide and she gasped, "Your bride doll! She's the most beautiful doll in the world!"

Aunt Helga had given me the bride doll for my last birthday. "A twelve-year-old girl is really too old to play with dolls," she had said, "but every girl should have a last doll, a very special doll to keep her company while she is growing up." The doll was beautiful, eight inches tall, with a white dress and veil of handmade lace. She wore a tiny pearl necklace and white high-heeled shoes.

I closed my eyes for a moment, picturing the little bride doll. I had packed it carefully this afternoon.

"If you promise," I told Annie slowly, "not to say a single word about America, not to *anybody,* I'll let you have my bride doll."

Annie gasped. "For keeps?"

"Yes."

"I promise! I promise!" Annie cried, hopping up and down.

"If you break your promise," I told her in my sternest voice, "I'll take the doll away from you, and you'll never even be able to touch her again."

"I won't say a word," Annie whispered, her eyes shining.

"Now go to bed. Tomorrow morning—no, I'll get her now."

When I brought the doll, Annie immediately tucked it into bed beside her, crushing the lace dress under her covers. She put her thumb in her mouth and smiled at me, a crooked, blissful smile.

Very early the next morning, when we were almost ready to leave, Annie sat quietly on the sofa, dressed for the journey, holding her baby doll in one arm and the bride doll in the other.

"Lisa," Mother called. "Did you know Annie has your bride doll? Weren't you going to pack it?"

"I gave it to Annie," I said, avoiding Mother's eyes. "I'm getting too old to play with dolls."

The Last Barrier

I T WAS BARELY DAYBREAK. The neighbors still slept. Their houses were dark and silent. I turned for a moment to look back at the house where I had lived almost all my life, at the small courtyard where I used to play with my dolls, at the low wrought iron gate, at the upstairs window of my bedroom and the white lacy curtains Clara had made. I glanced at the lilies that grew by the walk. I had planted them myself only a year before.

The taxi was waiting, and Clara, with her apron on, came with us to the waiting car. "Good-bye," she said loudly, just in case someone should be awake to hear, "have a good vacation. I'll see you in a few weeks." She reached into her pocket. "Here's something for you to have on the train." She gave each of us a small round tin of candies.

I put my arms around Clara. "Thank you, Clara." There was so much I wanted to say to her, but my voice broke at the word, "Good-bye."

"Don't cry, Lischen," she said, but her eyes, too, were full.

"Come, Lisa," Mother called me. "Help Annie into the taxi. We have to hurry. The train leaves in an hour."

The taxi sped down the street with the driver whistling softly to himself. I had never seen the city at dawn before. The streets were hushed and shadowy, with only a few merchants moving about, preparing for the day.

We drove past the big park, where we had spent many afternoons playing with friends and wandering along the paths of the zoo. The bandstand was deserted, the swings hung limp and silent. Later children would come to play while their mothers had coffee and cake on the terrace overlooking the playground, and nursemaids in white dresses would wheel fine baby carriages along the tree-lined paths.

I felt a tightness in my throat. Surely, I thought, surely it would always be this way. On every Sunday afternoon, long after we were gone, the band would play Viennese waltzes and boys would play ball on the lawn, and children would beg to ride the carousel. Families like ours would meet their friends and sit around the tables, laughing and talking.

How could it ever be different?

But already things were different. It had been a slow, gradual change, like a shadow crossing the sun, bringing a strange cold feeling that one could not quite explain.

At first it had been a curious sight to see men in uniform with their arm bands and high black boots. Little children would stand at a distance, staring and whispering. But soon even Annie knew that those men must be avoided.

Every day on the way to school Ruth and I saw the soldiers, their arms linked as they strode through the streets, laughing and singing loudly. It was the students, though, with their brown shirts and black ties bearing the swastika emblem who were the worst. They pushed their way through the busy streets, walking five and six abreast, as if they owned the city. They sang new songs, and one in particular was so horrible that I could not believe my ears.

> *When the blood of Jews spurts from our knives,*
> *Then things will be twice as good as before!*

On the street corners there were soldiers shaking their collection boxes, shouting in chorus, "Give, give, give to the Nazi party!" Every time I saw them I wanted to run, and the sound of those jangling coins pounded in my ears, but Ruth and I would walk past, keeping our faces blank.

Then one afternoon we had been forced to stop. We had been out shopping with Mother, and suddenly we could walk no further. The street was roped off, and swarms of people had gathered.

"There's going to be a parade," Mother had said, her face ashen. "Oh, children, if I had known! We'll have to stand here until it's over." She grasped Annie's hand tightly and said in her sternest voice, "Don't move, Annie, and don't you dare cry!"

All I could see through the crowd were the tops of helmets and black marching feet. Drums thundered; horns and trumpets made a deafening blast. Flags waved everywhere, not the German flag we loved, but the bright red Nazi flag with the black hooked cross.

Suddenly a tremendous roar came from the crowd. "Heil Hitler! Heil Hitler!" The whole street seemed to vibrate with it, "Heil Hitler!" and I trembled and wondered whether my legs would hold me upright. It seemed that we were the only people who did not join the shouting. We had stood motionless, surrounded by the roaring crowd, until finally it was over. We went home, but things were never quite the same again. Now the taxi slammed to an abrupt halt, and Annie nearly fell off the seat.

"What's the matter, driver?" Mother asked, frowning.

"Can't get through here," the driver muttered. "They're preparing for a rally and a parade."

"A parade at this time of the morning?" Mother exclaimed.

"See that poster? It's not starting until ten, but they're blocking off the street and setting up a platform for speakers."

From the window I could see soldiers inspecting the grounds. Some were hanging a huge Nazi flag behind the platform.

"Oh," Annie piped up with a little giggle, "how beautiful."

I wanted to pinch her.

"Herr Hitler himself will speak today," said the taxi driver proudly. "Too bad you have to miss it."

"Yes," Mother said faintly, and now I gave Annie a fierce look and nodded toward the bride doll.

A guard with a black pistol in his belt came over to the car. "You can't get through here," he said gruffly. "No cars allowed until after the parade."

The taxi driver yawned and scratched his head. "Guess I'll turn around and take the next street."

"You can't. It's barricaded too. You'll have to turn there," the guard pointed. "Where are you headed?"

"The railroad station."

"Then you'll have to go up about six blocks, then left . . ."

I saw Mother looking at her watch, shaking her head. Then she reached into her purse and suddenly got out of the taxi and walked up to the guard.

"How silly of me to forget about the parade today," I heard her say in a gay voice. "It's a shame. I know the children would love to see it." She smiled brightly.

"If you can wait," said the guard, "I could arrange to save some chairs for you and your children. Think what it would mean to them to see the Führer so close!" His eyes gleamed.

"You are very kind," Mother said. "Unfortunately we have relatives meeting us in Switzerland at the station. It's the only train today. I suppose the children will get over their disappointment. I told my girls that of course you couldn't move the barricade just for us."

The guard glanced over his shoulder. "I suppose they can see another parade soon," he said, "and they are probably excited about this trip."

He glanced inside the taxi. Annie's face was pressed against the window, and she waved and smiled happily.

Mother held out her hand. Between her fingers was a

folded and crumpled bill.

"I suppose I could let you through," he mused.

"You are very kind to take the trouble," Mother said.

"Not at all," he replied, taking the bill and putting it into his pocket. "I wouldn't want you to miss your train. I know how children look forward to these things—I have two of my own."

"Nice fellow," said the driver when the barricade had been moved and we continued along the street toward the station.

We had barely boarded the train before the engines began to hiss and puff and we were moving. Mother asked the porter to turn one of the seats around, so that we could all face each other. Then she leaned back, her eyes closed. Her face looked very white, and I wondered whether she had slept at all the night before.

Suddenly she sat up, coughing, and pointed to the water fountain at the end of the car.

Ruth ran to bring water in a paper cup. "You never did see Dr. Michels," she said.

"I know," Mother sighed. "There was so much to do. I'll be all right. Just let me rest awhile. You can tell Annie some stories."

"Come sit between us," Ruth said to Annie, and she began to tell Annie her favorite story, *Cinderella*.

Mother leaned toward us suddenly and whispered, "Listen, I forgot to tell you. At the border they might ask us whether we have any valuables. If they say you cannot take your rings, you'll have to give them up. Do you understand?"

Ruth and I nodded, but I really did not understand,

and I looked down at my beautiful ring and watched the light from the window shining through the stone.

It was a strange, long morning. I had brought a book to read, but I couldn't concentrate on anything except the click of the wheels and the sound of the engine.

I saw a little boy sitting on a fence, waving frantically as the train sped by, but I did not wave back.

Ruth came close beside me to look out of the window.

"We'll never come back," she whispered.

"Maybe—someday." I said.

Never, never, my thoughts repeated in rhythm to the clicking wheels. The train followed the course of the Rhine River—Frankfurt, where we went for winter vacation, Heidelberg, with the large old stone castle on the hill—all the places we had loved.

At last the train lurched and came to a stop. There was a great deal of grumbling. "Why are we stopping here?" a woman exclaimed crossly. "This stop isn't scheduled."

"Last stop before the border," the conductor shouted, passing through our car.

After a few minutes a man in uniform came onto the train. I recognized the black arm band and the high black boots.

"Jews out!" he shouted. "Jews out for inspection."

I stared at Mother, unable to speak.

"What a bother," someone complained. "We'll all be delayed."

"Jews out!" the Nazi shouted again. "Out!" He looked around the car.

"Come on, girls," Mother said in a low voice.

My hands were moist, and my face felt hot. I would

never be able to walk through that train. I shook my head blindly, wanting to scream, but the words came out in a whisper, "I can't."

"We must!" Mother took my arm. "You must obey, Lisa! Come, don't be afraid."

"Bring all your belongings," said the officer when he saw us standing.

"Take your coat, Lisa," Mother said, "and your violin, Ruth."

Ruth took the violin from under her seat, and I felt Mother pulling me toward the aisle. "Lisa, *please*," she whispered.

Numbly I began to walk. Everyone's head was turned toward us. We were the only ones in the car who had to leave. With every step I took the aisle seemed to stretch out longer, but I put one foot in front of the other and kept my eyes straight ahead.

But they were staring at us, all those eyes, and I wanted to scream at all of them, "Why do you look at us? We're no different than anyone else!" Dimly I saw Annie scampering ahead of me, then she turned and I saw her smiling, and I thought of the Mullers.

All the suitcases were piled at the end of the car. Mother began to search for ours. She told Ruth and me to carry our own, and then a man with gray hair came up to us.

"Allow me to help you," he said softly, taking a suitcase in each hand.

"Thank you," Mother murmured.

"It's beyond belief," he muttered under his breath.

Mother shook her head at him slightly, for the Nazi

strode past us, calling, "Quick! Quick!"

We were led into a small wooden shack with a few splintery benches along the walls and a large counter where another Nazi waited.

"Open the suitcases," he commanded.

With both hands he rummaged through my dresses, my underwear and pajamas, holding them up. He put his hand inside my shoes, then reached down to the bottom of the suitcase and took out the salami. His lips were pressed tightly together as he held up the salami. "Well?

Don't you know that food is forbidden?" he shouted.

"This child," Mother said, coughing slightly, "simply loves salami."

I heard the salami land in the waste can behind the counter. My clothes were pushed back inside the suitcase.

When all four bags were closed once more, the man turned to Mother. "Have you any jewels?" he asked.

"Only what I am wearing," Mother said, showing her watch, necklace and rings.

"You can tell me," he said with a forced smile. "You

won't be punished. Surely you own more jewelry than that!"

"I have taken only what is allowed," Mother insisted.

"We'll see," he said sharply. "Frau Krantz will make the personal inspection. This way."

She was a round-faced woman with braids wound around her head, wearing a dark blue uniform. "Remove your shoes and outer clothing," she said to Mother, when we were in the small, cold room. Ruth and Annie and I sat down on the bench, watching while the woman quickly searched through Mother's shoes, the pockets of her dress, the lining of her coat. Then she said, "Take everything out of your purse and put it on the table."

My flesh felt cold at the thought that this woman would touch me, examine me down to my skin as if I were a criminal.

"Now the children," she said. She hesitated. "The children need only take off their shoes and coats."

She put her hands inside my shoes and felt the folds of my dress and coat, then she looked at my ring, but said nothing. She opened the door and called out, "These people have nothing."

We stepped outside the shack into the sunlight, and again we saw the Nazi who had come onto the train. He held up his hand to stop us, then knelt down beside Annie.

"What a pretty doll you have," he said. "May I see her?"

Annie stared at him woodenly and clutched the bride doll more tightly against her chest.

"Show the officer your doll, Annie," Mother said.

Annie held the doll toward him, biting her lip as he searched through the dress and veil.

"Very well," he said, turning with a brisk click of his heels. "You may—wait! I see we have missed something. What is that?" he asked, pointing at Ruth's violin case.

"It's my violin," Ruth said in a whisper.

"It is forbidden to take musical instruments," he declared.

"But I only—I have to practice."

"Musical instruments are strictly *forbidden!*"

"Give it up, Ruth," Mother said in a low, urgent voice. "Give it!"

We walked back to the train, Ruth with her head down. I looked back for a moment and saw that he had taken the violin from its case and was stroking the smooth wood with his fingertips. Ruth did not notice, and all the way to Zurich she did not speak.

Zurich–
City of Refuge

I T WAS LATE AT NIGHT when we reached Zurich. At the railroad station, while Mother went to get a newspaper, Annie fell asleep with her head on a suitcase, and we could scarcely waken her to board the bus that would take us to the rooming house.

"I had hoped to rent an apartment," Mother sighed, "but everything is so expensive."

I could see the shining water of Zurich Lake as the bus traveled on, and behind it the hills, dotted with houses whose lights sent their reflection down to the lake. It was beautiful, almost unreal, like a picture postcard.

At the rooming house we climbed the sagging stairway two flights, followed by Frau Feldin, the landlady. She was very thin, and she reminded me of a bird, talking incessantly in a high, chirping voice.

"I hope your little girl doesn't wet," she said rapidly to Mother. "I don't have many sheets, you know, and you'll have to launder your own."

"Oh, Annie doesn't wet anymore," Mother replied. "She's nearly four."

"We have so many boarders now," Frau Feldin said, her hands fluttering. "We used to have only one man living with us, but times change, so many refugees now. You have one of the biggest rooms," she said, "with a stove and an icebox. The bathroom is down the hall. I'll leave you now. If you need anything . . ." her voice trailed off, and from the stairway she called, *"Grüss Gott,"* the Swiss phrase for greeting and parting, "God greet you."

The room had the musty odor of old, faded things, and I wondered, if this was one of the largest rooms, what the small ones were like.

"Where shall we put our things?" Ruth asked.

"Here." Mother pointed to a dark, heavy cupboard. "But wait until tomorrow to unpack."

I walked to the window and looked to the alley below, where garbage pails and old crates were the only view. The drapes on the window and across the tiny kitchen nook were heavy with soil and unevenly faded, the yellow and green patterns of ferns blending together.

"Let's go to bed," Mother said cheerfully, "and tomorrow we'll get acquainted with the city. Maybe we'll even find a larger room."

I felt vaguely hungry, but was too tired even to mention it, and I knew the cupboards were empty. Annie was put to bed on the sofa, while Ruth and I slept in the double bed beside Mother's cot. The sheets felt slightly damp, but after lying for a few moments in the darkness I fell asleep. Then, from far, far away it seemed, I saw a light and heard Mother's voice, "Oh, Annie, my darling, you did wet the bed, and I told the landlady . . ." But I was too tired to stay awake.

In the morning we took our first walk around the city, and in the days that followed Ruth and I became familiar with the streets and shops, for there was not much else to do. The children, free from school for summer vacation, were swimming in Zurich Lake and going in sailboats and motorboats, but this was not for us. Entrance to the lakeside beach cost money, and we could not spend the little that was left in Mother's purse.

There was no larger room to be had, nor any room that would not cost nearly twice as much as Frau Feldin's. "We'll manage," Mother said, when Ruth complained of the cramped quarters. "It probably won't be for long." But with Papa's next letters we began to realize that we might have to stay in Zurich for several months.

"There is a great deal involved," Papa wrote. "I must save enough money for your tickets, then find a sponsor for you. It will probably be several months, but remember that I am doing all I can."

I had not seen Papa for five months. Why should it take so long simply to go to another country? Mother said that Papa had to find witnesses who would swear that he could support us. There were forms to fill out, and each form meant that we had to wait a little longer. And there were thousands like us, people from all over the world, trying to get to America. It would take time, and everyone was fighting against time, trying to settle somewhere in safety before war overtook them.

People from Austria, Poland, Lithuania and Czechoslovakia had gathered a few possessions as we had done, and become refugees. I hated that word.

"There is an agency to help refugees," Frau Feldin told Mother. "I've heard that they sometimes find homes for refugee children. It is too crowded, the four of you in that room."

"I'll keep the children with me," Mother said. "I want us to stay together," and she added softly, "as long as possible."

Night after night, when Ruth and I were in bed, I saw Mother sitting at the table counting the money that was left. She scarcely ate, taking only a cup of tea for breakfast, while she gave us slices of bread and butter. And then one day I saw that Mother's diamond engagement ring was gone, and I asked her, knowing the answer beforehand, "What happened to your ring?"

"I sold it."

There was nothing left of value now, except for Ruth's ring and mine.

"Maybe we should sell them," I said to Ruth one day when we were out walking. Day after day we walked and looked at the shop windows filled with beautiful, tempting displays of toys, watches, pretty clothes and music boxes. I had never cared that much for owning things, but now, without a penny in my pocket, all I could think of was going in to buy something, anything. The bakery shop, with its little cakes all arranged and the wonderful sweet smells made me think of home, where the cooky jar was always full and the aroma of Clara's baking filled the house.

We hurried past the bakery, and in the next window we saw an odd assortment of gold watches, dishes, furniture and clothing.

"It's a pawnshop," Ruth told me.

"I know."

"Maybe we should . . ."

"Do you think so?"

"Papa said we should sell them when we needed money."

Before I could answer Ruth had stepped inside, and the little bell tinkled as I followed her into the small, dim shop.

We stood at the cluttered counter until the man, wearing thick glasses, approached us. "Yes?"

Ruth held out her hand. "I want to sell my ring," she said resolutely. "How much will you give me?"

"I'd have to look at it closely," he said, smiling as if someone had made a joke.

His expression changed to one of astonishment when he examined the ring under his glass. He came toward us, shaking his head and saying soberly, "I cannot buy this. This is a real stone. You would have to have your mother's permission."

Ruth's cheeks were flushed. "It's *my* ring" she said.

"I'm sorry, Fräulein," he replied. "If your mother agrees that you should sell it, I'll be glad to talk to her about it."

Outside Ruth's face was still rigid with anger, and when I stumbled into a puddle she lashed out at me, "Now look what you've done! You'll ruin your shoes. Why can't you be careful?"

I didn't answer, and she went on, nearly in tears, "If only he hadn't taken my violin!"

"I know," I whispered, taking Ruth's hand briefly. Then, as we walked past another toy shop, I suddenly remembered. Tomorrow was Annie's birthday, and we had nothing to give her.

"Of course I remembered Annie's birthday," Mother said later, when I mentioned it. "And we'll do something special. We'll all go to the park, and maybe we can take a ride on the funicular up to the Uetliberg. Frau Feldin says the view from the top of the mountain is wonderful, and it's a thrilling ride."

"I'll go tell Annie," I said, but Mother stopped me.

"No, let's surprise her."

"You think we might not be able to go," I said. "It costs money, doesn't it?"

"It does," Mother said rather sharply, "but I'm going to manage it. Tomorrow morning we're going to the agency. They will help us," she said confidently, but the look of concern she wore so often was still there.

I saw that same look on nearly every face when we sat waiting at the agency office the next day. We were lucky to have found seats on a wooden bench, for the room was filled with people, some leaning against the walls, little children sitting on the floor, all in a hot, humid room filled with the sound of typewriters, the ringing of telephones and the low, constant babble of voices speaking in foreign languages.

After nearly two hours of waiting, our turn came at last, and we were led into a small room cluttered with books and papers.

A woman with bright yellow hair and dark-rimmed glasses looked up at us from behind her desk.

"May I have your name, please?" She was ready to begin writing.

"Margo Platt," said Mother, "and my three daughters. We are here from Germany to join my husband in . . ."

"Wait until I ask you. I must fill out the form."

The woman wrote rapidly, while Mother sat down and we stood beside her.

"Ages of your children?" Her voice tapped out the words like a machine. "Husband's occupation? Present address?"

Finally the woman stopped writing and looked up at Mother.

"Did you leave Germany by your own choice?" she asked, blinking rapidly.

"Yes, of course," Mother replied. "You know how things are for us there."

"What is your problem, Frau Platt?"

"I have hardly any money left. We were allowed to take out only ten marks apiece."

"Have you family in Germany?"

"Yes—my mother, my husband's brothers. But you know they can't send any money out."

"Wouldn't they help you if you were in Germany?" She fixed her eyes keenly on Mother, then glanced briefly at us, and by her look I felt that surely my hair was untidy, and that maybe I had forgotten to wash my face.

"If we were in Germany," Mother said, breathing heavily, "we wouldn't need their help." She spoke slowly, distinctly, as if somehow this woman was unable to follow the point of the conversation. "We left all our money and all our possessions in Germany," Mother explained. "I was told that this agency would help me."

"Of course, there are funds for certain cases," the woman said, still looking at Mother intently, "but you left Germany by your own choice. You were not driven out."

"Not driven out!" Mother repeated.

"Many Jewish people are still living in Germany, and without harm."

Mother's eyes were wide, and I saw the tight grip of her fingers on the arms of the chair. "Don't you know what is going on? Don't you read the newspapers, the arrests, the beatings . . ."

"Frau Platt," she said, as if she were reasoning patiently with a stubborn child, "I would suggest very seriously that you take your children back to Germany. You have no way to support yourself here. Since you left Germany by your own choice, there is nothing we can do for you."

Mother's knuckles were white from her grip. "I am not going back," she said with soft fury, her eyes narrowing. "I'll never go back to Germany. We have come this far, and we will stay, even if you will not help. Come, girls!"

Mother swept out of the office so quickly that Annie had to run to keep up, and she panted, "Where are we going, Mama? Where?"

"To the park," Mother said, her voice strangely high-pitched. "To the park," she repeated, pulling Annie along beside her, while Ruth and I rushed to follow, not daring to speak.

Mother sat down on the park bench and told us, still in

that strange, high tone, "Go and play, girls. Leave me. I have to think."

I didn't want to walk away from Mother, even for a moment, but I went with Annie and Ruth to the swings. We pushed Annie higher and higher, until she giggled and squealed, and then we took her to play in the sand-box.

"We'll have to sell our rings now," I told Ruth softly.

"Mother probably won't let us," she replied. "I asked her last night. She said we have to save something for a real emergency."

"And isn't this a real emergency?" I demanded, but Ruth only shrugged. "Maybe we could get a job," I said, "washing dishes or delivering things."

"You always think everything is so *simple!*" Ruth snapped. "People can't work in a country when they're just visiting. If it were that easy, Mother would get a job."

"What can we do, then?"

"Nothing."

Ruth left me abruptly and went to help Annie build a sand castle. All around me children were laughing and shouting and playing on the bars, but I felt all alone, and I sat down on the warm grass with my eyes closed, wish-ing, pretending, half-praying, wanting to believe that the strength of my thoughts could reach out and make some-thing happen, make somebody care.

I opened my eyes and swallowed hard. I had made a resolution. *They* wouldn't make me cry. But as I looked toward the benches at my mother I saw, or I knew by the tilt of her body, that she was crying.

I ran to her. "Mother!" I sat beside her, my arms

around her. "Please don't cry, Mother. Don't be unhappy."

Mother tried to wipe the tears away. "I was so sure that the agency would help us," she said, shaking her head. "I just don't know where to turn."

"Should we write to Papa? Can't he help?"

"What help, child? Your father told me to go to the agency. If I only knew someone. If we had a friend or a relative."

"Ruth and I want to sell our rings," I said quickly. "We want to help."

"No. We must keep something. If you want to help, just sit here quietly and let me think."

I sat and looked all around at the trees and the lawns, past the playground and up to the hills. I thought of the psalm I had learned long ago, "I will lift up mine eyes unto the hills, from whence cometh my help . . ."

Softly I said to Mother, "I will pray."

"Yes, child, do," she murmured.

I might have prayed that something good would happen, but I had been taught that prayer is not for making wishes, but to seek strength and to praise God. "I will lift up mine eyes . . ."

"Lisa!" Mother said slowly, grasping my hand. "Maybe there is a way. At least I can try. Why didn't I think of it before? I'll go to a rabbi. He would know how to help. Ruth! Annie! Come, we're going."

At the rooming house Mother made a hasty telephone call, then she told us to stay and wait for her in the room. "Maybe I'll have good news," she said, with a faint light of hope in her eyes. "We'll have your birthday treat another day, Annie," Mother said, kissing her. "You're a big girl now, you understand."

"It's all right," Annie said gravely, and I thought how much she had grown in just a few months, until I saw her reach for her old, ragged blanket and rub it against her cheek.

New Faces

Y OU DON'T HAVE TO GO," Mother told us, "unless you want to."

"We'll go," Ruth said quickly. She had nodded to me as soon as Mother mentioned the camp that the rabbi had suggested. It was just an hour outside Zurich, and we would be able to visit Mother and Annie sometimes.

"Do you want to go, Lisa?" Mother asked me, watching my face intently.

I didn't want to go at all to this camp for refugee children, even though Mother spoke of having playmates there and said it was a chance for us to get away from our crowded little room.

"We'll go," I said. "It will be fun."

"No it won't," Annie shouted, bursting into tears. "I don't want you to go! I'll be all alone!"

"We'll come to visit you," I told her. "Maybe we'll come every week."

"Lisa, don't go!" Annie cried, flinging her arms around me. "Take me with you."

"It's just for older children," Mother tried to explain. "Someday you'll have a chance to go somewhere, too. Lisa and Ruth would like to make new friends and see other places."

"Let Ruth go, then!" Annie cried.

"I *want* to go," I told Annie. "And somebody has to stay with Mother to keep her company."

"That's right," Mother said quickly. "Think how lonesome I'd be with all my girls gone. Now you'll be the one to help me cook, Annie, and we'll go to the park together where you can play with other children."

"I don't love them. I don't want them. I want Lisa!" Annie sobbed.

I picked her up and put her on the sofa bed. "Lie down," I told her, "and I'll tell you a story. I'll tell you *Cinderella*." This time when I told of the wicked stepmother, Annie began to sob again, and I hurried through to tell about the king's ball, the glass slipper, and the prince coming to take Cinderella with him to his castle, where they lived happily ever after.

"It's not true," Annie said drowsily. "Things like that don't really happen."

"Yes they do," I said firmly. "Good things happen all the time. Now go to sleep!"

I wanted Annie to believe in the fairy tale, just as I wanted to make myself more cheerful, as I had promised Papa I would be. I glanced at Mother and saw for the first time how thin she had become, how loosely her dress fitted over her body. She was darning our socks again, patching our pajamas, making do.

The rabbi had told Mother that he would speak to the agency personally, that they must help us. But help would be slight; there simply wasn't enough money for everyone. Mother just couldn't afford to keep us with her, but I tried not to think of it that way.

"At least we'll be together," I whispered to Ruth, when we lay in bed. "We might each have been sent to a separate family."

"I wouldn't want to live with another family," Ruth whispered back. "I'd feel like a stepchild."

"I guess it will be nice at the camp," I said.

Ruth didn't answer. I realized how accustomed I had become to the little room. It was, in a way, home, and the thought of going to a strange place, sleeping in a strange bed, gave me a fluttering feeling in my stomach.

That feeling of dread was with me still in the morning when Mother took us to the agency office. This time we saw a different clerk, a pretty young woman who smiled and took Mother's hand and told Ruth and me that the cook from the camp would come to the agency to meet us. "He's a nice old man," she said. "He used to be chief cook at the Hofstaader Hotel in Vienna."

He came at last, limping slightly as if one leg pained him, but he was tall and stout and robust and wore a white shirt and white trousers. His head was completely bald, except for a few bristling white hairs along the back of his neck.

"What a sweet little one!" he exclaimed, seeing Annie, and he bent down close to her. He asked us our names, then nodded to Mother. "I'm Emil Wagner," he said, "but the children all call me Pop. I've almost forgotten my other name," he chuckled.

"Come along then," he said, taking up our suitcases. "Two more for dinner. It's a shame we can't take this little one too, but . . . " he seemed to have forgotten his train of thought. "Come along. We must hurry. There is supper to prepare. Ah, there was a time when supper was truly an event—fourteen main dishes to cook, hot rolls, pastries, glazed fruits. Everybody who was *anybody* came through those doors at the Hofstaader Hotel—dukes, counts, even princes, yes."

After we had said good-bye to Mother and Annie, and Ruth and I climbed into the cab of the battered old truck, Pop continued as if he had never left off remembering. "Six cook's helpers in my charge," he murmured, "and two underchefs. There will come a time again. Yes, it will be so again."

We bumped along the streets through the city, then up into the hills. The truck swayed so violently that I could hardly speak. Ruth and I looked at each other, and suddenly we both began to laugh; I'm not sure why. Maybe it was the sudden freedom of a truck ride though the country. Maybe because, inside, we were lonely. And for reasons of his own, Pop laughed with us. At last he wiped his bald head with a handkerchief and mopped his face, sighing, "Ah, such memories!"

Ruth and I sat silent. The old man was, somehow, transported into another time. At last Ruth asked him timidly, "How is it at the camp?"

"You will see," he replied. He did not speak the rest of the way, until after he had maneuvered the truck over a series of terrible ruts, he pointed past the trees to a small clearing. "There it is. We're home."

The air was sultry and heavy when we stepped out of the truck and hurried behind Pop, who carried our suitcases.

It occurred to me that travelers are always following their suitcases, always in fear that they will be lost or stolen. The suitcase is the last and only familiar thing.

But even as I hurried, I glanced about. There was only the one old wooden building, somebody's forsaken barn, perhaps, but all around it stood huge pine trees, and I could smell a deep scent of sap and pine needles, mingled with the dust from the road and the odor of earth that is damp even before the rains come.

I'm not certain what I expected. I had read *Jane Eyre,* and perhaps from this I dreaded an institution of any sort, and expected severe mistresses and hard little cots all in a row, with lists of rules posted on the walls, and children marching uniformly to lessons or gymnastics.

We walked through a large hallway, and I could only make out dull brown shapes of furniture in a room to one side, the kind that people give away when it is long past use. On the other side was the dining room, with three long wooden tables, and again I had the feeling that this place must once have been a stable.

Pop put down our suitcases and pointed to a door. "Just knock," he said. "Frau Strom is inside." He disappeared through a swinging door that must have led to the kitchen.

"Who's Frau Strom?" I whispered to Ruth, and Ruth replied, also in a whisper, "Probably the director."

Ruth's knock sounded loud and bold, and I wanted to crouch back into the shadows, but the door swung open. "Yes—yes, come in."

The voice sounded hurried, flustered, and as we entered Frau Strom gave us only a darting glance and continued to patter back and forth, plucking up an object here and there, searching aimlessly and with "tss-tss" sounds of despair. And it was no wonder that she couldn't find anything. I had never in my life seen such a mess, powder spilled on the dresser top, clothing draped over chairs, and every little space crammed with bottles and boxes and half empty cups of tea.

She snatched her curling iron from the hot plate, which was beginning to give off a bitter smelling smoke, and, holding a bit of hair tightly between the hot iron, she turned to us.

"So you are the new girls." She turned to the mirror, released a tight little curl and gave it a pat. Her face was marked with ruddy places, from little blood vessels that had burst, and her eyes were never still, her tone a little breathless, as if she had been rushing all day.

"Did you bring sheets?" she asked.

I shook my head, and Ruth answered aloud, "No, we didn't. We don't have any."

"Same old story." She began another curl. "They said you would come at noon."

"We waited for the cook," Ruth explained.

"Now I'll have to make out a new list," Frau Strom said accusingly. "They want it alphabetical. *Why* does everything have to be alphabetical? What is your last name?"

"Platt," I said.

"Our mother is in Zurich," Ruth supplied, "and our father is in America."

"I'll show you your beds." She went to the door and motioned for us to follow.

We went up the stairs, and I wondered at the silence. Where were the children? She led us into a room with eight beds, all different, but beside each was an identical unpainted low cabinet with half a dozen cubby holes where the children kept their things.

"You can sleep here," Frau Strom told Ruth. "It's the only bed available. Your sister will be in the next room. It's just as well. When sisters are together they usually fight."

In the next room a girl about my age was sweeping the floor, her long straight hair half falling over her face. She looked up briefly when we came in, then continued with her work.

I glanced around. All the cabinets were filled, except one that stood beside a crib. I looked at Frau Strom.

"We are overcrowded," she said. "The agency doesn't seem to understand that I can't *make* room. I have asked for more beds, but do they send them? Well, you're not so very tall. You'll fit. Put your things in the shelf, then. Emma, did you sweep under the beds?" she asked the girl.

"Yes," the girl said softly, pushing back her hair.

"Here, then." Frau Strom held out a chocolate bar, and the girl took it quickly. "Unpack your things, Lisa!" Frau Strom said, and I was surprised that she knew my name.

As soon as Frau Strom was gone, Emma began eating greedily, taking large bites of the chocolate.

"When is lunch?" I asked her.

"You missed it."

I began to unpack, and Emma watched me, still eating.

"I'm Lisa Platt," I told her, not at all sure that she cared.

"How do you do," she said with some sarcasm. "I'm Emma. Emma, the housemaid."

"What do you mean?"

"My wages," she said, holding out what was left of the chocolate bar. "Would you like some?"

"No thanks."

"Take a little piece, Lisa."

I accepted, and immediately longed for more, but it was gone. "Where are the others?" I asked.

"Out playing in the woods, I guess," Emma said. She fixed her keen blue eyes on me intently. "There's nothing to do here, you know."

"But what about Frau Strom?"

"What about her? She doesn't do anything either, except curl her hair and go out shopping. It's like a jail, you see. The worst thing about a jail," she said, pushing back her long hair, "is that there's nothing to do. We're all just waiting."

"For what?"

"Oh, different things. Some are waiting to leave Switzerland. I'm waiting to be adopted. Big chance—people only want babies. What are you waiting for?"

"To be with my father in America," I said.

"Ah well, that is something worthwhile, at least. You

won't mind it here," she said, smiling slightly. "The other kids aren't bad. Say, do you play the piano?"

I shook my head. "I dance, though."

"There's one boy here, Werner, who plays the piano. He won't do it anymore, though. Too many keys are stuck on that old thing in the parlor. We call Werner the professor. There's nothing to do, but he's always busy. He studies things, like bugs and flowers and rocks. I wish I could be that way," she said wistfully. "I'm too restless." She began to pace, as if to prove her words, and by her attitude it seemed that the only thing lacking were bars on the windows.

Ruth came in, looking as confused as I felt, asking, "Where is everybody?"

"Ruth, meet Emma," I said, still unpacking my things.

"What's that crib for?"

"Me." I felt a lump rising in my throat.

"You can take the mattress out," Ruth said at last, "and sleep on the floor."

"No," Emma said briefly. "There are mice."

I couldn't look at either of them. I dreaded the night, and when it came and the little room was noisy with girls all settling down into their beds, I climbed up into the crib. All talk ceased suddenly, and it seemed that everyone avoided looking at me. "Hey!" I cried out, unable to bear their silence, "look at me!" I clung to the bars and scratched violently and made faces like a monkey. Now there was laughter all around me, and they cried, "Oh, Lisa, do it again! That's the funniest thing I ever saw!"

"Quiet now!" came Frau Strom's voice from the corridor. The lights went out, and I curled up into sleeping position, the top panel of the crib pressing against my head.

I awakened ravenous. Supper the night before had consisted only of oatmeal and crackers and half an apple for each of us.

"When do we eat?" I asked Emma, climbing out of my bed.

"Never," she replied. "Never enough."

"What do you mean?" I demanded.

"We get oatmeal and beans, oatmeal and crackers, oatmeal and apples," Emma said, her jaw firm with anger. "Oatmeal is cheap, you see."

"I do *not* see!" I cried, feeling faint from hunger.

"You will," Emma replied.

As Emma had said, oatmeal appeared unfailingly at each meal that day and the next and the next. There was only one helping for each of us.

"Nobody complains," I said to Ruth incredulously.

"Maybe they're used to it," she answered. "But I'm not!" Her face had that look of angry determination I knew so well. "Come on," she said, yanking my arm.

She half pulled me through the dim corridor, and when we stood in front of Frau Strom's door, she knocked loudly. There was no answer, and she knocked again, harder, and we heard a shout, "Come in!"

The radio was blaring, and Frau Strom turned to look at us. "Well, what is it?" she shouted over the noise.

"My sister and I are hungry," Ruth said distinctly. "We would like something to eat."

Frau Strom stared at us, and her face turned redder still, as if she could not believe her ears. Deliberately she walked to the radio and turned it off, then faced Ruth. "What did you say?"

"We're hungry," Ruth repeated. "May we have something to eat?"

"I saw it from the first," said Frau Strom, her eyes blazing. "It shows in your face. You are a typical troublemaker. Have you not eaten three meals every day since you arrived? Do you hear any of the other children complaining? At least they are not rude. At least they have some gratitude. Did you expect the Ritz Hotel? This is a charity camp. *Charity!*" She almost screamed the word, and my hands were trembling.

"It's no good to give charity to some people," she went on, breathing heavily. "They're never satisfied. Well, I will tell you something, young lady. You will appreciate what you have here, and if you should dare to come to this room again asking for special favors," her voice shook with anger, and she stepped close to Ruth, "if you should dare, you will be punished. In other countries children are starving and you—you—*get out!*"

We fled, the door slamming after us, Ruth sobbing while I tried in vain to comfort her. Ruth flung herself down on her bed, and I sat down beside her. At last Ruth looked up, her face red and tear-stained, and she said between clenched teeth, "She steals the money the agency sends for our food. She uses it to buy clothes."

"Oh, Ruth," I began, and then we heard Emma's calm voice from the doorway.

"It's true, of course," Emma said. "She goes to town two or three times a week and comes back with boxes and boxes of clothes. She's going again this afternoon. She had Pop get the car out for her. It's our luck when she goes."

"What do you mean?" Ruth asked, wiping her eyes.

"Pop will give us something to eat when she's gone. He can never refuse us. He's a nice old man, but a little bit . . ." she tapped her finger on her forehead, "you know, strange."

As soon as Frau Strom's car was out of sight, all of us as if on signal walked down to the kitchen, with Emma and Werner in the lead. For the first time the house rang with the noise of twenty-three boys and girls all talking at once, and there was a great deal of pushing and laughing as we crowded into the kitchen.

Pop turned from the sink, where he was washing a large pot. "Yes, my children, come in, little ones."

There was laughter, for Werner, at sixteen was nearly as tall as the old man. "Do you have something for us, Pop?" Werner asked gravely.

"Well, chicken I do not have." The old man smiled, his head bobbing. "Nor do I have eggs nor chopped livers. If you had seen the luncheon spread at the Hotel Hofstaader, the buffet filled, and on an ordinary day, without even any dignitaries . . ."

"Do you have some bread, Pop?" Werner asked gently.

Pop opened the pantry and took out a long loaf. "That I have," he said, "and how about some applesauce on top?"

He cut a thick slice for each of us and spread it generously with applesauce. "It should have a touch of cinnamon," he said, shaking his head sadly, "but there is none.

The agency doesn't pay for frills, Frau Strom always says. A woman quite in a class by herself."

We all laughed, cheered by the food, and Werner said, "Tell us more about the hotel, Pop."

I couldn't understand Werner's interest or the eagerness of the other children as they crowded close around the stool where Pop sat and began dreamily to share his memories.

I noticed then finally that Werner turned and gave a slight nod to two of the other boys. I saw them take off their jackets and move slowly away from the group, circling toward the pantry. They slipped noiselessly into the small storeroom. When they came out, they moved toward the door, holding their jackets, now curiously lumpy, under their arms.

Now the group began to separate, and Werner said, "We'll go outside now, Pop. Thanks for telling us. It sounds very exciting."

"Ah, yes," Pop sighed, nodding and mopping his face. "That was a time, a time to remember."

Once outside, the boys began to run, and the girls, laughing wildly, followed. I was caught up in the excitement and ran with them, not knowing where we were going or why, thinking only how wonderful it was to be running in the sunshine through the woods, feeling the wind in my hair.

Ways Through
the Woods

Wʜᴇɴ ᴡᴇ ʀᴇᴀᴄʜᴇᴅ a small clearing everyone stopped before a circle of large, flat stones.

"What's happening?" I asked Emma, still panting.

"A cookout," Emma replied, smiling. "Come on, let's help gather some twigs."

"What is there to cook?"

"Potatoes."

"We stole them," Werner said, coming up with a large log. "What do you think of that?" he demanded, with a nod at Ruth.

Ruth's cheeks reddened, then she quickly looked away.

Soon a fire blazed in the circle of rocks, and we all sat around it until the potatoes were done. They were scorched and burning hot on the outside, half raw on the inside, but we feasted on them hungrily and called them delicious.

I looked around at the faces that had become familiar

in just a few days. There were the twins, Nick and Anton, who spoke only Italian but made themselves understood nevertheless. There were Lotte and her brother David, both pale and silent; they had fled from Vienna. We knew nothing more. There was Carla from Holland, always gay, her blond braids swinging. Her parents had sent her to Zurich alone, intending to follow later.

Ruth and I were the lucky ones, with our mother close by. I wondered what my mother and the parents of the others would think if they saw us sitting there eating stolen potatoes. And yet, they must have been intended for us. How could people steal from themselves?

For the first time in many days I felt peaceful and happy. I began to wander away from the group, thinking of Papa and how he would love the forest. I wanted to memorize it all, to tell him later and let him share it. Just beyond the campfire circle was a field of tiny yellow and pink wildflowers. The wild grass reached up to my knees, and I bent down to let the fragrance surround me. Nearby, in a large fallen log, a colony of insects was working, building, and I stopped to watch. Still further a clump of willows stood bent together, and between their leaves I could see a stream flowing down the hillside, wearing the large stones into smooth, glistening mounds.

"You like it?"

I was startled, then I smiled at Werner, who stood beneath a tree, closely examining the bark.

"It's beautiful," I sighed. "I didn't know there were so many beautiful places in the world. When we were leaving Germany, I looked out of the train window and I thought it was the end."

"I know," he nodded. "I felt the same. But that's wrong. There is always something more. Look at this." He motioned for me to come near. "See that perfect circle of holes? A woodpecker sits here every morning and makes these designs. This tree," he said gravely, "is sixty-eight years old."

"How do you know?"

"By counting the rings here where the branch was cut. It was cut with an axe," he said. "You can tell by the marks. See this dark mark and the hollow place?"

I nodded.

"The tree was struck by lightning some years ago, about ten, I think. New shoots are growing all around the scar."

"How do you know these things?" I asked him, feeling awed and privileged to be his pupil.

"I read," he said, "and I think about things. The secret is to concentrate, to forget about yourself."

"Are there books here?" I had not read for weeks, and I longed, now, for something new to fill my mind, as Werner's explanations had done.

"In the parlor," he said, "on the shelf behind the piano there are some books."

"Storybooks?" I asked eagerly.

"No. There are some on wildlife, a few about minerals and some almanacs. Don't look so sad! Maybe there is a storybook or two. But it doesn't matter. You can read about the wildlife or find facts in the almanac and make up the stories for yourself."

No boy had ever spoken to me this way. Actually, my cousins were the only boys I really knew well, and they

were always joking and playing pranks. Werner was much older than I, and yet I felt that he understood me, that he already knew whatever I would say.

"You're from Berlin, too, aren't you?" I asked.

"Yes," he said, stepping out into the clearing abruptly. "It's going to rain," he said. "I can feel it. Come on—we'd better get back."

Later, when we were indoors and the rain gushed down against the windows and thunder cracked in the distance, I asked Emma about Werner.

"Do you like him?" she asked with a slow smile.

I shrugged. "He's very smart."

"Yes, he is," Emma nodded. "He knows so many things; mostly he knows about people. I was crying once, and he saw me and we talked. He knew why I was crying, I think, even before I told him. That's when he told me about himself. He's from Berlin, you know. One day he was at a friend's house, and when he went home his parents were gone. He found out later that his father had been shot. He doesn't even know where his mother is. His parents had both spoken out against the Nazis at a meeting. Friends sent him here to Switzerland. I guess he's worse off than any of us, not knowing."

I went down to the parlor and groped along the shelf behind the piano. The parlor was always dark, for there were no bulbs in the light sockets. I took the first book that my hand grasped and sat with it on the stairway, where a dim light shone and the noise from upstairs was muted. It was a very old book about birds. The pages were badly warped, some of them stuck together with mildew, but I read with complete absorption all afternoon and into the night, not realizing until later that there was to be no supper at all.

Perhaps Pop had forgotten, hypnotized by his memories. Perhaps Frau Strom, returning late from the city, happened to investigate the pantry and discovered the half empty potato bin. Nothing was said, and although my stomach growled, I went to bed contented, calculating how wise I would be if I read a book every single day of my life.

I read almost constantly for the next few days, while outside the rain continued in torrents, and Frau Strom kept to her room, unwilling, as she put it, to catch her death by going to town in the rain. To us it meant simply that there would be no stolen treats, either from the pantry or from Pop.

But one day Frau Strom approached me as I sat on the stair reading a book about Catholic saints. She interrupted just as in my story the torches were being lit around the pyre where St. Joan was tied to the stake.

"Do you have a sweet tooth, Lisa?"

I looked up, started, and saw that she held out a bar of chocolate.

I nodded, still dazed from the story.

"There is dusting to be done," she said, "and the hall is thick with mud. You would think that people would wipe their feet, wouldn't you?"

My eyes were fastened on the chocolate, a thick, large bar. Suddenly I hated her tight little curls and ruddy face, and the temptation she put in front of me. Oh, I wanted to be a martyr like St. Joan and the others so clearly pictured in the storybook. I wanted desperately to resist the bribe, to cry out that I would not work for the food that certainly we were entitled to receive. But I dearly love sweets, and my mouth watered until I felt faint from the desire.

I stood up and said, "I'll do it."

"You will have your reward when you are finished," said Frau Strom, putting the chocolate back in her pocket.

I had never scrubbed before. What happens to the handle while you're wringing out the mop? I had watched Clara do it dozens of times, and I had never seen *her* get sopping wet or getting her feet tangled in the long wooden handle.

I had to laugh at my own awkwardness, but by the time I had finished mopping the long hallway twice over, I was so tired and miserable that I sat down on the stair, feeling truly like a martyr. I dreaded the thought that anyone would walk on that floor. I remembered how Clara used to say, "Now, don't you stamp mud all over my clean kitchen!" But she always said it with a twinkle in her eyes, and she was never really cross. Why hadn't I ever told Clara how much I loved her while there was still time? The last time I said good-bye, I knew I would probably never see Clara again. Now I realized what that meant.

When Frau Strom came to inspect the hallway, she only nodded and handed me the chocolate, saying, "This is only for you. Don't give any to your sister."

I wouldn't look at her. I wouldn't let her see that I had been crying. She would have thought I was crying about the work—if she had noticed at all—but it was for Clara, only for Clara. I went up and found Ruth and divided the chocolate bar in half.

"Keep it," she said, twisting her hair. "You shouldn't have to work for me. I'm the oldest."

I held it out to her again and again, but Ruth wouldn't budge. At last I ate every bit of the chocolate myself, but it tasted dull and almost sickening. The next time Frau Strom came to me with that forced little smile on her face, offering me candy if I would wash the floor, I shook my head. "I don't like chocolate anymore," I told her.

She went off with a snort. "Stubborn little mule!"

As the days dragged on I realized how right Emma had been, for we were like prisoners with nothing to do, nothing to plan or look forward to. We tried to make up games, and I read a great deal, but all I really thought about was leaving, going back to Mother. Yet, if we went to Zurich for a visit, how could we ever make ourselves return to the camp?

When the rains were finally over, Ruth decided we should go to see Mother.

"Can we?" I cried. "Will Frau Strom let us?"

"She won't care," Ruth replied. "The woman at the agency said we could visit."

"But how do we get there?"

"We'll walk," Ruth said. "Emma told me the way. She's walked to Zurich several times. We just go straight through the woods—there's a dirt road behind the campfire place. Past the woods there are some houses, then a paved road leads right into the city. It's really a short cut," she explained. "It should take us only an hour or so."

"I still think we should tell Frau Strom," I insisted.

"Tell her if you like," Ruth said. "She won't care."

Ruth was right.

"Go ahead," Frau Strom said, with a wave of her hand. "You'd better be back by dark, because nobody is going to come out looking for you."

I couldn't stand to wait another moment. "Let's go now," I begged Ruth.

"We'll miss lunch," Ruth reminded me.

"I don't care. It's only porridge anyway. I can't stand the sight of it anymore."

"All right," Ruth agreed. But on the way she warned me again and again, "Don't you say a word to Mother about being hungry, do you understand? Don't you say a word about the oatmeal or the potatoes."

"I won't," I muttered, wanting only to enjoy the walk and the thought of seeing Mother, but still Ruth lectured.

"Mother can't afford to keep us with her, you know that. If she thinks we're not getting enough to eat, she'll feel that she ought to keep us in Zurich, and then she'll worry, and then . . ."

"Oh, stop it," I snapped. "I won't say anything."

We made our way through the woods, careful to keep to the narrow dirt path. I was afraid of getting lost out in the forest, and I think Ruth was too, for she kept chattering incessantly. The sudden, cackling call of a large bird made us jump, and then we laughed at our foolishness. Midway down the mountain we came upon a small log cabin, leaning downhill as if with the next big wind storm it would collapse completely. On the roof was a short chimney of stones, and the door had a hole where the latch had once been.

Ruth and I gazed at each other, our feet still firmly on the path. "Just an old cabin," she said, sounding very, very uninterested. "Some old woodsman probably used it."

"Yes," I said. "We'd better go on. We still have a long walk ahead of us."

But still I looked at that dark cabin, wishing so very much for the courage to go inside, horrified at the things my imagination told me lay behind that door, ashamed of the dryness in my throat and of my terror.

"I can't go in," I whispered to Ruth.

"Who said you should? Come on. Don't be silly."

Still I brooded, until we came upon the small cluster of houses that showed we were at the city's edge. Then we ran the rest of the way down the hill, faster and faster, until at last the streets were familiar, the distant mountains, the lake, the shops exactly the same as before. I felt, suddenly, that we had been away for months. It had been less than three weeks.

"Remember," Ruth told me sternly when we approached the rooming house, "not a word."

Annie's shouts and hugs and tears and Mother's kisses made it seem that we had truly been gone a long time.

"Oh, tell me about the camp," Annie cried, climbing onto my lap. "Are there games? Are there stories? Do you get to swim?"

"No," I said. "No swimming."

Ruth spoke about the other girls and where they were from, and I told about the forest and the flowers and streams, but then there was nothing more to tell.

"You're probably tired from the long walk," Mother said. She looked at us intently, and all through the afternoon it seemed that she was about to ask a question, but then she would only sigh and shake her head and press my hand or Ruth's. Finally she went to the little kitchen and asked cheerfully, "Are you hungry?"

"No," Ruth said quickly in a loud voice.

"Did you have lunch?"

"Oh, yes," I said.

"I went to the market this morning and bought a nice German sausage," Mother said. "I was going to fix some anyway, with eggs. Won't you try a little?"

The smell of that sausage frying was overpowering. We sat down at the table.

"Come on, Ruth," Mother coaxed, "eat."

"Well, just a little," Ruth said softly, flushing.

"Just a little for me, too," I added. I was, I thought in disgust, becoming a glutton, thinking of nothing but food.

When we had finished, Mother took me aside, and I was afraid for a moment that she would ask a question that I would not be able to answer without telling a direct lie. But she only handed me an envelope, saying, "This letter from Rosemarie came for you a few days ago."

I looked for a long moment at Rosemarie's handwriting, the letters so round and neat. Then I went to sit by the window and opened it.

My dearest Lisa,

I was so happy to get your letter. How pretty Zurich must be from your description. I can really picture it all, the lake, the hills, the houses. Wouldn't it be wonderful

*if we were there together? Can you send me some post-
cards?*

I glanced up and saw that Mother and Ruth busied
themselves in the tiny kitchen, leaving me alone with my
precious letter. How would I explain to Rosemarie that I
had no money to buy picture postcards?

*The summer seems very long without you. Mother says I
keep to myself too much, and I have tried going places
with some of the other girls, but it just isn't the same. So I
read a lot, and I have been painting again.*

*I hear that Hanna and her parents have left the city. I
don't know where they went. My parents speak of taking
a trip someday, maybe to Palestine. Wouldn't it be wonderful to see Jerusalem? But for now Father is so busy
with his patients that he can't even think of it.*

I knew how it was for Rosemarie, that her parents
would sit up late into the night puzzling over what to do,
whether to leave, whether to stay, as my parents had sat
up talking and wondering.

*For myself I'd be happy never to see or hear our "off-
key chimpanzees" again.*

It was our private name for those brown-shirted students who went through the streets singing their hateful
songs. They seemed to us like apes, and Rosemarie and I
used to scorn them in private, "They swing their arms like
chimpanzees, and they sing off key!"

I was in the park roller skating one day last week, and a group of the apes came along, shouting and calling insults to an old man. You must know what names they called him. They told him to get down on his hands and knees and pick up the papers there in the park—that old, old man. And when he just stood there, shaking and confused, they started reaching into the trash can and they threw the garbage at him, but still the old man couldn't move. They closed in on him, and I knew they were going to beat him. Lisa, what could I do? I felt so sick inside. How could I help that man?

I saw what they were doing to him, but the old man didn't even cry out. What good would it have done? A group of little kids came running up, and they stood there watching, as if it were an entertainment. I couldn't stand it, and I ran home. I must have been pretty hysterical. For the first time in my life I was sick to my stomach. I shouted at my mother to call the police. Then I realized that there are no policemen that we can call.

I read over this letter and I realize how dismal I must sound, but you know I'm never sad for long. I'm sure everything will be fine. Fifi says to tell you, 'Go out and play!'

I smiled to myself, remembering Fifi, her parrot, who always, at any time of the day or night, shouted in that peculiar voice, "Go out and play!" and for some inexplicable reason added, "Dirty dishes! Dirty dishes!"

I showed Mother the letter, and she read it, her lips pressed tightly together. "Rosemarie should be careful of what she writes," Mother said softly. "If only they would decide to . . ." but she left the thought unfinished and asked me instead, "When do you have to be back?"

"Before dark," I told her, remembering Frau Strom's warning.

"Then we have time," Mother said, "to take that ride up the Uetliberg. Annie's been waiting so eagerly."

I had never been on a funicular. We stood at the little station house and looked up, straight up, it seemed to where the cable climbed the mountainside to the top and out of sight. It seemed unbelievable that the little car would actually be pulled up that mountain clear to the top.

People piled in, the four of us sitting close together, and when the climb began we looked down, clutching at each other, laughing and gasping, for never in this world was there a mountain so steep or a car so rickety making its way upward like a determined alpine goat. The houses and people below shrank smaller and smaller, and I kept my eyes fastened on them, determined not to miss the thrill, though my stomach felt as if I were riding an elevator clear up to the sky.

The car creaked to a stop, and we all rushed out into the cold air, giggling with excitement. How clear it was! All of Zurich lay at our feet, the boats on the lake were tiny white dots, the houses like mere wooden blocks of different colors, and the people—they were not to be seen at all. "We're the only people in the world!" I exclaimed, laughing. "It's wonderful."

"I can see clear to America!" Annie shouted. "Papa!" she called, as if she were inside a cave. "Hello-oo."

The ride down seemed shorter, but no less exciting, and when we arrived I felt that we had been up in a balloon and back again.

Too soon it was time to go back, and Mother and Annie walked with us to the houses where the real climb began. Then Annie hugged us and called, "Come back. Come back soon." Mother kissed us solemnly, and I wondered that she did not say, as usually she did, "Be good. Remember all you've been taught."

Three days later I knew why. Frau Strom came into the dormitory and said in a rigid voice, "Pack your things, Lisa. Your mother is here."

"Why?" I exclaimed. "What's the matter?"

"Pack your things. You're leaving."

Erica

A TAXI WAITED outside. In a moment our bags were put into the trunk, the car turned around and we barely had time to wave to the boys and girls who stood curiously at the windows.

"What is it!" I exclaimed, feeling caught up in confusion. Mother had barely spoken to Frau Strom, but rushed us into the taxi and away. "Are we leaving Switzerland? Did Papa send for us?"

"No, darling. I couldn't leave you at that place."

"What do you mean?" Ruth stammered. "We didn't—we didn't say anything."

"You didn't have to," Mother replied. "A mother knows. Don't you think I could see that you weren't getting enough to eat? No routine, no care at all—like little lost souls, all those children looking out of the windows!" She took up her handkerchief and wiped her eyes, hard, as if some speck of dust irritated them.

I felt numb from the abruptness of our departure.

"Where's Annie?" I asked, wanting her, somehow, to make it seem real.

"When I went to the agency and told them that I was taking you away from the camp," Mother said, "they gave me the names of several families who have offered to take children to live with them for a while. I went to see one of the families this morning. They want Annie to stay with them."

"Tell me about them," I said, trying to conceal my disappointment.

"I had to send her, Lisa," Mother said seriously. "Don't think I wanted to let her go. But I haven't been feeling very strong lately, and Annie needs playmates too." She sighed.

"Do they have children?" I could imagine Annie playing and laughing, and I wanted her with me.

"There are children Annie's age next door to the Zeilers," Mother told me. "They have a baby boy. Actually, Frau Zeiler wanted an older child; but when she saw Annie and talked to her, she couldn't bear to let her go. And Annie was happy to stay."

"What about us?" Ruth asked, biting her lip.

"I have found homes for you," Mother said. "It won't be for long, I hope. Papa has saved almost enough money to buy our tickets. You'll be staying with families right here in Zurich. You'll be able to visit me as much as you like."

All that afternoon and late into the evening we sat in the little room talking, and this time Ruth and I told everything. Mother listened, shaking her head, now and then reaching for her handkerchief, murmuring, "Oh, why didn't you tell me? What if I hadn't suspected?"

Now I began to think of Emma and Werner and all the others who had no place to go, nobody who would come for them.

"I keep thinking about the others," I said hesitantly, "that we should do something."

"What can I possibly do?" Mother asked wearily. "I can report this to the agency, and there will be an investigation, I suppose, but such things take time. And probably at the end they'll say, 'Well, it's not a perfect place for children, but it's the best we can do right now.'" Mother sighed deeply. "There are too many needs, too few people who know and want to help. Well, I'll make the report, girls. We'll see if something comes of it."

But we all knew that we were completely helpless to bring any real change.

To sleep that night in the spacious double bed beside Ruth was like a special gift. I had never been so happy before simply to go to bed and stretch out, and to turn without bumping my head or my elbows. I said to Ruth, "How wonderful to sleep in a real bed!" Mother heard, and for some reason this, more than anything we had told her, made her break down and weep.

"I'm so sorry, so sorry," she said again and again. "I shouldn't have sent you. I didn't know. You don't deserve this, really, such good children."

I made my voice light. "Oh, so what. It didn't hurt me. Actually, it was funny. Imagine me in a crib, at my age!" I made my monkey faces, and mother began to smile faintly, and then she kissed us goodnight.

We did not even unpack our clothes the next morning, for we were to go to the agency that afternoon, to meet the families that would be taking care of us. After breakfast Mother asked us to go to the grocery store for her.

"I've made out the shopping list," she said, "but I think I'd rather stay here and rest a little. I feel so tired," she added apologetically.

"It's all right," Ruth and I said. "We like to shop."

We got our coats and the money, but just as we reached the door Mother called out in a strange, trembling voice,

"Oh, don't go, girls! I need you. I feel so—so . . ."

We rushed toward her, for Mother was moving unsteadily toward the bed, and then her body seemed to

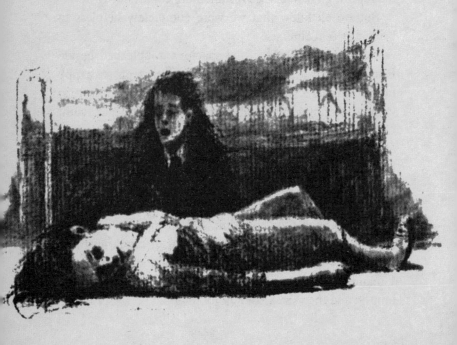

crumple, and she lay on the floor, motionless.

Ruth crouched beside her calling, "Mother! Mother! Mother!" and I raced down the stairs, shouting for Frau Feldin. My heart made loud thumps in my ears, and I heard my own voice as a strange, dull sound as I pounded on Frau Feldin's door. "A doctor! Get a doctor! My mother has fainted."

I had never seen anybody faint, but I knew, and somehow I knew what to do. Something inside moved me without my willing it or thinking of it. I stood beside Frau Feldin while she screeched her message into the telephone. Then I went upstairs. Somehow Mother had gotten onto the bed, conscious now, her hand reaching out slowly toward Ruth, who knelt beside the bed looking completely dazed.

"I'll be all right, Ruth," I heard Mother whisper.

I threw open the window to let in some fresh air. I took off Mother's shoes and she sighed faintly. Then I began, mechanically, to put the kettle on for some tea, and I gave Mother a cold cloth for her head.

"Thank you, Lisa," she whispered, reaching again toward Ruth who still had not moved from the spot.

I was feeding Mother spoonfuls of hot tea when we heard voices coming from the stairs, Frau Feldin's highpitched, distracted chatter, and the strong, calm voice of the doctor.

When he stepped into the room, I suddenly felt that I had always known him, and that he knew us, knew exactly what we felt and needed. He filled the room completely, moving about as if all this were most natural and familiar. He was not a tall man, but broad-shouldered and solidly built. His face was deeply creased, and his eyes were keen with life, his hair and eyebrows thick and shaggy. I wanted to go to him, but I waited.

He felt Mother's pulse, then took her temperature and asked to wash his hands. I ran to get a clean towel, and he smiled and put his arm briefly around my shoulder.

"I'm Doctor Gross," he said.

"I'm Lisa Platt," I told him, "and my sister Ruth." I waved toward Ruth, and he went to her, touching her face gently. "Go and sit down on the sofa now, Ruth," he said softly. "I must have room to tend to your mother. Go, child. I'll take care of your mother. You needn't be afraid."

Ruth moved to the sofa, and we sat there together, watching Dr. Gross.

"When did you eat last?" he asked Mother.

"Breakfast," Mother murmured. "I had a cup of tea."

"No more," he stated, shaking his head. "I'm afraid you have a touch of pneumonia, Frau Platt. It probably began with an ordinary cold and you must have been under considerable strain."

"Yes," Mother whispered. "We are from Germany—refugees."

"I understand," he said. "Don't try to talk now. I'm going to send for an ambulance to take you to the hospital," he said in his deep, steady voice. "It's nothing to be alarmed about, just a convenience. I know you're feeling very weak, Frau Platt, and it probably hurts a bit when you try to breathe deeply, doesn't it?"

Mother only nodded, and her eyes filled with tears.

"The children," she whispered. "They were supposed

to go to stay with some people this afternoon. The addresses are in my purse. The Resettlement Agency . . ."

"I'll call the agency and inform them," said the doctor. "We'll arrange to have your girls taken care of. Now you rest for a moment while I talk to Lisa."

"Where is your father?" he asked me softly.

"In America," I replied. "And my little sister Annie is staying with another family."

"Your Mother will be in the hospital for several weeks," Doctor Gross said, frowning. "But she'll be all right."

"Will we be able to visit?" I asked.

"Not for a while. It's contagious. It's a wonder you and your sister haven't caught it."

I explained that we had just returned from camp, pointing to our suitcases still unpacked.

"Well, you're certainly having your share of experiences," he said, and I was thankful that he did not sympathize. It would have made me cry.

He turned to Ruth. "Are you better now? Your mother is in no danger. I'm going to see to it that she receives the best possible care, that she gets lots of rest and good food. You'll be able to telephone her every day."

"I'm all right now," Ruth said, standing very straight. "Thank you."

Mother asked me to find the note in her purse. On it were written two names, "family Kunst and family Werfel." My name was written beside the latter.

"You will like it," Mother whispered to me. "I met Herr Werfel. He has a daughter, too."

The next few hours passed in a haze, with the ambu-

lance sending its terrible wail along the streets, doctors in
white coats rushing in with a stretcher, Mother reaching
out to touch our faces as they took her away. I felt that
somehow I had lived all this before, and my body re-
sponded automatically, without feeling.

"How can you be so calm?" Ruth asked me again and
again, as we walked to the agency office, where we were
to meet the people who were taking us to their homes.
Mother had forgotten to leave money for bus fare, and
we hadn't thought to ask. "How can you be so calm? My
whole body is shaking."

"I don't know," I replied.

"I wish we could be together," she said, biting her lip.

"I'll call you tonight," I promised.

"Mother said they have a boy my age," Ruth told me.
"I don't want to go."

I laughed slightly. "He won't bother you. Don't you
like boys?"

"Don't tease now, Lisa," she said gravely. "You know
what I mean. Oh, this suitcase is heavy. I feel like a
gypsy."

I still felt nothing at all. I might have been watching
from a distance. It was the same feeling I had the night
Papa left, that the real me was only looking on. I put one
foot in front of the other until we reached the agency
office, and suddenly I found myself in the arms of the tall,
graying man who was Herr Werfel.

"My child!" he exclaimed. "Come, let me take that
suitcase. They didn't tell us you had to walk all this way.
Come, come to the car, my dear. We'll take you home."

Ruth, too, was leaving, walking beside a tall thin boy

speaking with him shyly. She turned back to wave good-bye and I knew that she was satisfied to go.

In the car something inside me gave way. I began to tremble violently, and tears slid down my cheeks, although I hardly realized I was crying.

Frau Werfel put her arms around me, and I lay against her while she murmured, "There, there. Let it all go, my child. Don't try to hold back. There is a time for tears—now, now all will be well."

I looked up at last and saw their daughter, Erica, looking at me with such consternation that I had to smile. "I'm fine," I said. "Really, I'm sorry."

"When we get home," Erica said, with a smile that made her whole face glow, "I'll show you the rabbits. We have eight altogether, six babies. We keep them in the barn. Would you like to have one of the bunnies to keep?"

I didn't know what to say, and she continued, "We can sleep together in my room—if you want to, that is."

"I want to," I said. She was so sweet, not pretty like Rosemarie, but her face was so frank and filled with feeling that I knew we would be friends, really friends, although she was nearly two years younger than I.

"Let Lisa rest a while," Frau Werfel told Erica when we reached the large old farmhouse. "Lie down here on the sofa, dear. Erica, don't tire Lisa with too much talk. We'll have many days together, I hope." She bent down and kissed me, as if I were her own. I looked from one to the other, at Frau Werfel's plump, motherly face, at Herr Werfel, tall as a reed, but gentle in his movements, and I could see that they really wanted me.

The sofa was old and comfortable, like the house itself. I lay down against the soft cushions, and Erica sat beside me, fingering her long dark braids and smiling but not speaking.

"I have never been on a farm," I told her. "What do you grow?"

"It's not really much of a farm," Erica said. "We have a few chickens and pigs, and a vegetable garden."

"Do you have a horse?"

"Oh, yes. There's the barn, you see, and it wouldn't do to leave it empty, so we got the horse."

I laughed slightly. She was so serious, so eager to please, it seemed.

"My cousins live just up the hill," she said. "They have a large apple orchard. I'll take you there one day, and you can drink all the apple cider you want. And you can ride the horse if you like horses, which I guess you do, because you asked about it. We have a hayloft. Have you ever been in a hayloft? Oh, there are a few little mice under the hay, but they won't bother you. Sometimes you can hear them squeak, and sometimes they pop out, but then they run away and hide again very quickly."

She gazed at me for a long moment. "Do you want to sleep? Am I talking too much?"

"No, not at all."

"I don't suppose you play with dolls," she said. "I don't either, never did much. I've always had little animals, instead, like the bunnies. Do you like to play ball?"

I nodded.

"I do too. It's something you can do alone. There

aren't many children in the neighborhood. That's why I'm so glad you came to stay with us. It must have been exciting to live in Berlin. I have always lived right here."

Frau Werfel came in with mugs of hot chocolate. "Erica!" she reprimanded. "You're talking too much." But her eyes were gay, and she said to me, "I can't really blame her. We're all so excited about having you with us."

Frau Werfel thought of everything. After dinner she telephoned the hospital, and I was allowed to talk to Mother, but only for a few minutes.

"Do you like the Werfels?" she asked me in a soft, weak voice.

"Yes, yes," I assured her, "very much."

She sighed. "I have a nice room," she said. "The nurses bring me food every two hours." She paused, as if speaking were an effort. "The doctor says I'm undernourished. But I'll be well soon," she added hastily. "Be a good girl, Lisa, and remember—remember all you have been taught."

I went into the kitchen, where Frau Werfel was setting out bread dough to rise overnight. Her movements as she kneaded the dough and the smell of yeast reminded me of home and of all the times I had sat at the kitchen table watching Clara.

From the next room I could hear Erica and her father talking softly, laughing now and then. There was music from the radio, a pretty tune I had never heard before, but somehow everything seemed familiar, too familiar. I was not really a part of it. How could I be? I could belong to only one family, and mine was scattered in different directions. I knew that I was wanted here, and welcome, but my mind and heart were divided into too many places, and I could not feel whole.

Frau Werfel turned to smile at me. "Would you like to write to your father, Lisa? I've put out some stationery and stamps. You can sit here at the kitchen table."

I thanked her, marveling that she seemed to know just how I felt. I had wanted to write to Papa for weeks, but had not been able to for lack of paper and a stamp.

It grew dark outside while I wrote, but I was too engrossed to notice anything around me. I gave no thought whatever to the organization of my letter. I simply wrote and wrote, leaping from one thing to the other, from one place to another, but always picturing Papa here beside me.

When at last I was finished Herr Werfel called to me. "Come and sit with us awhile, Lisa," he said. "Tell us about your family. Tell us about your father."

I began slowly, almost reluctantly. How could I possibly describe Papa? I told them some of the funny little stories Papa had told me, never make-believe stories, but real incidents that happened to him. He had told me many things about his childhood, and I could picture him and his four brothers turning the house inside out with their pranks. I told of the time when Papa, as a young boy, had eaten nearly a whole bushel of cherries, just to prove to his brothers that he could do it. I told how, at the age of fourteen, he was apprenticed to a tailor in another town, and how he ran back home one night, overcome with loneliness. I told about the time Papa had invented a new cleaning fluid, and how the bottle had exploded in the garage. And I told how, before our trip to Brazil, Papa had to go to Czechoslovakia to pick up Ruth from boarding school.

"He needed money to pay for her school and to get to Italy, but he wasn't allowed to take any money out. He had to hide it in some way."

Herr Werfel nodded, and Erica asked, "What did he do?"

"He bought some grapes," I answered. "He put them in a double bag, with money between the two bags. When the inspector came onto the train, Papa was sitting there eating grapes. He offered some to the inspector, too."

"What if he had been caught?" Erica gasped.

"He would have gone to jail, I guess," I said. "But he's a good actor, my father. Oh, he can make anybody laugh!"

I felt closer to Papa than ever, and when it was time to go to bed I was contented and whole.

Frau Werfel had unpacked my clothes and laid my pajamas out on the bed beside Erica's. My dresses were hung neatly in Erica's closet, and now I saw how shabby they had become. I got into bed quickly, self-conscious about the patches on my pajamas.

Frau Werfel did not seem to notice. She kissed us both, then tucked the blankets around me, saying, "Goodnight, Lisa dear. We're so lucky to have you with us."

I watched as Erica knelt beside her bed to say her prayers, and I looked up at the picture of Jesus, the shepherd, that hung on the wall. When she had finished, Erica turned to me with her glowing smile and said, "Goodnight."

What was it, I wondered, that made these people so good?

In the darkness I said my own prayer, ending as always, "and please let us all be together again soon."

Questions and Quotas

IT HAD BEEN a wonderful week, each day filled with new, exciting things to do. I rode the horse every morning, a sweet, gentle old mare that had probably never received a cross word in her life. Her name was Stella, for she had a white patch, almost the shape of a star on her forehead. Sweet Stella, I called her, as she rubbed her nose against my hands and clothing, searching for the carrots and sugar lumps we always brought.

That week opened a new world to me. Who in Berlin had ever picked peas fresh from the garden, or gathered eggs in a hen house? How could I ever have dreamed that a hayloft could be such a marvelous place for play, or for lying down and looking out of the loft window, or for jumping down onto the slippery, fresh smelling stacks below?

I had never seen apples growing on trees. I had certainly never seen a cider press. We trooped up the hill,

Erica and I, to her cousin's house, about a mile along the country road, and then we went into the orchards, where the apples hung ripe on the trees and bushel baskets of picked fruit stood in rows. We brought a gallon jug with us, and Frau Werfel always said with a twinkling smile, "Now this time bring the cider *home*." Erica's aunt would fill the jug with cider, and on the way down the hill we were always tempted to take just a little taste, then another and another, passing the jug back and forth, until when we arrived back at Erica's house the jug was empty. "Now go back," Erica's mother would say, giving her a playful swat, "And this time bring the cider *home, you imps!*"

Then the last week before school would begin arrived. There is something about that last week of vacation—it is always the very best time of the whole summer. I remarked about it to Erica. "Haven't you found it so?"

"Only since you are here," she answered, giving me a smile. "I wish . . ." She stopped abruptly.

"What do you wish?" I urged her.

"It's selfish of me," she said wistfully. "But I—I wish you could stay with us for a long, long time."

I didn't want to think beyond that day.

"Do you think your mother will let you stay with us," Erica asked hesitantly, "until you leave Switzerland?"

"I think so," I replied.

"My father will ask her today," Erica said, for that afternoon they were taking me to the hospital to visit Mother. I had spoken to Dr. Gross on the telephone.

"Yes, I think it would be good for your mother to see you girls," he had said, "but only one at a time, and just for a few minutes. She still needs plenty of rest."

Doctor Gross was in Mother's room when we arrived. I was struck with how fragile Mother looked in the great bed among the white linens and wearing a hospital gown. I rushed to her, but she held me away. "Not too close, darling. I don't want to take any chances. Sit down there on the chair. Let me look at you. Your cheeks are rosy again!" She smiled and her eyes shone.

"Your mother's getting along fine," Dr. Gross said, taking up his bag. "She'll be up and around in ten days or so, but," he turned to Mother, "you'll still have to take it easy, and remember that people can't live on tea and toast—not if they want to stay healthy."

"I'll remember, Doctor," Mother said meekly, half-smiling.

"And you'd best try to keep your daughters right where they are. No use shuffling those girls around like library books!"

"And what would I do all day?" Mother asked him boldly.

"You'll visit them," the doctor said promptly, patting me on the shoulder as he turned to go. "Just a few minutes, now, Lisa."

The Werfels had left me at the door to Mother's room, unwilling to tire her with too many visitors. They were to come back for me in ten minutes. My head was filled with things I wanted to say, but in my rush to tell everything I was, for a moment, speechless.

"You like the Werfels, don't you?" Mother asked.

"They are the most wonderful people I've ever known," I replied promptly. "Frau Werfel made me some pajamas to match Erica's. She said it would be fun for us to have something alike, as if we were real sisters. She's so kind!" Frau Werfel never made it seem that she was giving me a gift or supplying something I desperately needed. It was the same when she made us each dresses. "She says it's just as easy to make two," I told Mother. "How can that be?"

Mother laughed, and her face looked pink and healthy again. "Have you been helping around the house?"

"Oh, yes," I said quickly. "But it's fun. I mean, we get to feed the chickens, and Frau Werfel taught me how to darn socks. I made the *nicest* little patch in one of Herr Werfel's."

"Marvelous!" Mother exclaimed. "You're turning into a young lady after all. And today? What did you do today?"

I took a deep breath, then said rapidly, "We went to church. I—I went too. Is it all right?"

"Of course it is," Mother said, nodding.

"The Werfels are Catholic," I said.

"I know."

"It was a Catholic mass," I explained insistently.

"You can pray wherever you are," Mother said soberly, "and still be a good Jew. God is everywhere. I have prayed in many churches. But what's the matter, Lisa? Were you uncomfortable?"

"No," I murmured. "It was beautiful." I sighed, not wanting to ask, but needing to talk about the thoughts that had haunted me. "Do you think that's what makes them so good? Going to church, I mean, and being Catholic?" Our eyes met intently, and there was silence for a moment. Then Mother lay back against the pillows, hesitating before she faced me fully and asked, "What do *you* think?"

"I don't know," I said, shaking my head. I did not ask that nagging question, If I were a Catholic, would I be better, too? How could I ask it, even of myself? I loved the synagogue, the songs and prayers, the closeness to God. How could I question the faith of my fathers?

There wasn't time to pursue it, for a nurse came bustling into the room. "There's a letter for you, Frau Platt," she said.

"A letter? But it's Sunday."

"Special delivery," the nurse answered briskly, already on her way out. "From America."

Mother ripped open the envelope.

"Is it from Papa?" I asked, rushing to see.

"Of course." Mother quickly scanned the page, then she cried out, "Oh, no! He mustn't."

"What? What is it?"

"Papa says—he—he wants to leave America!" she said in a stricken tone. "He mustn't! He says he got a letter from you and one from Frau Feldin, saying that I was very sick and in the hospital. Lisa, what did you write to Papa?" Her voice was shaking.

"I don't remember, exactly. I told him about Erica."

"What did you say about me?" Mother demanded fiercely. "Tell me!"

"Just that you are sick and in the hospital. Just what you told me, and what Doctor Gross said. I told him you would get better soon. I *told* him you were getting special care and medicine to make you better."

"That Frau Feldin, such a scatterbrain. I never should have given her Papa's address. It was only in case of an emergency."

"She probably thought it *was* an emergency!" I exclaimed. "With the ambulance coming and everything. Wouldn't *you* have thought so?"

"Lisa, for heaven's sake, don't argue with me now. I have to stop him. He says he's making arrangements to come to Zurich. Listen," she read from the letter, "Benjamin says I am a fool even to think of leaving, but I must come to you and take my chances. I can't sleep for worrying about you, Margo, thinking of you alone in a foreign city and sick. No matter what happens, at least we'll be together. I can't stand . . ."

She put the letter down, her eyes brimming.

The very thought of seeing Papa filled me with such great excitement that I couldn't think of anything else. Why couldn't he come? Why couldn't we all stay in Switzerland and make it our home? Why America?

"Let him come," I begged, half kneeling beside Mother's bed. "Oh, please, don't stop him."

Mother sat upright and snapped, "Don't be foolish, Lisa. You just don't understand. We can't stay in Zurich. There would be no work for Papa here. Switzerland is a tiny country. They can't take immigrants, and it's too close, too close to Germany."

"You mean the Nazis might come *here?*" I cried.

"I don't know." Mother shook her head, then took my hand gently. "I'm sorry, darling. It wasn't your fault— that Frau Feldin, stupid woman! I'll send a cablegram to Papa," she said. "Ring for the nurse."

When the nurse came, she shook her head firmly. "You are not allowed to get out of bed, Frau Platt."

"Nonsense!" Mother scolded, swinging her feet onto the floor. "Hand me my robe, Lisa."

"It is against my orders," the nurse said, standing in Mother's way. "I'd have to check with Doctor Gross.

Now you wait here, Frau Platt," she said. "I'll try to find him."

Mother sat back on the bed. "I'll wait five minutes," she said firmly. "That's all."

"Now just relax," the nurse soothed. "Look, you've another visitor." She whispered something to Herr Werfel and he nodded, then strode over to Mother and took her hand.

"Grüss Gott," he said, smiling. "I hope you're feeling better, Frau Platt. Oh, your Lisa is a jewel. We want to keep her with us, if we may, until you leave Switzerland. But you look troubled, and the nurse said I am to keep you here. What is it? What can I do?"

When he had heard about the letter, Herr Werfel began to pace back and forth, frowning deeply. "You're right, of course," he said to Mother. "If he once leaves America, your husband may have a hard time re-entering. In fact, I've just read in the newspapers about the quota system, and how many people are waiting to go to the United States."

"That's exactly it," Mother said quickly. "As long as my husband is there already, the girls and I don't have to come under the quota system. If he were to leave now, the whole thing would have to be started over again, with new forms, new waiting lists. Now all he has to do is send one more certificate. Oh, Herr Werfel," Mother said pleadingly, "we've waited so long. Everything we've waited for would be undone!"

The nurse came to the door to announce, "Doctor Gross has left the hospital, I'm afraid. You just have to . . ."

"Never mind," Herr Werfel told her. "Frau Platt just wants to send a cablegram. I'll take care of it for her."

He pulled the chair over beside Mother's bed and took a small notebook and pencil from his vest pocket. "Now, take your time," he said gently. "I'll write down exactly what you want to say, and I'll ask for an answer immediately, so you won't have to worry. It will take a few hours, but at least you'll be able to sleep tonight in peace."

Together they composed the message. "DO NOT LEAVE AMERICA. RECOVERING QUICKLY. ALL IS WELL. LOVE. MARGO."

"You have more than ten words," Herr Werfel said. "You can omit the word 'love,' or pay extra for it."

"I'll pay extra," Mother said, smiling slightly. "It's worth it."

"I agree," Herr Werfel smiled. "I'll ask for a reply immediately."

"Lie down again now, Mother," I coaxed, and by the time Herr Werfel returned she was settled once more under the blankets, but I knew she would not rest easily until she had Papa's reply.

"We'd better leave you now, Frau Platt," Herr Werfel said. "Try to rest. We'll call you tonight. Oh, I nearly forgot, and Erica will be waiting to know. May I tell her that Lisa will stay with us until you leave?"

"Of course," Mother said gratefully. "You are so kind."

Erica and Frau Werfel were waiting in the car, and now we told them what had happened. "We'll call the hospital right after supper," Frau Werfel said. But it was not until after our third call that we knew Papa's answer. "Will stay. Sending last form this month. Love to girls."

"It's long past bedtime," Frau Werfel announced, "and you two have school tomorrow."

But neither Erica nor I could sleep. I was thinking about going to a strange new school again, and about Papa. As for Erica, I didn't know what was keeping her awake until she asked in the darkness, "What is a quota, Lisa?"

"I think it means that only a certain number of people can get into a country at any particular time. America has a quota," I told her.

"Does Switzerland?" she asked.

"I don't know. But we can't stay here anyway."

She was silent for a time, then asked, "Have you ever seen a Nazi, Lisa?"

I sighed. "Yes."

"Are they really so terrible?"

"Yes."

Again Erica was silent, and then she sat up to look at me by the faint light that shone through the window. "Lisa," she said urgently, "I have to ask you something."

"What is it?"

"Well, I have never known anybody who was Jewish before, and it seems to me that you are—I mean," she faltered, "are all Jewish girls as good as you? And are they all so brave?"

I smiled to myself, and my heart beat faster. How strange it was that she asked me such a question, but no stranger, I realized, than my question to Mother that afternoon. I understood now why Mother had not answered. It was something I had to figure out for myself.

"Some are good and some aren't," I told Erica. I didn't say more. She would have to think it through on her own.

After a long pause Erica spoke again. "You know, Switzerland is surrounded on all sides by high mountains. The German soldiers wouldn't even try to come here. We've never been conquered. It couldn't happen."

"Of course not," I said, but to myself I thought, anything could happen. Hadn't it happened in Germany?

But even at school, in the geography and history classes, the teachers spoke of Switzerland's natural barriers. When they introduced me to the class as having come from Germany, they spoke of the Nazis there, and I suppose I became somewhat of a celebrity in the little school, having escaped. At recess the other girls crowded around me, wanting to hear all about Berlin. I tried to tell them that Berlin was just a city, my home. I only wanted to remember the good things, before the Nazis. Finally the yard duty teacher came and started us all in a ball game. To me she said, "You don't have to talk about it, dear."

There was talk about Germany every night on the radio that September. While Erica and I were doing our homework at the kitchen table, we would hear the news broadcasts in the background. Afterward Herr Werfel's face was always very grave, and he and his wife would talk together in low tones.

"It looks bad," he would say, "very bad. Hitler's going to make a grab for Czechoslovakia. The Czechs can't possibly hold out against the German army. And what next? He won't stop, that madman, until he's plunged the whole world into war."

"Maybe not," Frau Werfel replied. "Maybe other nations will help Czechoslovakia. What about England and France and even America? Don't they have treaties? Maybe, if Hitler sees they are all against him, he'll stop."

"Only force will stop him," said Herr Werfel grimly. "And that means war, world war."

I froze in my seat. America at war? How, then, could we go there? Where else in the world could we go to be safe? My imagination gave me no answers. I could only picture countries the way they looked on the large wall map at school. The black boundaries, to me, represented walls, with gates to let people in or keep them out. If there was a war, I was certain, all the gates would be closed. People did not travel freely during war. Hadn't we learned that in Germany?

All that month and into the next we waited. Even at school, where the teachers gathered in the halls to whisper together, there was a shadow over us, the same feeling we had known in Berlin. People would forget for a time and go on about their business, but then someone would ask a question or make a remark and we would remember that everyone waited, as if for a time bomb to tick to an end. And then the news changed. It was nearly winter, the news announcers said. Hitler wouldn't move in winter. He would wait at least until spring. Perhaps, they added hopefully, the big scare was over.

Mother got out of the hospital as Dr. Gross had promised and I visited her two or three times a week at the rooming house. On Sundays we were all together at the

Werfels, the whole family except Papa. Annie simply went wild over the rabbits and chickens. She promptly named them all Susan.

On Sunday afternoons Frau Werfel never seemed to stop serving food, smiling and saying, "This house *should* be filled with children."

"But with such noisy children?" Mother would protest, chuckling.

"Oh, let them run and shout," Frau Werfel would say. "That's what childhood is for."

Even Ruth, who usually considered herself too grown-up for such things, romped with us in the hayloft and took leap after leap onto the stacks. She swung higher and longer than any of us on the rope swing that Herr Werfel had tied to a huge oak.

But there were other times when Ruth sat apart from us, thinking troubled thoughts, I guessed, for she wound a lock of hair around and around her finger.

"Leave Ruth alone," Mother would say, when the three of us tried to make her join in some game. "She needs some time to herself. She's growing so fast. In Berlin she would be going out with other young people, going to parties and dances."

Erica and I couldn't understand Ruth's sullen moods, or her sudden temper when we interrupted them. Once Annie, holding one of the bunnies in her arms, ran toward Ruth, who was sitting under a tree in the garden.

"Leave Ruth alone, Annie," I called teasingly. "She's in one of her 'moods' and doesn't want to be disturbed."

I knew that Ruth had heard, but she ignored me, just as she ignored Annie, who sat down beside her.

"I love it here," I heard Annie say. "Don't you love this little bunny? Don't you want to hold him?"

"No," Ruth replied shortly. "He smells."

"He smells nice," Annie insisted, burying her nose in the soft fur. "I love him. I can't take him to America, can I?"

"Of course not," Ruth retorted.

"Maybe we won't go to America," I heard Annie say. "Maybe Papa won't send for us. Maybe Papa's dead and we'll never see him again."

Suddenly Ruth's hand shot out and Annie lay screaming on the lawn. Everyone rushed over. Ruth made another grab at Annie, shaking her furiously, shouting, "She'd rather have that rabbit than ever see Papa again! She wishes Papa were dead!"

"Ruth, Ruth," Mother cried, "stop it! She's just a baby. She didn't mean that. *Leave her alone.* Just look what you've done. There, there, Annie, Ruth didn't mean it. She didn't mean it."

On Annie's cheek there was a large red mark, where Ruth's hand had struck.

"She did mean it!" Annie cried. "She hates the bunny. She hates me, too."

"No she doesn't hate anybody. She's lonesome for Papa, that's all. She's upset from waiting and wondering." I knew that Mother was speaking more to me than to Annie. "Still, it's dreadful to make such a scene," she said to Ruth, "and especially when you are a guest here. What must Frau Werfel think?"

But Frau Werfel had gone into the house and not a

word was said about the episode. It was so like her to pretend that nothing at all had happened. In all the weeks I was with them, I never saw Frau Werfel lose her composure—except one terrible day in November.

Passport to Freedom

WE HAD JUST SAT DOWN to breakfast early that Sunday morning when the telephone rang. Frau Werfel went to answer, looking perplexed that anyone should call so early. We all knew, I think, that something dreadful had happened, even before we heard Frau Werfel's outcry and saw her face creased with sorrow and pain.

"Oh, dear God!" I heard her exclaim. "But of course you must come to us right away, my dear Frau Platt. Let us help you. My husband will leave immediately. No, no —of course it's no trouble. We'll be there in fifteen minutes, my dear."

My heart was beating frantically. I couldn't speak. I only looked at Frau Werfel, my eyes asking the question.

"A terrible thing has happened," she said weeping, "in Germany."

Inwardly I sighed with relief. At least it wasn't Papa! Frau Werfel's voice was choked with sobs, and she would not look at any of us. "The Nazis," she began, "they have murdered . . ."

"What is it?" her husband cried. "Tell me!"

"They have murdered many—Jews—many," came the halting reply. "We must go to Frau Platt. You girls stay here," she said, throwing off her apron and wiping her face with it. "We'll be back in half an hour. Stay here," she said again, and then in silence Erica and I went into the living room to wait.

My hands were icy cold, but I didn't notice until Erica said, "Lisa, you're shivering," and she gave me Frau Werfel's knitted shawl to put around my shoulders.

As we sat there, only one vision was fastened in my mind—not of murder, for murder is something too shocking to be realized even in the imagination—but of the young Nazis in their brown shirts and black ties, stamping through the streets singing in loud, bold voices, "When the blood of Jews . . ."

Before the Werfels' car had stopped, we were outside, and in a moment I was in Mother's arms.

"Lisa!" Through all the bad times and fearful moments, I had never seen Mother look like this. "Do you know? Did Frau Werfel tell you?"

I shook my head, and beside me Frau Werfel murmured, "No. I couldn't."

"Come inside, Lisa." For several long moments Mother could not seem to begin. I only looked at her, waiting, not wanting to hear, yet needing to know.

"Lisa, there is no way I can prepare you," Mother said. "Your Uncle Arnold is dead. And Tante Helga too."

"How?" My voice sounded strange to my own ears,

hollow and high.

"The Nazis."

"No." Again that toneless voice. "You must be wrong, Mother." I shook my head and covered my ears. It's a mistake, something inside me cried; it's someone else she's talking about, not my Aunt Helga, not Uncle Arnold. I love them, and they're alive, *alive*.

"It's true. Lisa, my darling come here to me, please."

But I couldn't move. Helga, my beautiful aunt who was always so gay, making jokes even on the day of parting.

"I know what you are feeling," I heard Mother's voice as from a distance, "and I cannot spare you the pain. You would know someday, you would hear of it. Look at me, Lisa! Grandmother telephoned me from Berlin. They didn't suffer, Lisa. Remember that. It was fast, and it is over for them."

Mother must have telephoned Ruth, for later she came, and we all sat together in the parlor, and through that whole long day I could not get warm, even when I stood by the fire wrapped in the knitted shawl. Late in the afternoon the sun came out, but still the room seemed gray and dim. Somewhere people were going on about their ordinary day, making plans, doing work and taking pleasures. But for us time had stopped, and we stood still looking backwards, only backwards to this thing that had happened even without our knowing.

Yesterday. It was yesterday, and I was playing then, playing ball with Erica, while in Berlin the madness had already begun. Little by little, then over and over again it was told, as if by telling we could understand. It had begun with a small, angry mob, rampaging through the streets, smashing windows, smearing paint on doors and windows, hurling bricks. As night fell there were more men in the streets, some with guns, some with knives, and some with kerosene.

But there had to be a *reason*. It couldn't just have begun so suddenly, this killing of Jews.

Mother told us, and we heard it again and again on the radio all through the day. "A German official was killed in Paris. The Nazis have taken vengeance on the Jews in Germany."

Because someone in Paris had been shot, Uncle Arnold and Aunt Helga had paid with their lives. All our talk about it still left us with the same impossible question, *"Why?"*

They didn't suffer. Someone had thrown a homemade bomb into their house. An explosion ended everything. But how could we be sure? How many moments are there between life and death?

"Just believe it, Lisa," Mother said, holding me close. "It was fast and final. We will learn to live with this, somehow."

That night I went back with Mother to the rooming house, but the next day I returned to school and to the Werfels. I was glad for the routine of school, for the girls all around me at recess, and for Erica with me after school and in the evening. I did not want to be alone or idle, but at night there were always those minutes before sleep, when I had to think of it.

On one of Mother's Sunday visits to the Werfels, she brought me another letter from Rosemarie. This time the postmark was English. I tore open the letter. It was dated two weeks past, just before that terrible time in Berlin. They were safe, then! They had left in time!

I read the words hastily, then again, and wordlessly I handed the letter to Mother, looking over her shoulder to see the words once more, for Rosemarie and her sister were in England, all alone.

We have been here nearly a week, both my sister and I. Father could not bring himself to leave, with so many people needing him. My parents decided, at last, to send us to England, and we are at a kind of boarding school here. It's very crowded, but the ladies in charge are nice to us, although only one of them speaks German, and when she is not here I feel lost. So I will have to learn to speak English, just like you, Lisa, when you get to America.

"She doesn't say anything about her parents!" I cried out to Mother.

"She says that they will send for her when it's safe," Mother replied quietly.

"But what if it isn't safe? What if there *is* a war?"

"Then they will go to her in England," Mother said.

"But, Mother, it's awful for Rosemarie—she's so alone!"

"She has her sister," Mother said, "and thank God she's out of danger. Her parents did what they had to do. It isn't easy for a mother to send her child away." Her voice broke, and then she said, "We've been very lucky, Lisa. We've been able to stay together, at least in the same city."

I answered Rosemarie that night, sitting over my letter for over an hour. I told her about Erica and the farm and the school, avoiding any mention of Tante Helga or what had happened in Berlin.

Just a few days later came the message we had been waiting for. "There's a telegram from Papa!" Mother told me joyously over the telephone. "He has sent the last form. We can buy our boat tickets!"

Mother had an appointment to see the American consul the following day, and I begged her to let me go with her. She came for me that afternoon.

"Lisa's my adventurer," she told Frau Werfel, smiling broadly. "She wants to know everything that's going on."

"I just want to see for myself," I said. "I want to be sure it's really true."

"When do you think you will leave?" Frau Werfel asked Mother.

"It could be just a couple of weeks," Mother answered. Her whole face was radiant. "My husband has sent this form—they call it number 575—to Zurich. Now all we have to do is get our passports and ship reservations."

"What a grand day for you!" Frau Werfel exclaimed. "Tonight we'll have chocolate cake to celebrate," she said to me.

In the office of the American consul we waited. I was used to waiting, and it was easy now, for I felt that here in this office we were already halfway to America.

"Margo Platt!" a clerk called out suddenly, and we jumped up. A young secretary led the way. "You have only ten minutes," she said, then opened the door to a warm, comfortable room with deep leather chairs and a highly polished desk. Behind it sat the consul, a broad-shouldered, full-faced man with crisp dark hair.

He looked up, then rose to shake Mother's hand. "Sit down, please," he said, smiling at me.

In one corner of the room stood the American flag and above it hung a picture of the President. All the while Mother and the consul were talking, I looked at that flag and the picture.

"You like that flag, don't you?" the consul said suddenly, and I blushed.

"Yes," I said softly. "And the man in the picture, the President. Do you know him? He looks so—so kind."

The man chuckled, and in place of the weariness, there was a sparkle in his eyes. "I can't say that I know him personally, but I know enough about him to tell you honestly, yes, he is kind."

"When can we go to America?" I asked, and Mother motioned to me and said "Shh."

The man folded his hands together and faced Mother. "We have a problem," he said.

"A problem?" Mother echoed.

"Form 575," he stated. "Maybe you weren't informed, but unless we have it we can't give you a passport, Frau Platt. Now, you must write to your husband and tell him to send . . ."

"But he *has* sent it!" Mother exclaimed. "He sent me a telegram telling me that he sent the form two weeks ago, and that everything is ready now."

"My secretary has checked the files," he said, shaking his head slowly, "and we have no such form for you."

I felt that I had been running hard and couldn't quite

catch my breath. I wanted to tell him that of course Papa had sent it if he said he did! Papa would never make a mistake like that.

"All I can suggest," said the consul, "is that you have your husband send another form."

"But that might take weeks," Mother objected, "and I know he sent it. It *must* be here. We've been apart for ten months already, nearly a year, and all this time he's worked and saved and we have waited . . ."

"Please, calm yourself, Frau Platt," he said, half-rising from his chair. "We are trying to do all we can. Please understand. Hundreds of people come through this office every day, hundreds of papers are sent. We don't have enough help, and everybody wants to leave immediately. I'm helpless without that form. I have to follow regulations. If it were up to me . . ."

"I'm sorry," Mother said more calmly, "but I know that somewhere in this building there is a form for us. Please, please look again."

"Very well," the man sighed. "I suppose we could check. I'll call you."

"No," Mother said, her eyes blazing with determination. "We'll wait in the other room."

"But it could take hours, or even days."

"We'll wait."

We waited. "What if they close?" I asked Mother.

"We'll wait."

I knew better than to argue when I saw the determined look in her eyes.

It was nearly five o'clock when once more the secretary called us and we were shown into the consul's office.

"You were right," he declared, beaming. "Your form was in another part of the office. What can you expect, with all this confusion? Well, now all you have to do is get some photographs of your children and yourself, and then you shall have your passports."

"Oh, good heavens, I forgot all about that," Mother groaned.

"One more day won't really matter," the consul said, smiling. "You can have it done first thing in the morning, and by noon you'll have your passports in your hands."

The next morning we were waiting outside the door when the photographer opened his shop. We waited impatiently as purposefully, slowly, he drew up the shades, turned on the lights and unlocked the door. He was a small man, hardly taller than I, with thin stooped shoulders and a stiff moustache.

"We must have passport photographs immediately," Mother told him, when we were shown inside.

He took off his glasses and began to wipe them slowly with a tiny piece of cloth, over and over again. "No, you cannot. You cannot have them until—well, perhaps near the end of the week," he said, lingering over each word.

"Come now," Mother said pleasantly, "it must be a fairly simple process. Don't you develop the pictures right here?"

"Oh, yes, that we do," the man replied. "I have all the newest equipment—yes, I have a darkroom, just newly outfitted. Would you like to see?"

Mother sighed and gave a helpless look at the ceiling.

"We must have the pictures today," she repeated. She reached inside her purse, took out a bill and pressed it

into the man's hand. "Perhaps you can make an exception and have the pictures ready today. You see, these children have not seen their father for a very long time."

"Ah, well, so," the man mused, "I suppose it could be done. I do suppose I could—try. But at least two hours. Absolutely, I cannot do it any faster."

"Fine," Mother said, smiling.

Each of us in turn sat on the high stool that stood in front of a large white screen, waiting while the photographer fussed over his lights and his camera until finally he was satisfied.

With Annie he spent so much time trying to get her to smile, wriggling his fingers and clicking his tongue, that I blurted out, "Honestly, Annie, if you don't smile I'm going to shake you!"

Annie gave me the funniest silliest grin I have ever seen, but the photographer thought it was perfect, and he let the lens click.

While we waited, we walked until we were shivering with cold. It had snowed in the night, not heavily, but enough to leave mounds of snow against the buildings.

"Let's make a snowman," Mother said suddenly, and I stopped to stare at her. "Right here?" I asked. "On the street?"

"Why not?" she said, laughing. "Come on. Don't be so stuffy, Lisa!"

Annie and Ruth had already begun, and although we had no mittens, we rushed to form the snow into a huge ball, patting it down, adding more, until our man was as tall as Mother.

"We need eyes," Mother directed. "Annie, find some

little pebbles. Look, we'll use this twig. It's his cigar!" She took off her brown felt hat and put it on the snowman's head and stood back, laughing.

Since we had left Germany, I had not seen Mother so gay.

People stopped to smile as they went by, and several nodded, "*Grüss Gott!*"

It ended, of course, with Ruth and Annie and I throwing snowballs at each other, and even Mother tossed a few, one landing right on my head. I laughed until my eyes were blurred. It was so funny to see Mother standing there, wearing her prim traveling suit, but her hair flying in all directions, and her hat crumpled under her arm, sending snowballs flying with perfect aim.

I wondered what the photographer must have thought of us when we returned to the shop, our clothes damp and rumpled, all of us still laughing.

Our photographs were ready. Outside Mother opened the small envelope to see our pictures. "They do resemble us," Mother said, laughing again, "but what expressions!" Then, neatly folded among the photographs, Mother found the bill she had given the photographer to encourage him to hurry.

"How very nice of him," she exclaimed.

"Shouldn't we go back and thank him?" I suggested.

Mother paused, then shook her head. "No," she said. "I don't think he would like that. He wanted me to find the money later."

"Everybody is nice to us," Annie said, beaming.

"You be nice in the consul's office," Mother told her, "and don't chatter."

But the moment we entered the office, Annie ran around the desk, and the consul held out his arms and took her onto his lap.

"Can I go to America now?" Annie asked. "Can I see my Papa?"

"And who are you, Miss?" the consul asked with mock surprise.

"Annie Platt. My Papa's waiting for me in America. But," she added soberly, "I don't think I remember his face."

"I'm sure he remembers yours," the consul said.

He took up four slim green books and handed them to Mother. "Your passports, Frau Platt," he said, smiling. "You're on your way."

Mother held the passports tightly in her hand and looked at them for a long moment before she put them in her purse.

"Do you know," she said softly, "how it feels to have these in my hands?"

He nodded. "I know."

We had all supposed that we would leave on the very next ship, but it was already filled, and the next one too. We were to wait five more weeks, until the middle of January.

"That means you'll be here for Christmas!" Erica said happily, and for days before the holiday Frau Werfel baked and cleaned and hustled off to town, returning with gaily wrapped packages. With Herr Werfel, Erica and I went to the edge of a pine grove to cut down the Christmas tree. On Christmas Eve Mother and Ruth and Annie and I helped the Werfels trim the tree. It was a new experience for me, since we do not celebrate Christmas. But we all knew the Christmas carols and sang them together, watching the candles shine on the beautiful tree.

"It's good to have you with us," I heard Frau Werfel say to Mother, and Mother nodded.

"We are lucky," she said. "So many people have helped us."

There were gifts for everyone, cologne for Mother, and for me and Ruth, matching sweaters of light blue with a white snowflake design. For Annie there was a doll with real hair.

"What are you going to name her?" we all asked, laughing.

"This one," she said promptly, "will be *Erica.*"

At school I had made felt bookmarks for everyone, cut into animal shapes with beads for eyes. Frau Werfel's was in the shape of a poodle, with tufts of black wooly curls.

"I'll always treasure this, Lisa," she said softly. "Someday you'll come back to Switzerland, I hope. Maybe you'll be grown-up then. What a wonderful reunion we'll have, eh? And you'll see, I'll still have your lovely gift."

The next day we went to visit Erica's aunt, and she had a present for me too, a little pocket diary bound in red leather. "This new year will be one adventure after the other for you," she said. "You'll have much to tell in your diary."

All the months away from Papa I had thought only of seeing him again, but as the day of leaving drew closer, I realized how hard it would be say good-bye once more. In America I would be truly a foreigner. How would I speak to the people there? In Switzerland we were at least familiar in language, and we were near enough to Germany to telephone.

Mother did telephone Berlin the day before we were to leave. She called from the Werfels' house, telling me in a casual tone, "I just want to talk to my mother again before we sail." From the other room I heard her speaking, and she said again and again, "Yes, truly I will send for you, Mother. Yes, of course you'll be able to leave. It won't be difficult, since I'll be in America already. Now don't you worry, Mother. I'll send for you. Good-bye, Mother. Good-bye."

For a long time afterward Mother walked by herself in the garden. I wanted to go to her, but Frau Werfel stopped me gently with a hand on my shoulder. "I think your mother would like to be alone with her thoughts for a while, Lisa."

I knew what she must be thinking. Every minute on that ocean liner would take us further away from the danger that awaited Europe, taking us to safety, with no help to give those who stayed behind.

Are You My Papa?

DURING THE LAST WEEK before we left Frau Werfel sat for hours at her sewing machine, and when it was time to pack, my suitcase was filled with new clothes. Everything I had brought from Germany was threadbare, except for my coat. On the last day Herr Werfel took me to Zurich to buy new shoes, sturdy brown oxfords and also a pair of white party slippers.

"But do you think I'll need party shoes?" I asked hesitantly.

"A young lady like you?" he said. "Of course!"

Annie, too, was newly outfitted, and when we all met at the station, I saw to my surprise that Ruth was wearing silk stockings and shoes with a slight heel. She wore a new traveling suit, and her hair had been cut and curled. My sister, incredibly, my sister had grown up, and I hadn't even noticed! It seemed so strange to see her like this, more absorbed than ever with her own thoughts; and

when she said good-bye to the Kunst family, I saw the
boy lean toward her briefly for a kiss.

The railroad station was filled with the commotion of
arrivals and partings. Great engines steamed, and their
shrill whistles pierced the air, while the loudspeaker rum-
bled continually, "Last call . . . train for Paris leaving
on track 17 . . . all aboard, please. All aboard."

"Grüss Gott! Grüss Gott!" Our Swiss friends kissed us
good-bye, and just before I mounted the high iron steps
of the train, Frau Werfel pressed a large box of choco-
lates into my hands.

I saw Erica waving as the train moved down the track,
and I waved back until she was out of sight. Annie chat-
tered to herself as she looked through her new picture
book, but for Mother and Ruth and me there was nothing
we could say. I took out my little diary and wrote, "At
last we are on our way to America." I looked at the
words, repeated them to myself, but I felt no excitement
and no joy—only a great lump in my throat.

I slept and awakened to the confusion of another arrival.

"We're in Paris!" Ruth cried, shaking me. "Oh, I can't
wait to see it. Will we see the Eiffel tower?" she asked
Mother. "Oh, I want to see everything. I've heard it's so
beautiful."

To me it was just the same as any railroad station—
dirty and old and busy, and the many porters sped right
past us, although Mother signaled and tried to speak in
her halting French. At last Mother caught the arm of one
of the porters and showed him an address that someone
from the ticket office had scribbled on a piece of paper.

The man glanced at the note, nodded briskly and scooped up our bags. We ran behind him and soon found ourselves in a bus filled with travelers.

The sun was just setting, and Ruth and I strained to see the sights, crowding together at the window. "Can't we get off, Mother?" she begged. "Can't we *see* Paris? What good is it looking from a window?"

"We're not in Paris for sight-seeing, Ruth," Mother said. "We're to go to a special place overnight, and to-morrow morning we'll take the train to LeHavre. Oh, Ruth, don't be disappointed. Just think, we're sailing to-morrow!"

But Ruth was scowling, and suddenly she gave me a sharp pinch and grumbled, "Quit pushing, Lisa. Honestly, you're a pest."

Mother gave me a warning look. Don't fight, it said, not now. I moved away from the window.

The bus stopped beside a row of flat wooden buildings, like army barracks, set in a grim, dusty enclosure of wire fencing.

"It looks like a prison!" Ruth gasped as we followed the others through the narrow corridors of the building.

"This room." Someone pointed, and we went in.

Inside there were three iron beds, each covered with a single army blanket. There was nothing else in the room, no chair, no shelf, only a bulb hanging down from a long black wire to show the raw timbers of the walls.

"I'm freezing," Ruth muttered.

"Can't you stand it for one night?" Mother demanded.

We lined up to receive our supper: a stew of potatoes and green beans with slivers of meat. After that we lined up again for the washroom. People did not speak to each other or introduce themselves. By tomorrow they would be strangers again, sailing on different ships to different places.

Annie slept with me, and we kept each other warm by huddling close together. We were awakened by a sharp blast, like a factory whistle, and I jumped out into the cold.

Mother was already dressed, and she hastily packed our pajamas. "Hurry!" she told us repeatedly. "Ruth, hurry up. Stop combing your hair, for goodness sake. Lisa, help Annie get dressed."

Annie was still half-asleep, and I had to push and pull to get her clothes on, for she kept popping her thumb back into her mouth. As soon as we were on the bus, Annie began to wail. "I have to go to the bathroom!"

"You can't. You'll have to wait," I told her, "until we're on the train."

It was still pitch black outside, and it felt as if we were driving through a tunnel all the way to the station. In the train there were dim night lights.

It was a short ride to LeHavre, where the ship waited. Again we were in a huge station room, and again our luggage and papers had to be inspected.

"I'll never travel again," Ruth mumbled, "never. I've had enough. It's nothing but waiting and getting up at the crack of dawn to go to another waiting room."

I had never seen so many people rushing and shouting, all carrying bundles. Even the little children were laden with bags and boxes, Annie, too, with her dolls and things.

"I want to go see the ship," Annie said, hopping up and down impatiently.

"We have to wait here for Mother," I told her. "Just sit down."

Through the windows I could see the huge ship bobbing up and down like a giant cork in the gray water. I could see barrels and boxes being brought up the ramp, and others being hoisted aboard with a huge crane. "Just look at it," I said. "Look, Annie."

Annie! She had been there, right beside me! "Ruth, where's Annie?" I shouted above the noise.

Ruth stared at me. *"Where? You* were watching her. I don't know where she went. Why didn't you watch her? Why didn't you hold on to her?" Her voice rose sharply, and I strained to see through the crowds, my panic mounting. How, among all those people, could we find her? And Mother—what would I say to Mother?

"Find her! Find her!" Ruth shouted at me.

"Maybe she's at the candy stand," I said, steadying my voice. "I'll go and look."

"No! Mother told us to . . ."

"You stay here and tell her . . . tell her."

I broke away and rushed over to the candy stand, but no Annie. I called, but my voice was lost in the sounds of other voices, and when I came back to Ruth, Mother was standing beside her, her face white and hard.

"You two sit here," she said, "and this time obey me!"

I wanted to explain. She had been there and then she was gone. I wanted to tell Mother I was sorry, for all the good that would do!

"Just stay here. I'll find her," Mother said.

"They'll sail without us," Ruth said over and over again while we waited. "They won't wait. I knew something like this would happen."

I tried to concentrate on looking for Annie, and on ignoring Ruth's accusing moans. "They'll sail without us. It's all your fault."

At last I couldn't bear it and I wanted to shake Ruth with all my might. "Stop it!" It was not a shout, although inside I felt that I was bursting. "You are the oldest. Just stop that awful moaning and behave yourself!"

She only gasped, and in that instant Mother was beside us, grasping Annie tightly by the arm. Annie was silent,

red-eyed, sniffling only a little, and rubbing the place where she had been spanked.

"Now," Mother said, drawing a deep breath, "we will go to the ship."

Our ship was a large French ocean liner, as large as several city blocks, and in every way like a whole town afloat. Whatever we wanted, there it was: games on the deck, meals we had once dreamed about, music in the lounge at night, and dancing. There were movies, and we all went to see them at night, even Annie. They were the first films I had seen in nearly a year, wonderful, funny films and stories that I loved.

It was like one long vacation from day to day, until on the fifth day the air grew cold, the wind began to blow, whistling along the deck, and the ship tipped and swayed from side to side.

Annie thought it was a joke to try to walk on the rolling, pitching deck, until at lunch she became very pale and whispered, "I think I'm going to be sick."

"Nonsense," Mother said quickly, giving her a piece of bread to eat. "You're just hungry. Only babies get seasick."

I didn't say anything, but it was clear by the empty places in the dining room that nearly half the passengers couldn't face the thought of a meal, and even as we ate our lunch others left hastily, their hands over their mouths.

At the evening meal only a handful of people appeared. Glasses slid clear across the table. We clutched at the hand rails as we walked, sometimes being tilted from one side of the passageway to the other.

Everywhere there was talk of the storm, and passengers crowded around the purser's desk, anxiously wanting to know when it would end, when we would arrive in America. A sign was posted announcing a delay in our arrival. We would be a whole day late, due to the storm, and maybe two.

All the next day the wind blew in fierce gusts, and by noon Ruth lay in her bunk, unable to rise. "Go away," she moaned. "I can't eat. Go away. I'm dying."

"Seasick," Mother said lightly; and Annie sang out, "Only babies get seasick, Ruth," whereupon Ruth threw down a slipper, which Annie dodged.

Again we stood at the purser's desk, and this time the people were all talking at once, frantic about the delay. Two elderly women were in a state of near-hysteria. "We'll sink, I know it," one cried out.

And the other wept, "How can fate be so cruel? We'll never see America. Never."

"I'd like to send a message," Mother told the purser when our turn had come. "My husband will be planning to meet the ship, and I want to tell him about the delay."

"I'm sorry," said the purser. "We cannot send any private messages. Your husband will probably be in touch with the steamship company, or he will find out through the newspapers."

"He'll check with the company," I told Mother. "Papa always checks things like that. Don't worry."

"I hope so," Mother said, frowning. Then she smiled at me. "You're right, dear. It's silly to fret about it."

By morning the winds had settled, the sea was calm. People began to sit on the deck again. The next day, it was said, the next day we would see land.

Night brought a change in mood, a great excitement, an air of celebration. People danced in the dining room and the ship's orchestra played gay tunes, while newly found friends exchanged addresses.

The next morning everyone was up early, crowding at the rails, straining to see the first glimpse of land. We stood close together, the four of us, and several times there was a false cry—land!—then disappointment and Annie's questions, "When? When?"

For nearly two hours we stood. Then, suddenly there began a murmur, rising to a shout, until it spread the length and breadth of the ship. "America! America! I see it! Look!"

People shouted wildly as they pressed closer and closer to the rail to see the dim, distant outline of the Statue of Liberty. Parents held their little children high on their shoulders that they might see, and I strained on tiptoe, shouting at the top of my lungs while I stared at the statue and the buildings in the distance, thinking it might be a dream, but the throbbing inside me was real, very real.

"I'll never forget this sight," Mother whispered.

Beside us an old woman wept, her head pressed against her husband's shoulder. "America! God be praised!"

On and on the shouting, the waving, the tears. The ship seemed to rock and sway with it, and then I heard the first strains of music from the ship's orchestra. If people didn't know the words, they sang the tune,

"America! America! God shed His grace on thee."

Amid the streaming crowd we made our way down the gangplank, and when we stood on firm ground, my legs still swayed from the motion of the sea. I saw a bearded young man beside me stoop down and gather up a handful of soil, and everything he felt showed in his eyes.

For a few moments we stood lost in the tangle of people, all waiting for someone, all wondering where to go. We began to walk, following painted arrows. We passed through many rooms and saw many people who looked at our papers, and then, suddenly, Mother stopped short.

I can't remember what I said or did, but I heard the shriek from Ruth, and I suppose my own voice mingled with hers, "Papa! Papa!" It was as if I had been hurled through space and dropped here, straight into Papa's arms.

With all the crowd milling past, Mother and Papa drew close in a long embrace. At last Papa exclaimed, "Annie, darling, don't you know me?" For Annie hung back, clutching Mother's hand.

Now Annie came forward and said with a strange, shy look, "Are you my Papa? Are you really?"

"Oh, yes, my little Annie! I am, and I love you." Papa scooped her up into his arms, and Annie buried her face in his neck. "Yes," she sighed. "Oh, Papa!"

"Come now," Papa said, with his arm around me. "There's time for talk later. I want to hear everything. But now," he said, his voice husky, "let's go home. It's just a little apartment, and I don't have much furniture yet."

"It will be beautiful," Mother whispered.

Home, I thought, home was a feeling more than a place. I gave Papa's hand a squeeze and he smiled down at me. Yes, we were home.

The Varieties of the Meditative Experience

DANIEL GOLEMAN

*A Dutton
Paperback*

E. P. DUTTON
New York

Library of Congress Cataloging in Publication Data

Goleman, Daniel.
   The varieties of the meditative experience.

   Includes bibliography and index.
   1. Meditation.   I. Title.
BL627.G66   1977   291.4'3   76-46306

ISBN: 0-525-47448-X

Published simultaneously in Canada by Clarke, Irwin & Company Limited,
Toronto and Vancouver

10 9 8 7 6 5 4 3 2 1
First Edition

To Neemkaroli Baba,
for Anasuya, Govinddas, and Hanuman

CONTENTS

FOREWORD

Swiftly arose and spread around me the peace and
joy and knowledge that passes all the art and argument of the earth; and I know that the hand of God
is the elder hand of my own, and I know that the
Spirit of God is the eldest brother of my own . . .
                                    —Walt Whitman
                                    Leaves of Grass

I have been in that heaven the most illumined
By light from Him, and seen things which to utter
He who returns hath neither skill nor knowledge;
For as it nears the object of its yearning
Our intellect is overwhelmed so deeply
It can never retrace the path that it followed.
But whatsoever of the holy kingdom
Was in the power of memory to treasure
Will be my theme until the song is ended.
                                    —Dante
                                    Inferno

Most of us do not have quite such a vivid and compelling experience as did Dante or Whitman, yet you and I do have moments when we become disoriented in time and/or space; moments when we seem to be at the doorway to another state of being; moments when our own personal viewpoint seems trivial and we sense a greater intuitive harmony in the universe. Perhaps your experiences have come after becoming "lost" in a compelling film, book, piece of art or music, or church service; perhaps after a period of reverie near a brook, a mountain, or the ocean; possibly as the result of a high fever; at the moment of a traumatic event; through drugs or childbirth; from looking at the stars or falling in love. What is so provocative about these moments is that we are out of personal control, and yet all seems harmonious and all right.

In these experiences we sense, though usually cannot articulate, a more profound meaning to our lives. The *sine qua non* of these experiences is that they are not mediated by our intellect. Often, however, immediately after they pass, we return to our analytic minds and attempt to label what has happened. And there is where the trouble begins. Disputes about labels have led to incredible human misunderstandings, even culminating in religious wars. Once we have labeled our experiences, these labels take on power of their own through their association with profound moments and, in addition, they give our egos the security that we know what's what, that we are in control. Some labels treat the experiences as psychological apparition: "I was out of my mind," a "hallucination," a "dissociated state," "surfacing of the unconscious mind," "hysteria," "delusion." Other labels, focusing on the content, imply a mystical or spiritual event: "God came to me"; "I came into the spirit"; "I felt the Presence of Christ," or "a spirit guide"; "I understood the Tao," or "the Dharma," or "the Divine Law."

In 1961 I became involved in a labeling dispute. Having ingested psilocybin, I had the most profound experience of my life to date. The context was religio-mystical, and a spiritual label seemed appropriate. However, I was at the time a social science professor at Harvard, and thus was quite sympathetic to labels that implied that the chemical was a psychotomimetic—that is, it made you crazy. If the chemical didn't make me crazy, I suspected the labeling conflict (often within myself) would ultimately do so. Carl Jung describes the insanity of Richard Wilhelm, translator of the *I Ching*, to be the result of his attempt to incorporate two disparate cultures into his being simultaneously.

Outwardly, the battle revolved around the little psilocybin mushroom. The Mexican Curanderos labeled it *Teonanactyl*—the flesh of the Gods—useful for divinitory and mystical experiences. Humphry Osmond made the labeling a little more palatable for the Western mind by inventing the word *psychedelic*, meaning "mind manifesting." The psychiatric community's label of the same mushroom was "a psychotomimetic triptomine derivative," of interest only for the experimental induction of pseudo-schizophrenic states. Using one labeling system, we were explorers into the mystical realms tried by Moses, Mohammed, Christ, and Buddha. According to the other, we were damn fools, driving ourselves insane.

There was an intuitive validity to the use of the spiritual metaphors. Corroboration for these interpretations came from obvious parallels between the immediate experiences with psychedelics and the mystic literature. I resolved the almost unbearable dissonance by shifting in the direction of a spiritual interpretation. For five years we attempted to find labels that would optimize the value of these experiences for mankind. The issue had significant implications for the politics of human consciousness. Using one set of metaphors, every state of mind not continuous with rational, normal, waking consciousness was to be treated as deviant—as a reflection of lack of adjustment. The other set of metaphors treated altered states of consciousness as rare and precious opportunities for humanity to delve into greater realms of its own potential awareness. As such, these experiences ought to be cultivated rather than suppressed, even if they create a threat to existing social institutions. By raising this issue we were following in the footsteps of William James who, in 1902, wrote of altered states of consciousness in *Varieties of Religious Experience:*

> No account of the universe in its totality can be final, which leaves these other forms of consciousness quite disregarded. How to regard them is the question, for they are so discontinuous with ordinary consciousness. Yet they may determine attitudes, though they cannot furnish formulas, and open a region though they fail to give a map. At any rate, they forbid a premature closing of our accounts with reality.

We came to appreciate the sophistication and sensitivity of Eastern systems of labeling altered states of consciousness. For approximately 4000 years Eastern religions had been evolving maps and charts for the terrain of inner exploration. We could understand some of these, while others were based on cultural perspectives too alien to our own to be useful. In 1967 I went to India because of the attraction of these maps and I wanted to find a way—or perhaps a teacher—through which I could utilize the maps more effectively. I hoped then to be able to stabilize these altered states of consciousness and integrate them with normal everyday life. None of us had been able to do so with psychedelics.

In India I met Neemkaroli Baba, who was far more than I could have hoped for. He lived in the state called sahaj samadhi, in which altered states of consciousness were an integral part of his life. In his presence one had the feeling of boundless space and timelessness, as well as vast love and compassion. Maharaji, as we called him, once ingested a huge dose of psychedelics and, to my complete surprise, nothing happened. If his awareness was not limited to any place, then there was nowhere to go, for he was already here, in all its possibilities.

Seeing one and being one are two different things—and I'd much rather be one than see one. The question was how to effect the transformation from whom I thought I was to whom or what Maharaji was or wasn't. I took everything that came out of Maharaji's mouth as specific instruction, although I wasn't capable of following all of them. But then it got more complicated because he gave conflicting instructions. Now I realized I was confronting a teacher, like a Zen koan, who was not effective so long as one remained bound to the rational. From where I was standing, in my rational, righteous, analytic mind, I couldn't get to where I thought I was going. What to do?

In the presence of Maharaji I experienced my heart opening and felt previously unexperienced waves of ever more consuming love. Perhaps this was the way—drowning in love. But my mind would not be quiet. The social scientist—that skeptic—was not to be drowned without a struggle. Using all the tools, including my sensual desire and intellect, as well as guilt and sense of responsibility, my ego structure fought back. For example, in the temples in which Maharaji stayed, there were statues of Hanuman, a monkey-God who had all power due to his total devotion to God. Hanuman is deeply loved and honored by Maharaji's devotees. I sat before an eight-foot cement statue of a monkey, painted red, and I sang to him and meditated upon him. Every now and then a voice would observe, "Ah, sitting worshipping a cement monkey idol. You've really gone over the edge." This was the inner battle, for which the Bhagavad Gita is a metaphor.

My Buddhist friends said that the problem was a matter of discipline of mind and, upon questioning, Maharaji affirmed that if you brought your mind to one-pointedness you would know God. Perhaps that was what I had to do. So I started to meditate in earnest. The devotional path allowed too much play of mind, and I had to get tough with myself. In 1971 I began serious meditation practice in Bodh Gaya, where Buddha had been enlightened. In a series of ten day courses I, along with about 100 Westerners, was gently guided into Theravadan Buddhist meditation techniques—the ultimate in simplicity of practice.

During this period I met Anagarika Munindra, a Therevadan teacher who seemed, in his almost transparent quality, to reflect the mindful, light equanimity to which the method pointed. I was exhilarated by my first tastes of a new deep tranquility. I asked to learn more, and he introduced me to the Visuddhimagga, part of Buddhism's scholastic tradition. Finally, I, a Western psychologist, was truly humbled intellectually. For I saw what *psyche logos* was really about. Here, in this one volume, was an exquisitely articulated and inclusive category system of mental conditions, plus a philosophy and method for extricating your awareness from the tyranny of your own mind. Here was the labeling system I had been looking for since 1961. It was amazingly free of value judgments and thus lent itself to serving as a way of comparing disparate metaphorical systems concerning altered consciousness. I drank the book like a fine brandy.

Though my intellect was delighted by the system underlying the practices, I found myself becoming dry and resistant to the meditation itself. Was this an error in the way I was practicing the method, or was it a clue that this form of spiritual practice was not my way? I happily left Bodh Gaya to fulfill a promise to attend a bhakti celebration and also to find Maharaji, who was my Guru. You may ask why, if Maharaji, a Hindu, is my Guru, I would go to study Buddhist meditation in the first place—rather than stay with him. Well, the answer was that he wouldn't let me stay with him, and he continuously reiterated "*Sub Ek*" (all is one). He spoke at length of Christ and Buddha, and then threw me out. Therefore, when I was away from Maharaji, it did not seem inconsistent to pursue other traditions. For in the method of Guru, all of the other methods fed the process of purification that would allow me to merge with my beloved Maharaji. To merge would be the end of the journey.

When I left Bodh Gaya I had arranged to spend the summer with Munindra in Kosani, a small Himalayan village. At the last minute he could not come, so Dan Goleman and I, and about twenty others, practiced a collection of Buddhist, Hindu, and Christian methods during that summer. In the course of it, in conversation with Dan, I found that he and I held much in common. We were both trained as psychologists; both connected with Harvard; both had the same Guru; and both had an appreciation of Buddhist theory and meditation practice. He was struggling, as I had been, to integrate these disparate parts of our lives.

There were important differences between Dan and me. Among them was the fact that he was motivated to bring what he could, from these experiences and practices, home to the scientific community. I, on the other hand, had long since left academia. Dan could do the intellectual task of integration. His astute scientific mind, his devotion to Maharaji, and his appreciation of the Buddhist tradition ideally prepared him to provide a needed overview of spiritual paths and the states of consciousness they traverse. As you will find in this book, he has done just that.

When I seek to understand what has happened to me, where I am going, or what is becoming of me, then this book delights me. On the other hand, when I meditate upon my guru in my heart, such books as this are irrelevant. Just as you can't make love if you think too much about it, so you can't *be* love if you think too much about it.

Some will be unhappy with this book, feeling that Dan has given short shrift to the subtleties of their particular method of meditation. For example, from my point of view, nothing he has said here has much to do with the quality of grace which comes from my guru to me. But this is not his intent, for his is an impractical view of the unity of paths that holds no special brief for any one of them. Those who consider their path the only way will be especially upset. Here I refer not only to obvious cases, such as Christian fundamentalists or the Krishna Consciousness organization, but to the subtle snobbery that permeates almost all traditions. Apparently each of us, in our insecurity, must feel that his or her way is *the* best way. A more mature perception is that one method is the best way for me, but other paths suit other people. This book exemplifies that open attitude.

Once we get beyond the emotional attachments to our own methods, we will be able to appreciate this work. It is the beginnings of a systematic semantic foundation for appreciating the universality of the spiritual journey, similar to the philosophical foundation set forth by Aldous Huxley in his *Perennial Philosophy*. And, certainly, when we can recognize the commonalities, then we can honor the differences.

RAM DASS

Barre, Massachusetts

PREFACE

I WROTE the major part of this book while living in a tiny Himalayan village during monsoon season, 1971. For the previous several months I had been studying with Indian yogis and swamis, Tibetan lamas, and southern Buddhist laymen and monks. Strange terms and concepts assailed me: "samadhi," "jhana," "turiya," "nirvana," and a host of others used by these teachers to explain their spiritual paths. Each path seemed to be in essence the same as every other path, but each had its own way of explaining how to travel it and what major landmarks to expect.

I was confused. Things first began to jell in my understanding, though, with a remark by Joseph Goldstein, a teacher of insight meditation, at Bodh Gaya. It's simple mathematics, he said: All meditation systems either aim for One or Zero—union with God or emptiness. The path to the One is through concentration on Him, to the Zero is insight into the voidness of one's mind. This was my first guideline for sorting out meditation techniques.

A month or two later I found myself sitting out the monsoon rains in that hilltop village. Five of us had come there to study with a meditation teacher during the rains. He never showed up. Instead, there came a steady trickle of Westerners, sent by my Guru, Neemkaroli Baba, to "be with Ram Dass," one of the five of us there. By the end of monsoon season there had gathered thirty or forty Western pilgrims. Among them were students of virtually every major spiritual tradition: of the various kinds of Indian yogas, of different sects of Tibetan Buddhism, of Sufism, of Christian contemplation, of Zen, of Gurdjieff, of Krishnamurti, and of innumerable individual swamis, gurus, yogis, and babas. Each brought his or her own small treasure of favored books and his trove of private anecdotes. From these literary and personal sources, I sorted out for myself the main similarities and differences among all these meditation paths.

The writings that evolved into this book began as explanations to myself. I needed maps, and each of these traditions had its own to offer. At various times each of these maps has helped me find my way in meditation or made me feel safe in unfamiliar territory. None is complete of itself, for all of them together will fail to explain every facet of any one meditator's experience. Each of us has his own private road to follow, though for periods we may cover well-traveled paths. The maps included here are among the best traveled. These are popular routes but by no means define the whole terrain. This mental territory is mostly unmapped; each of us is an explorer.

Foremost among my debts in writing this book is to Neemkaroli Baba, who inspired me to take seriously my own path. My understanding owes much to conversations and encounters with Ram Dass, Anagarika Munindra, Chogyam Trungpa, Bhagavan Das, Ananda Mayee Ma, Kunu Rinpoche, Krishnamurti, S. N. Goenka,

Swami Muktananda, Nyanaponika Mahathera, Bhikku Nyanajivako, Joseph Goldstein, Herbert Guenther, K. K. Sah, Father Theophane, Yogi Ramagyadas, Charles Reeder, and many others who actively follow these paths themselves. The editors of the *Journal of Transpersonal Psychology* encouraged me to put my work into the form of articles, from which parts of this book are abridged. My travels in Asia were as a Harvard predoctoral fellow and then as a research training fellow of the Social Science Research Council. My wife and children have suffered with me the long hours required to put this book into its final shape. To all those who have helped me, I am deeply grateful.

Daniel Goleman

Woodstock, New York
Guru Poornima Day, 1976

INTRODUCTION

MEDITATION HAS COME to the West in a big way. At this writing, more than a thousand people a day are starting Transcendental Meditation (TM), the largest group in America. An estimated 775,000 people have been instructed in TM. It is telling that "TM" is a registered trademark: Meditation has become big business.

Such forms of meditation offer us something this culture needs but lacks: While we have mastered the environment, we have just begun to tame our inner world. But meditation has been for millenia the path for the person who seeks to go beyond the limiting goals of the everyday world. Ironically, meditation is now touted as the best way to fulfill those everyday goals and live out worldy visions.

In the rush to capture the market of would-be meditators, some organizations have spread distortions about meditation. The notion, for example, that only one kind of meditation can change one for the better, while others cannot, masks the basic sameness of all meditation techniques. I hope to straighten out such confusions by de-

scribing a dozen major meditation techniques, recogniz-
ing genuine differences as well as similarities.

All these meditation traditions promise to change us;
all agree meditation is the path to that change. In the first
section, I describe the specifics of these changes and the
major landmarks of altered states of consciousness along
the way, from the viewpoints of a dozen major traditions.

A word of caution: These states are quite rare. They
never happen to the majority of meditators. Their likeli-
hood increases with one's length of experience in meditation and a host of other factors, such as depth of concentration, purity and stillness of mind, zeal and energy.
The everyday meditative struggles and pleasures of most
of us are not altered states, though they sometimes approach the limits of our ordinary awareness. Those few
among us, however, who have undergone some of these
altered states will find in the second section reassuring
guideposts to events for which our culture knows no safe
context.

A true altered state requires a qualitative break with
the normal range of one's consciousness. The striking experiences that come to most of us during meditation—deep relaxation, intense body pain, or vivid day-
dreams—are not altered states in this sense, just
unusually intense feelings. The so-called "relaxation response," for example, is simply another term for a normal physiological state in which the body is relaxed, re-
storing itself from stress or exertion. This calm state is a
pleasant experience, but it has little to do with the meditative states that transcend the normal limits of sensory
awareness and that are the basis of religious mysticism.

The founder and early followers of every world religion had altered-state experiences. Moses receiving the

Ten Commandments, Jesus' forty-day vigil in the wilderness, Allah's desert visions, and Buddha's enlightenment under the Bo Tree all bespeak extraordinary states of consciousness. These transcendental states inspired churches, monasteries, and orders of monks and have spawned theologies. But too often the institutions and theologies outlive the transmission of the original states that generated them. Without these living experiences, the institutions are pointless, the theologies empty. In my view, the modern crisis of established religions is due to the absence in our age of the personal experience of these transcendental states, the living spirit at the common base of all religions.

The unity of this transcendental experience is veiled by the different names given it by various religions. The "Kingdom of Heaven," the "Other Shore," and the "Pure Land" are all geographical metaphors for this transcendental mental space. As we learn more about states of consciousness, such seeming differences turn out to reflect discrepancies in outlook rather than in the innate nature of the states themselves. Idiosyncracies of belief create false differences. In meditation, as elsewhere, people apply the names they know to what they see. A turn-of-the-century example is R. M. Bucke, who spontaneously entered an altered state while riding home after an evening of reading Whitman's poetry and subsequently saw his experience in terms of "cosmic consciousness." In the present book, by showing clearly the unity of that experience, we can help to reduce the confusion created by the numerous terms.

As an old Zen saying puts it:

From of old there were not two paths. "Those who have arrived" all walked the same road.

THE VARIETIES OF THE
MEDITATIVE EXPERIENCE

PART ONE

THE VISUDDHIMAGGA:
A MAP FOR INNER SPACE

THE CLASSICAL Buddhist *Abhidhamma* is probably the broadest and most detailed traditional psychology of states of consciousness. In the fifth century A.D., the monk Buddhaghosa summarized the portion of Abhidhamma about meditation into the *Visuddhimagga*, the "Path to Purification" (Nanamoli, 1964).* Buddhaghosa explains that the ultimate "purification" should be strictly understood as *nibbana* (sanskrit: *nirvana*), which is an altered state of consciousness.

The Visuddhimagga was for centuries part of an oral textbook of Buddhist philosophy and psychology that aspiring monks memorized verbatim. Because it is so detailed and complete, the Visuddhimagga gives us a comprehensive picture of a single viewpoint regarding meditation. As such, it will give a good background and basis of comparison for understanding other kinds of meditation, the subject matter of Part II. The Visuddhimagga begins with advice on the best surroundings and attitudes

* Full references to these and other books mentioned in the text can be found in the Bibliography.

1

for meditation. It then describes the specific ways the meditator trains his attention and the landmarks he encounters in traversing the meditative path to the nirvanic state. It ends with the psychological consequences for the meditator of his experience of nirvana.*

The Visuddhimagga is a traditional recipe book for meditation, but it does not necessarily tell us about the specific practices of contemporary Theravadan Buddhists. The progression it describes is an ideal type and as such need not conform to the experiences of any given person. But experienced meditators will most certainly recognize familiar landmarks here and there.

1. PREPARATION FOR MEDITATION

Practice begins with *sila* (virtue or moral purity). This systematic cultivation of virtuous thought, word, and deed focuses the meditator's efforts for the alteration of consciousness in meditation. Unvirtuous thoughts, for example, sexual fantasies or anger, lead to distractedness during meditation. They are a waste of time and energy for the serious meditator. Psychological purification means paring away distracting thoughts.

The purification process is one of three major divisions

---

* In addition to the excellent translation from the original Pali by Bhikku Nanamoli (1976), other contemporary commentaries on the Visuddhimagga consulted include: Bhikku Soma (1949), E. Conze (1956), Kalu Rimpoche (1974), Kashyap (1954), Lama Govinda (1969), Ledi Sayadaw (1965), Mahasi Sayadaw (1965, 1970), Narada Thera (1956), Nyanaponika Thera (1949, 1962, 1968), Nyanatiloka (1952a and b, 1972), P. V. Mahathera (1962).

of training in the Buddhist schema, the other two being *samadhi* (meditative concentration) and *puñña* (insight). Insight is understood in the special sense of "seeing things as they are." Purification, concentration, and insight are closely related. Efforts to purify the mind facilitate initial concentration, which enables sustained insight. By developing either concentration or insight, purity becomes, instead of an act of will, effortless and natural for the meditator. Insight reinforces purity, while aiding concentration; strong concentration can have as by-products both insight and purity. The interaction is not linear; the development of any one facilitates the other two. There is no necessary progression, rather a simultaneous spiral of these three in the course of the meditation path. Though the presentation here is of necessity linear, there is a complex interrelation in the meditator's development of purity, concentration, and insight. These are three facets of a single process.

Active purification in the Visuddhimagga tradition begins with the observance of codes of discipline for laity, novices, and fully ordained monks. The precepts for laity are but five: abstaining from killing, stealing, unlawful sexual intercourse, lying, and intoxicants. For novices the list expands to ten, the first five becoming stricter in the process. For monks there are 227 prohibitions and observances regulating every detail of daily monastic life. While the practice of purity varies with one's mode of life, its intent is the same: It is the necessary preparation for meditation.

On one level these are codes for proper social behavior, but that is secondary in importance to the motivational purity that proper behavior foreshadows. Purity is understood not only in the ordinary external sense of propriety but also as the mental attitudes out of which proper speech, action, and thought arise. Thus, for example, the Visuddhimagga urges the meditator, should lustful thoughts arise, immediately to counter those thoughts by contemplating the body in the aspect of loathsomeness. The object is to free the meditator from thoughts of remorse, guilt, or shame, as well as from lust. Behavior is controlled because it affects the mind. Acts of purity are meant to produce a calmed and subdued mind. The purity of morality has only the purity of mind as its goal.

Because a controlled mind is the goal of purity, restraint of the senses is part of purification. The means for this is *sati* (mindfulness). In mindfulness, control of the senses comes through cultivating the habit of simply noticing sensory perceptions, not allowing them to stimulate the mind into thought chains of reaction. Mindfulness is the attitude of paying sensory stimuli only the barest attention. When systematically developed into the practice of *vipassana* (seeing things as they are), mindfulness becomes the avenue to the nirvanic state. In daily practice, mindfulness leads to detachment toward the meditator's own perceptions and thoughts. He becomes an onlooker to his stream of consciousness, weakening the pull to normal mental activity and so preparing the way to altered states.

In the initial stages, before firm grounding in mindfulness, the meditator is distracted by his surroundings. The Visuddhimagga accordingly gives instructions to the would-be meditator for the optimum life style and setting. He must engage in "right livelihood" so that the source of his financial support will not be cause for misgivings; in the case of monks, professions such as astrology, palm reading, and dream interpretation are expressly forbidden, while the life of a mendicant is recommended. Possessions should be kept to a minimum; a monk is to possess only eight articles: three robes, a belt, a begging bowl, a razor, a sewing needle, and sandals. He should take food in moderation, enough to ensure physical health but less than would make for drowsiness. His dwelling should be aloof from the world, a place of solitude; for householders who cannot live in isolation, a room should be set aside for meditation. Undue concern for the body should be avoided, but in case of sickness, the meditator should obtain appropriate medicine. In acquiring the four requisites of possessions, food, dwelling, and medicine, the meditator should get only what is necessary to his well-being. In getting these requisites, he should act without greed, so that even his material necessities will be untainted by impurity.

Since one's own state of mind is affected by the state of mind of one's associates, the serious meditator should surround himself with likeminded people. This is one advantage of a *sangha*, narrowly defined as those who have attained the nirvanic state and, in its widest sense, the community of people on the path. Meditation is helped by the company of mindful or concentrated persons and is harmed by those who are agitated, distracted, and immersed in worldly concerns. Agitated, worldly people are likely to talk in a way that does not lead to detachment, dispassion, or tranquility, qualities the meditator seeks to cultivate. The sort of topics typical of worldly, unprofitable talk are enumerated by the Buddha as (Nyanaponika Thera, 1962: p. 172):

> . . . about kings, thieves, ministers, armies, famine, and war; about eating, drinking, clothing and lodging; about garlands, perfumes, relatives, vehicles, cities and countries; about women and wine, the

gossip of the street and well; about ancestors and various trifles; tales about the origin of the world, talk about things being so or otherwise, and similar matters.

At later stages, the meditator may find to be obstacles what once were aids. The Visuddhimagga lists ten categories of potential attachments, all hindrances to progress in meditation: (1) any fixed dwelling place if its upkeep is the cause of worry, (2) family, if their welfare causes concern, (3) accruing gifts or reputation that involves spending time with admirers, (4) a following of students or being busy with teaching, (5) projects, having "something to do," (6) traveling about, (7) people dear to one whose needs demand attention, (8) illness necessitating undergoing treatment, (9) theoretical studies unaccompanied by practice, and (10) supernormal psychic powers, the practice of which becomes more interesting than meditation. Release from these obligations frees the meditator for single-minded pursuit of meditation: This is "purification" in the sense of freeing the mind from worrisome matters. The life of the monk is designed for this kind of freedom; for the layman, short retreats allow a temporary reprieve.

These ascetic practices are optional in the "middle way" of the Buddha. The serious monk can practice them, should he find any of them helpful. But he must be discreet in their observance, doing them so that they will not attract undue attention. These practices include wearing only robes made of rags; eating only one bowl of food, and just once a day; living in the forest under a tree; dwelling in a cemetery or in the open; sitting up throughout the night. Though optional, the Buddha praises those who follow these modes of living "for the sake of frugality, contentedness, austerity, detachment," while criticizing those who pride themselves on practicing austerities and look down on others who do not. In all facets of training, spiritual pride mars purity. Any gains from asceticism are lost in pride. The goal of purification is simply a mind unconcerned with externals, calm and ripe for meditation.

Entering the Path of Concentration

Purity is the psychological base for concentration. The essence of concentration is nondistractedness; purification is the systematic pruning away of sources of distraction. Now the meditator's work is to attain unification of mind, one-pointedness. The stream of thought is normally random and scattered. The goal of concentration in meditation is to focus the thought flow by fixing the mind on a single object, the meditation topic. In the later stages of concentrative meditation, the mind is not only directed toward the object but finally penetrates it; totally absorbed in it, the mind moves to oneness with the object. When this happens, the object is the only thing in the meditator's awareness.

Any object of attention can be the subject for concentrative meditation, which is simply sustaining a single point of focus. But the character of the object attended to has definite consequences for the outcome of meditation. The Visuddhimagga recommends forty meditation subjects:

—ten *kasinas:* colored wheels about a foot in circumference: earth, water, fire, air, dark blue, yellow, blood-red, white, light, bounded space

—ten *asubhas:* loathsome, decaying corpses; for example, a bloated corpse, a gnawed corpse, a worm-infected corpse, etc., including a skeleton

—ten reflections: on the attributes of the Buddha, the Doctrine, the sangha, peace, one's own purity, one's own liberality, one's own possessions of godly qualities, or on the inevitability of death; contemplation on the thirty-two parts of the body or on in-and-out breathing

—four sublime states: loving-kindness, compassion, joy in the joy of others, and equanimity

—four formless contemplations: of infinite space, infinite consciousness, the realm of nothingness, and the realm of "neither perception nor non perception"; the loathsomeness of food

—the four physical elements: earth, air, fire, water as abstract forces (i.e., extension, motility, heat, cohesion)

Each of these subjects has specific consequences for the nature, depth, and by-products of concentration; meditation on a corpse, for example, becomes very different from contemplating loving-kindness. All of these subjects are suitable for developing concentration to the depth necessary for attaining the nirvanic state. The concentration produced by those of a complicated nature—for example, the attributes of the Buddha—is less unified than that produced by a simple object—for example, the earth kasina, a clay-colored wheel. Apart from the depth of concentration produced by a given meditation subject, each has distinct psychological by-products. The meditation on loving-kindness, for example, has several results: The meditator sleeps and wakes in comfort; he dreams no evil dreams; he is dear to all beings; his mind is easily concentrated; his expression is serene; and he dies unconfused.

The Buddha saw that persons of different temperaments are more suited to some meditation subjects than to others. His guidelines for matching people to the best meditation subject is based on these main types of temperament: (1) one disposed to hatred; (2) the lustful, deluded, or excitable; (3) one prone to faith; (4) the intelligent.

Subjects suitable for the hateful type are: the four sublime states and the four color kasinas; for the lustful, the ten corpses, the body parts, and the breath; for the faithful, the first six reflections; and for the intelligent, reflection on death, the loathsomeness of food, and the physical elements. The remaining subjects are suitable for everyone. The Visuddhimagga also specifies the appropriate physical surrounding for each type. The lustful meditator, for example, should be assigned a cramped, windowless hut in an ugly location in the neighborhood of unfriendly people; the hateful type, on the other hand, is to be given a comfortable and roomy cottage in a pleasant area near helpful people.

The Teacher

The ideal meditation teacher was the Buddha, who, it is said, had developed the power to know the mind and heart of others. He perfectly matched each person with the appropriate subject and circumstance for concentration. In lieu of such an ideal teacher, the Visuddhimagga advises the would-be meditator to pick his * teacher ac-

* For "he" and "him" throughout this book, read "he/she" and "him/her." The path of meditation is clearly not closed to members of any sex, race, or creed.

cording to level of attainment in meditation, the most highly accomplished being the best teacher. The teacher's support and advice are critical to the meditator in making his way through unfamiliar mental terrain. The pupil "takes refuge" in his teacher, entering a contract of surrender to him.

The pupil surrenders egoism, the source of hindrances that prevent him from pursuing meditation to the point at which egoism is transcended. But the responsibility for salvation is laid squarely on the student's own shoulders, not on the teacher's; the teacher is merely a "good friend" on the path. The teacher points the way; the student must walk for himself. The essence of the teacher's role is given in the lines from the Japanese *Zenrin:*

If you wish to know the road up the mountain,
You must ask the man who goes back and forth
    on it.

2. THE PATH
OF CONCENTRATION

In describing the path of concentration, the Visuddhimagga map suffers from a serious oversight: It begins with the description of an advanced altered state, one that many or most meditators may never once experience. It skips the ordinary—and much more common— preliminary stages. This gap can be filled from other Buddhist sources, which start with the meditator's normal state of mind rather than with the rarefied states the Visuddhimagga elaborates in detail.

At the outset, the meditator's focus wanders from the object of meditation. As he notices he has wandered, he returns his awareness to the proper focus. His one-pointedness is occasional, coming in fits and starts. His mind oscillates between the object of meditation and distracting thoughts, feelings, and sensations. The first landmark in concentration comes when the meditator's mind is unaffected both by outer distractions, such as nearby sounds, and by the turbulence of his own assorted thoughts and feelings. Although sounds are heard, and his thoughts and feelings are noticed, they do not disturb the meditator.

In the next stage, his mind focuses on the object for prolonged periods. The meditator gets better at repeatedly returning his mind to the object as it wanders. His ability to return his attention gradually increases as the meditator sees the ill results of distractions (e.g., agitation) and feels the advantages of a calm one-pointedness. As this happens, the meditator is able to overcome mental habits antagonistic to calm collectedness, such as boredom due to hunger for novelty. By now, the meditator's mind can remain undistracted for long periods.

On the Verge of Absorption

In the early stages of meditation, there is a tension between concentration on the object of meditation and distracting thoughts. The main distractions are sensual desires; ill will, despair, and anger; sloth and torpor; agitation and worry; and doubt and skepticism. With much practice, a moment comes when these hindrances

are wholly subdued. There is then a noticeable quicken-
ing of concentration. At this moment, the mental attributes, such as one-pointedness and bliss, that will mature
into full absorption simultaneously come into dominance.
Each has been present previously to different degrees,
but when they come, all at once they have special power.
This is the first noteworthy attainment in concentrative
meditation; because it is the state verging on full absorption, it is called "access" concentration.

This state of concentration is like a child not yet able
to stand steady but always trying to do so. The mental
factors of full absorption are not strong at the access
level; their emergence is precarious, and the mind fluctu-
ates between them and its inner speech, the usual rumi-
nations and wandering thoughts. The meditator is still
open to his senses and remains aware of surrounding
noises and his body's feelings. The meditation subject is
a dominant thought but does not yet fully occupy the
mind. At this access level, strong feelings of zest or rapture emerge, along with happiness, pleasure, and equanimity. There is also fleeting attention to the meditation
subject as though striking at it, or more sustained focus
on it, repeatedly noting it. Sometimes there are luminous
shapes or flashes of bright light, especially if the meditation subject is a kasina or respiration. There may also be
a sensation of lightness, as though the body were floating
in the air. Access concentration is a precarious attainment. If not solidified into fuller absorption at the same
sitting, it must be protected between sessions by avoiding distracting actions or encounters.

Visions

Visionary experiences can occur on the threshold of this level when factors such as rapture have ripened but discursive thought continues, and so long as sustained focus on the object of concentration remains weak. Were sustained concentration to achieve full strength, mental processes necessary for visions would be cut short as long as attention remains with the primary object. Access and deeper levels of absorption are for this reason antithetical to visions, but as the access level is approached (or on emerging from deeper absorption), visions are most likely. Visions can be frightening—an image of oneself as a corpse, for example, or the form of a threatening and terrifying beast—or quite benign, such as the figure of a benevolent deity or a Buddha. Meditative visions are quite vivid; the Visuddhimagga says they are as realistic as talking to a guest who comes on a visit. Timid or anxious persons who have a terrifying vision, it is warned, can be driven mad. Another danger to the meditator is becoming enraptured by beatific visions and so halting further progress by making them the goal of one's meditation, failing to further strengthen concentration. The meditator's goal is beyond visions. In Zen, they say, "If you meet the Buddha, slay him."

Full Absorptions or Jhana

By continually focusing on the object of meditation, there comes the first moment marking a total break with normal consciousness. This is full absorption, or *jhana*. The mind suddenly seems to sink into the object and remains fixed in it. Hindering thoughts cease totally.

There is neither sensory perception nor the usual awareness of one's body; bodily pain cannot be felt. Apart from the initial and sustained attention to the primary object, consciousness is dominated by rapture, bliss, and one-pointedness. These are the mental factors that, when in simultaneous ascendance, constitute jhana.

There is a subtle distinction between rapture and bliss. Rapture at the level of the first jhana is likened to the initial pleasure and excitement of getting a long-sought object; bliss is the enjoyment of that object. Rapture may be experienced as raising of the hairs on the body, as momentary joy that flashes and disappears like lightning, as waves showering through the body again and again, as the sensation of levitation, or as immersion in thrilling happiness. Bliss is a more subdued state of continued ecstasy. One-pointedness is the property of mind that centers it in the jhanic state. The first taste of jhana lasts but a single moment, but with continued efforts, the jhanic state can be held for longer and longer intervals. Until the jhana is mastered, it is unstable and can be easily lost. Full mastery comes when the meditator can attain jhana whenever, wherever, as soon as, and for as long as he wishes.

Deeper Jhanas

In the course of meditation, one-pointedness becomes more and more intensified by the successive elimination of the jhanic factors. One-pointedness absorbs the energy invested in the other factors at each deeper jhanic level (Fig. 1). Becoming even more one-pointed after mastery of the first jhana requires eliminating initial and repeated returning of the mind to the meditation object. After

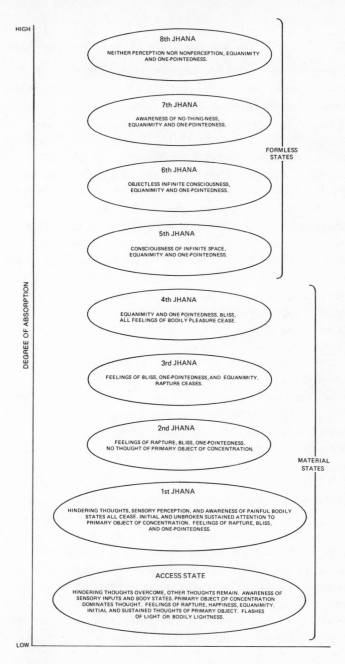

Fig. 1. Landmarks on the Path of Concentration.

emerging from the jhanic state, these attentional processes seem gross in comparison to the other more subtle
mental factors of jhana. Just as the hindrances were overcome on the way to the access level, and just as thoughts
were stilled in attaining the first jhana, initial and repeated attention to the primary object are abandoned at
the threshold of the second jhana. To go beyond these
kinds of attention, the meditator enters the first jhana by
focusing on the primary object. But then he frees the
mind of any thought of the object by instead turning the
mind toward rapture, bliss, and one-pointedness. This
level of absorption is more subtle and stable than the
first. The meditator's mind is now totally free of any verbal thoughts, even that of the original primary object.
Only a reflected image of the object remains as the focus
of one-pointedness.

Third Jhana

To go still deeper, the meditator masters the second
jhana as he did the first. Then, when he emerges from
the second jhana, he sees that rapture—a form of excitement—is gross compared to bliss and one-pointedness.
He attains the third level of jhana by again contemplating
the primary object and abandoning first thoughts of the
object, then rapture. In the third level of absorption,
there is a feeling of equanimity toward even the highest
rapture. This even-mindedness emerges with the fading
away of rapture. This jhana is extremely subtle, and
without this newly emergent equanimity, the meditator's
mind would be pulled back to rapture. If he stays in the
third jhana, an exceedingly sweet bliss fills the meditator,
and afterward this bliss floods his body. Because the bliss

of this level is accompanied by equanimity, the meditator's mind is kept one-pointed in these subtle dimensions, resisting the pull of a grosser rapture. Having mastered the third jhana as those before, the meditator can go deeper if he sees that bliss is more disturbing than one-pointedness and equanimity.

Fourth Jhana

To go deeper still, the meditator has to abandon all forms of mental pleasure. He has to give up all those mental states that might oppose more total stillness, even bliss and rapture. With the total cessation of bliss, equanimity and one-pointedness gain their full strength. In the fourth jhana, feelings of bodily pleasure are fully abandoned; feelings of pain ceased at the first jhana. There is not a single sensation or thought. The meditator's mind at this extremely subtle level rests with one-pointedness in equanimity. Just as his mind becomes progressively more still at each level of absorption, his breath becomes calmer. At this fourth level, the meditator's breath is so still he cannot sense the least stirring; he perceives his breath as ceasing altogether.

Formless Jhana

The next step in concentration culminates in the four states called "formless." The first four jhanas are attained by concentration on a material form or some concept derived therefrom. But the meditator attains the formless states by passing beyond all perception of form. To enter the first four jhanas, the meditator had to empty his mind of mental factors. To enter each successive formless jhana, the meditator substitutes progressively more subtle objects of concentration. All the formless jhanas share the mental factors of one-pointedness and equanimity, but at each level these factors are more refined. Concentration approaches imperturbability. The meditator cannot be disturbed but emerges after a self-determined time limit set before entering this state.

Fifth Jhana

The meditator reaches the first formless absorption and the fifth jhana by entering the fourth jhana through any of the kasinas. Mentally extending the limits of the kasina to the largest extent imaginable, his attention is then turned away from the colored light of the kasina and toward the space occupied by it. With this infinite space as the object of contemplation and with the full maturity of equanimity and one-pointedness, the meditator's mind now abides in a sphere in which all perceptions of form have ceased. His mind is so firmly set in this sublime consciousness that nothing can disrupt it. Still, the barest trace of the senses exists in the fifth jhana, though they are ignored. The absorption would be broken should the meditator turn his attention to them.

Once the fifth jhana is mastered, the meditator goes still deeper by first achieving an awareness of infinite space and then turning his attention to that infinite awareness. In this way, the thought of infinite space is abandoned, while objectless infinite awareness remains. This marks the sixth jhana. Having mastered the sixth, the meditator obtains the seventh jhana by first entering the sixth and then turning his awareness to the nonexistence of infinite consciousness. Thus, the seventh jhana is absorption with no-thing-ness, or the void, as its object. That is, the meditator's mind takes as its object the awareness of absence of any object.

Mastering this seventh jhana, the meditator can then review it and find any perception at all a disadvantage, its absence being more sublime. So motivated, the meditator attains the eighth jhana by first entering the seventh. He then turns his attention to the aspect of peacefulness and away from perception of the void. The delicacy of this is suggested by the stipulation that there must be no hint of desire to attain this peacefulness or to avoid perception of no-thing-ness. Attending to the peacefulness, he reaches an ultrasubtle state in which there are only residual mental processes. There is no gross perception here at all: This is a state of "no perception." There *is* ultrasubtle perception: thus, "not nonperception." The eighth jhana, therefore, is called the "sphere of neither perception nor nonperception." No mental states are decisively present: Their residuals remain, though they are nearly absent. This state approaches the ultimate limits of perception. As with mind, so with body; the meditator's metabolism becomes progressively stiller through the formless jhanas. "The eighth jhana," says one commentator, "is a state so extremely subtle that it cannot be said whether it is or is not."

Each jhana rests on the one below. In entering any jhana, the meditator's mind traverses upward each level in succession by eliminating the gross elements of each one by one. With practice, the traversal of jhanic levels becomes almost instantaneous, the meditator's awareness pausing at each level on the way for but a few moments of consciousness. As grosser mental factors are eliminated, concentration intensifies. The grossness of a med-

itation subject limits the depth of jhana the meditator can
reach through it. The simpler the subject, the deeper the
jhana (Table 1).

TABLE 1
JHANA LEVEL ATTAINABLE ACCORDING TO
MEDITATION SUBJECT

	Highest Jhana Level *Attainable*
Reflections; elements; loathsomeness of food	Access
Body parts; corpses	First
Loving-kindness; selfless joy; compassion	Third
Equanimity	Fourth
Infinite space	Fifth
Infinite consciousness	Sixth
No-thing-ness	Seventh
Kasinas; mindfulness of breath; neither perception nor nonperception	Eighth

3. THE PATH
OF INSIGHT

The Visuddhimagga sees mastery of the jhanas and tast-
ing their sublime bliss as of secondary importance to
puñña, discriminating wisdom. Jhana mastery is part of a
fully rounded training, but its advantages for the medita-

tor are in making his mind wieldy and pliable, so speeding his training in puñña. Indeed, the deeper jhanas are sometimes referred to in Pali, the language of the Visudhimagga, as "concentration games," the play of well-advanced meditators. But the crux of his training is a path that need not include the jhanas. This path begins with mindfulness (*satipatthana*), proceeds through insight (vipassana), and ends in nirvana.√

Mindfulness

The first phase, mindfulness, entails breaking through stereotyped perception. Our natural tendency is to become habituated to the world around us, no longer to notice the familiar. We also substitute abstract names or preconceptions for the raw evidence of our senses. In mindfulness, the meditator methodically faces the bare facts of his experience, seeing each event as though occurring for the first time. He does this by continuous attention to the first phase of perception, when his mind is *receptive* rather than reactive. He restricts his attention to the bare notice of his senses and thoughts. He attends to these as they arise in any of the five senses or in his mind, which, in the Visuddhimagga, constitutes a sixth sense. While attending to his sense impressions, the meditator keeps reaction simply to registering whatever he observes. If any further comment, judgment, or reflection arises in the meditator's mind, these are themselves made the focus of bare attention. They are neither repudiated nor pursued but simply dismissed after being noted. The essence of mindfulness is, in the words of Nyanaponika Thera, a modern Buddhist monk, "the clear and single-minded awareness of what actually happens *to* us and *in* us, at the successive moments of perception."

Whatever power of concentration the meditator has developed previously helps him in the thorough pursuit of mindfulness. One-pointedness is essential in adopting this new habit of bare perception. The best level of jhana for practicing mindfulness is the lowest, that of access. This is because mindfulness is applied to normal consciousness, and from the first jhana on, these normal processes cease. A level of concentration less than that of access, on the other hand, can be easily overshadowed by wandering thoughts and lapses in mindfulness. At the access level, there is a desirable balance: Perception and thought retain their usual patterns, but concentration is powerful enough to keep the meditator's awareness being diverted from steadily noting these patterns. The moments of entry to or exit from jhana are especially ripe for practicing insight. The mind's workings are transparent in these moments, making them more vulnerable to the clear gaze of the mindful meditator.

The preferred method for cultivating mindfulness is to precede it with training in the jhanas. There is, however, a method called "bare insight" in which the meditator begins mindfulness without any previous success in concentration. In bare insight, concentration strengthens through the practice of mindfulness itself. During the first stages of bare insight, the meditator's mind is intermittently interrupted by wandering thoughts between moments of mindful noticing. Sometimes the meditator notices the wandering, sometimes not. But momentary concentration gradually strengthens as more stray thoughts are noted. Wandering thoughts subside as soon as noticed, and the meditator resumes mindfulness immediately afterward. Finally, the meditator reaches the point at which his mind is unhindered by straying. When he notices every movement of the mind without break, this is the same as access concentration.

Kinds of Mindfulness

There are four kinds of mindfulness, identical in function but different in focus. Mindfulness can focus on the body, on feelings, on the mind, or on mind objects. Any one of these serves as a fixed point for bare attention to the stream of consciousness. In mindfulness of the body, the meditator attends to each moment of his bodily activity, such as his posture and the movements of his limbs. The meditator notes his body's motion and position regardless of what he does. The aims of his act are disregarded; the focus is on the bodily act itself. In mindfulness of feeling, the meditator focuses on his internal sensations, disregarding whether they are pleasant or unpleasant. He simply notes all his internal feelings as they come to his attention. Some feelings are the first reaction to messages from the senses, some are physical feelings accompanying psychological states, some are by-products of biological processes. Whatever the source, the feeling itself is registered.

In mindfulness of mental states, the meditator focuses on each state as it comes to awareness. Whatever mood, mode of thought, or psychological state presents itself, he simply registers it as such. If, for instance, there is anger at a disturbing noise, at that moment he simply notes "anger." The fourth technique, mindfulness of mind objects, is virtually the same as the one just described save for the level at which the mind's workings are observed. Rather than noting the quality of mental states as they arise, the meditator notes the attentional objects that occupy those states, for example, "disturbing noise." As each thought arises, the meditator notes it in terms of a detailed schema for classifying mental content. The broadest category on this list labels all thoughts as either hindrances to or helps toward enlightenment.

Any of these techniques of mindfulness will break through the illusions of continuity and reasonableness that sustain our mental life. In mindfulness, the meditator begins to witness the random units of mind stuff from which his reality is built. From these observations emerge a series of realizations about the nature of the mind. With these realizations, mindfulness matures into insight. The practice of insight begins at the point when mindfulness continues without lag. In insight meditation, awareness fixes on its object so that the contemplating mind and its object arise together in unbroken succession. This point marks the beginning of a chain of insights—mind knowing itself—ending in the nirvanic state (Fig. 2).

The first realization in insight is that the phenomena contemplated are distinct from mind contemplating them: Within the mind, the faculty whereby mind witnesses its own workings is different from the workings it witnesses. The meditator knows awareness is distinct from the objects it takes, but this knowledge is not at the verbal level as it is expressed here. Rather, the meditator knows this and each ensuing realization in his direct experience. He may have no words for his realizations; he understands but cannot necessarily state that understanding.

Continuing his practice of insight, after the meditator has realized the separate nature of awareness and its objects, he can, with further insight, gain a clear under-

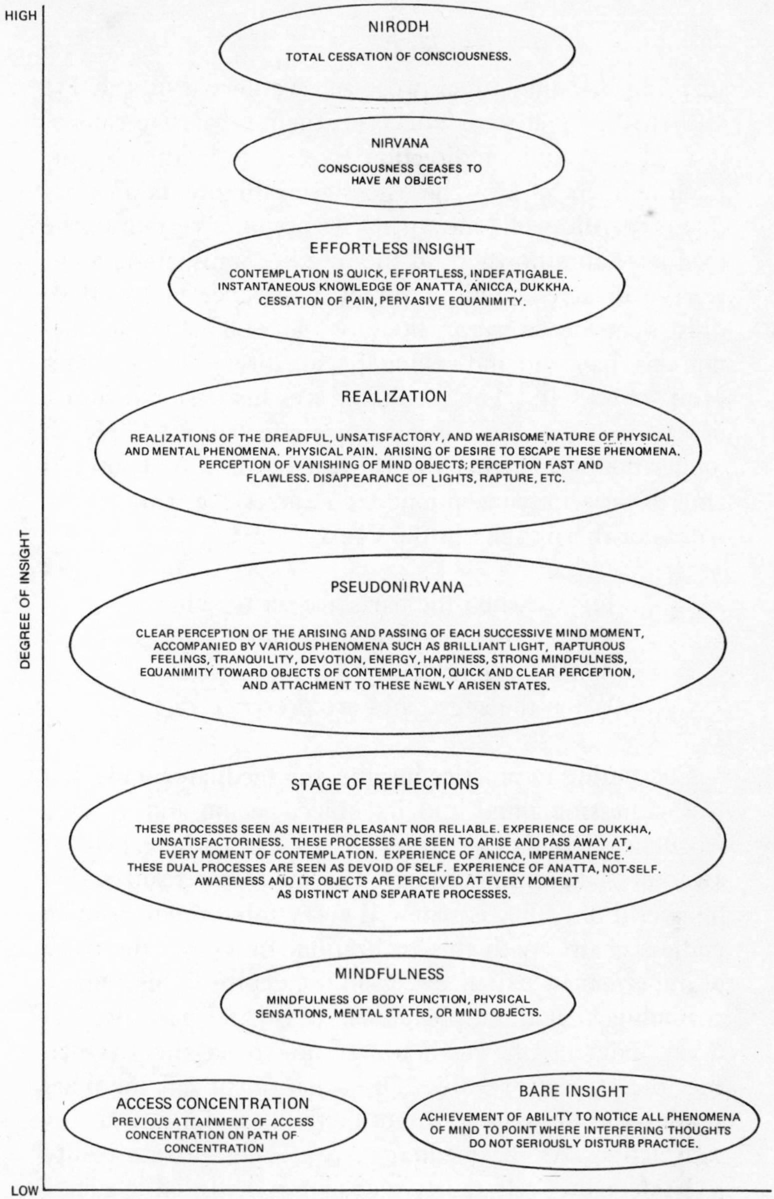

Fig. 2. Landmarks on the Path of Insight.

standing that these dual processes are devoid of self. He sees that they arise as effects of their respective causes, not as the result of direction by any individual agent. Each moment of awareness goes according to its own nature, regardless of "one's will." It becomes certain to the meditator that nowhere in the mind can any abiding entity be detected. This is direct experience of the Buddhist doctrine of *anatta*, literally "not self," that all phenomena have no indwelling personality. This includes even "one's self." The meditator sees his past and future life as merely a conditioned cause-effect process. He no longer doubts whether the "I" really exists; he knows "I am" to be a misconception. He realizes the truth of the words of the Buddha in the Pali Canon:

> Just as when the parts are set together
> There arises the word "chariot,"
> So does the notion of a being
> When the aggregates are present.

Continuing to practice insight, the meditator finds that his witnessing mind and its objects come and go at a frequency beyond his ken. He sees his whole field of awareness in continual flux. The meditator realizes that his world of reality is renewed every mind moment in an endless chain. With this realization, he knows the truth of impermanence (Pali: *anicca*) in the depths of his being.

Finding that these phenomena arise and pass away at every moment, the meditator comes to see them as neither pleasant nor reliable. Disenchantment sets in: What is constantly changing cannot be the basis for any lasting satisfaction. As the meditator realizes his private reality to be devoid of self and ever changing, he is led to a state of detachment from his world of experience. From this detached perspective, the impermanent and impersonal qualities of his mind lead him to see it as a source of suffering (Pali: *dukkha*).

Pseudonirvana

The meditator then continues without any further reflections. After these realizations, the meditator begins to see clearly the beginning and end of each successive moment of awareness. With this clarity of perception, there may occur:

—the vision of a *brilliant light* or luminous form

—*rapturous feelings* that cause goose flesh, tremor in the limbs, the sensation of levitation, and the other attributes of rapture

—*tranquility* in mind and body, making them light, plastic, and wieldy

—*devotional feelings* toward and faith in the meditation teacher, the Buddha, his teachings—including the method of insight itself—and the sangha, accompanied by joyous confidence in the virtues of meditation and the desire to advise friends and relatives to practice it

—*vigor* in meditating, with a steady energy neither too lax nor too tense

—sublime *happiness* suffusing the meditator's body, an unprecedented bliss that seems never-ending and motivates him to tell others of this extraordinary experience

—*quick and clear perception* of each moment of awareness: Noticing is keen, strong, and lucid, and the characteristics of impermanence, nonself, and unsatisfactoriness are clearly understood at once.

—*strong mindfulness* so the meditator effortlessly notices every successive moment of awareness;
mindfulness gains a momentum of its own
—*equanimity* toward whatever comes into awareness:
No matter what comes into his mind, the meditator maintains a detached neutrality.
—a subtle *attachment* to the lights and other factors
listed here and pleasure in their contemplation

The meditator is often elated at the emergence of these
ten signs and may speak of them thinking he has attained
enlightenment and finished the task of meditation. Even
if he does not think they mark his liberation, he may
pause to bask in their enjoyment. For this reason, this
stage, called "Knowledge of Arising and Passing Away,"
is subtitled in the Visuddhimagga "The Ten Corruptions
of Insight." It is a pseudonirvana. The great danger for
the meditator is in "mistaking what is not the Path for
the Path" or, in lieu of that, faltering in the further pursuit of insight because of his attachment to these phenomena. Finally, the meditator, either on his own or
through advice from his teacher, realizes these experiences to be a landmark along the way rather than his
final destination. At this point, he turns the focus of insight on them and on his own attachment to them.

Higher Realizations

As this pseudonirvana gradually diminishes, the meditator's perception of each moment of awareness becomes
clearer. He can make increasingly fine discrimination of
successive moments until his perception is flawless. As
his perception quickens, the ending of each moment of

awareness is more clearly perceived than its arising. Finally, the meditator perceives each moment only as it vanishes. He experiences contemplating mind and its object as vanishing in pairs at every moment. The meditator's world of reality is in a constant state of dissolution. A dreadful realization flows from this; the mind becomes gripped with fear. All his thoughts seem fearsome. He sees becoming, that is, thoughts coming into being, as a source of terror. To the meditator everything that enters his awareness—even what might once have been very pleasant—now seems oppressive. He is helpless to avoid this oppression; it is part of every moment.

At this point, the meditator realizes the unsatisfactory quality of all phenomena. The slightest awareness he sees as utterly destitute of any possible satisfaction. In them is nothing but danger. The meditator comes to feel that in all the kinds of becoming there is not a single thing that he can place his hopes in or hold onto. All of his awareness, every thought, every feeling, appears insipid. This includes any state of mind the meditator can conceive. In all the meditator perceives, he sees only suffering and misery.

Feeling this misery in all phenomena, the meditator becomes entirely disgusted with them. Though he continues with the practice of insight, his mind is dominated by feelings of discontent and listlessness toward all its own contents. Even the thought of the happiest sort of life or the most desirable objects seem unattractive and boring. He becomes absolutely dispassionate and adverse toward the multitude of mental stuff—to any kind of becoming, destiny, or state of consciousness.

Between the moments of noticing, it occurs to the meditator that only in the ceasing of all mental processes is relief possible. Now his mind no longer fastens on to its contents, and the meditator desires to escape from the suffering due to these phenomena. Painful feelings may flood his body, and he may no longer be able to remain long in one posture. The comfortless nature of mind stuff becomes more evident than ever; the desire for deliverance from it emerges at the root of his being.

With this strong desire for surcease from mental processes, the meditator intensifies his efforts to notice these processes for the very purpose of escaping them. Their nature—their impermanence, the element of suffering, and their voidness of self—become clearly evident. The meditator's body will sometimes undergo severe, sharp pains of growing intensity. His whole body and mind may seem a mass of suffering; restlessness may overwhelm his insight. But by systematically noting these pains, they will cease. At this point, the meditator's ability at simply noticing becomes strong and lucid. At every moment, he knows quite clearly the three characteristics of mental phenomena. One of these three comes to dominate his understanding.

Now the meditator's contemplation proceeds automatically, without special effort, as if borne onward of itself. Feelings of dread, despair, and misery cease. Body pains are absent entirely. The meditator's mind has abandoned both dread and delight. An exceedingly sublime clarity of mind and a pervasive equanimity emerge. The meditator need make no further deliberate effort; noticing continues in a steady flow for hours without his tiring. His meditation has its own momentum, and insight becomes especially quick.

Insight is now on the verge of its culmination; the meditator's noticing of each moment of awareness is keen, strong, and lucid. The meditator instantly knows each moment to be impermanent, painful, or without self as he sees its dissolution. He sees all mental phenomena as limited and circumscribed, devoid of desirability, or alien. His detachment from them is at a peak. His noticing no longer enters into or settles down on any phenomena at all. At this moment, a consciousness arises that takes as its object the "signless, no-occurrence, no-formation": *nirvana*. Awareness of all physical and mental phenomena ceases entirely.✓

This moment of penetration of nirvana does not, in its first attainment, last even for a second. Immediately following this, the "fruition" moment occurs, when the meditator's mind reflects on the experience of nirvana just past. That experience is a cognitive shock of deepest psychological consequence. Because it is of a realm beyond that of the common-sense reality from which our language is generated, nirvana is a "supramundane reality," describable only in terms of what it is not. Nirvana has no phenomenology, no experiential characteristics. It is the unconditioned state.✓

Nirvana: Subsequent Changes

The word "nirvana" derives from the negative prefix "nir" and the root "vana," to burn, a metaphorical expression for the extinction of motives for becoming. In nirvana, desire, attachment, and self-interest are burned out. Decisive behavior changes follow from this state of consciousness, and the full realization of nirvana actuates a permanent alteration of the meditator's consciousness per se. With the meditator's realization of nirvana, aspects of his ego and of his normal consciousness are abandoned, never to arise again.

The path of insight differs significantly from the path

of concentration on this point: Nirvana destroys "defiling" aspects of mental states—hatred, greed, delusion, etc.—whereas jhana merely suppresses them. The fruit of nirvana for the meditator is effortless moral purity; in fact, purity becomes his only possible behavior. Jhana smothers the meditator's defilements, but their seeds remain latent in his personality as potentialities. On his emergence from the jhanic state, impure acts again become possible as appropriate trigger situations arise. To attain effortless purity, the meditator's egoism must "die," that is, all of his desires originating from self-interest must cease to control his behavior.

After insight has culminated in the nirvanic state, the meditator's mind remains free of certain motivations and psychological states, which no longer arise. On full maturation of insight, his purity is perfected. By then, he will have utterly given up the potential for impure acts. What was in the early stages effortful for the meditator becomes a self-maintaining state in which attitudes of purity are effortless, choiceless by-products of the state itself.

The number of times the meditator enters the nirvanic state determines his level of mastery, that is, his ability to attain nirvana whenever, wherever, as soon as, and for as long as he wants. But his level of mastery is not the same as nirvana-caused personality changes. He can enter nirvana with a given degree of insight countless times without any subsequent change of his being. The deeper he develops insight prior to entering nirvana, the greater the subsequent changes will be. The nature of nirvana itself is identical at each level of attainment. Since nirvana is the complete extinction of consciousness, it is always the same, though beyond experience. But there are differences between levels of nirvana-caused change. The differences are reckoned in terms of the meditator's consequent loss of ego and alteration in his normal consciousness after he has emerged from nirvana. Entering the nirvanic state is his "awakening"; these subsequent changes are his "deliverance."

The first level of deliverance is that of *Sotapanna*, "stream enterer," the "stream" entered being that leading to the total loss of his selfish ego, the cessation of all his strivings to become. The meditator becomes a stream enterer at the moment of reflection after his first penetration of nirvana. He remains a stream enterer until his insight deepens to the degree necessary to break through to the next level of attainment. This final liberation, it is said, is sure to occur "within seven more lifetimes." The stream enterer loses the following personality traits: his greed for sensory objects; any resentments strong enough to make him agitated; greed for his own gain, possessions, or praise; his inability to share with others; his failure to perceive the relative and illusory nature of whatever may seem pleasurable or beautiful; his mistaking for permanent what is impermanent (anicca); his seeing a self in what is devoid of self (anatta); his adherence to mere rites, compulsive ritualism, and any belief that this or that is "the truth"; and his doubts in the utility of the path of insight meditation. The stream enterer by nature can also no longer engage in lying, stealing, sexual misconduct, physically harming others, or earning his livelihood at the expense of others.

When the meditator's insight deepens so that the realizations of dukkha, anatta, or anicca more fully pervade his awareness, his insight intensifies a quantum level deeper. At this deeper level both his greed for sense desires and his ill will weaken further. In addition to what he abandoned with stream entry, the meditator lets go of gross desires for sense objects and strong resentment. He is now a *sakadgami*, "once returner," who will be fully liberated in this lifetime "or the next." The intensity of his feelings of attraction and aversion diminishes: He can no longer be strongly impelled toward or put off by anything. The pull of sex, for example, lessens; he can still have intercourse for procreation, but he will have no compulsive sexual needs. Impartiality typifies his reactions toward any and all stimuli.

At the next phase in the deepening of his insight, he abandons altogether both greed for sense desires and ill will. What was diminished when he reached the level of once returner is now wholly extinguished. The meditator is an *anagami*, "nonreturner," and he will be totally liberated from the wheel of becoming in his present lifetime. In addition to what he previously abandoned, his last remaining residual propensities toward greed or resentment drop away. All aversion to worldly states, such as loss, disgrace, pain, or blame, ceases. Maliciousness in motivation, volition, or speech becomes impossible for the nonreturner. He can no longer even have a thought of ill will toward anyone, and the category of "enemy" vanishes from his thinking, along with that of "dislike." Similarly, even his subtlest desire for sense objects disappears. Sexual activity, for example, is unlikely for the nonreturner because his feelings of lust are gone, as are his desires for sensual pleasures. Equanimity prevails toward all external objects; their valence to the nonreturner is absolutely neutral.

When the meditator's insight fully matures, he overcomes all remaining fetters to liberation. He is now an *arahant*, an "awakened being" or saint; the word arahant means "one who is worthy" of veneration. The arahant is free from his former socially conditioned identity; he sees consensual concepts of reality as illusions. He is absolutely free from suffering and from acting in a way that would further his karma. Having no feelings of "self," his acts are purely functional, either for maintenance of his body or for the good of others. The arahant does everything with physical grace. Nothing in his past can cause thoughts of greed, hatred, and the like to come to mind. His past deeds are erased as determinants of behavior, and he is free of his past conditioned habits. He lives fully in the moment; all his actions bespeak spontaneity. The last vestiges of egoism the meditator relinquishes in this final stage include: his desire to seek worldly gain, fame, pleasure, or praise; his desire for even the bliss of the material or formless jhanas; mental stiffness or agitation; covetousness of anything whatsoever. For the arahant, the least tendency toward an unvirtuous thought or deed is literally inconceivable.

With the full extinction of "unwholesome" roots—lust, aggression, and pride—as motives in the meditator's behavior, loving-kindness, altruistic joy, compassion, and equanimity emerge as bases for his actions. Behavior stemming from unwholesome motives is seen as "unskilled"; the arahant's acts are in this sense "skilled." His motives are totally pure. Dreaming, too, changes for the arahant; he has no dreams due to bodily states (e.g., dreams of being chased, being hot or cold) or because of his impressions of daily happenings, but he may have premonitory dreams that foreshadow future events. Though the arahant can experience bodily pain, he bears it with equanimity. A prominent trait of the arahant is unselfishness, likened in the Pali Canon to motherly love:

Even as a mother watches over her only begotten child, so let his heart and mind be filled with boundless love for all creatures, great and small, let him practice benevolence towards the whole world, above, below, across, without exception, and let him set himself utterly free from ill-will and enmity.

One who has "awakened" in this way is capable of a dual perception: "Knowing how everything actually is, and how everything appears." For the arahant, normal reality is perceived simultaneously with the validity of the "noble truths" of impermanence, suffering and non-selfhood. Both these perceptual levels are evident at every moment. For example, even worldly pleasures are a form of suffering. Wei Wu Wei (1968: p. 61) says of the meaning of suffering at the arahant's level of consciousness:

When the Buddha found that he was Awake . . . it may be assumed that he observed that what hitherto he had regarded as happiness, as compared to suffering, was such no longer. His only standard henceforward was *ananda* or what we try to think of as bliss. Suffering he saw as the negative form of happiness, happiness as the positive form of suffering, respectively the negative and positive aspects of experience. But relative to the noumenal state which now alone he knew, both could be described . . . as *dukkha* (suffering.) *Dukkha* was the counterpart of *sukha* which implied "ease and well-being," . . . to the Buddha nothing phenomenal could appear to be *sukha* although in phenomenality it might so appear in contrast to *dukkha*.

The way the arahant might understand the truth of nonself is more straightforward. As D. T. Suzuki (1958:

p. 293) puts it, the arahant finds "by immediate knowledge that when one's heart was cleansed of the defilements of the ordinary ego-centered impulses and desires, nothing was left there to claim itself as ego-residuum." More simply, after the meditator has let go of his selfish ego to become an arahant, he finds he has no "self" left.

For the arahant, perception in insight meditation is perfected: He witnesses the most minute segments of his mind's working, the chain of mind moments. According to this tradition, the Buddha witnessed 17×10^{21} mind moments in "the wink of an eye," each one distinct and different from the one preceding and the one following it. Like him, the arahant sees that the smallest pieces of the mosaic of consciousness are changing at every moment. Nothing in the universe of his mind is constant. Since his external reality flows from his internal universe, nowhere can he find any stability or permanence.

Total Cessation

There is a state similar to nirvana (little known in the West) called *nirodh* (cessation). In nirvana, awareness has as its object the cessation of consciousness; in nirodh, awareness ceases altogether. This absolute cessation of consciousness is extremely difficult to attain. Nirodh is accessible only to a nonreturner or an arahant, and only if he has also mastered all eight jhanas. Neither a stream enterer nor a once returner has given up enough ego-bound attachments to muster the superconcentration required for nirodh. In gaining access to this state of total nonoccurrence, even the slightest sense desire is an obstacle.

On the path to nirodh, the meditator practices insight,

using as a base each jhana in succession up to the eighth, "neither perception nor nonperception." With the cessation of this last state of ultrasubtle consciousness, he enters nirodh. The cessation of nirodh is said to be "differently real," for all the data of our experience of reality, even the most subtle states, are absent.

Although nirodh can last for up to seven days of the human time rhythm, there is no time sequence in the state itself: The moment immediately preceding and that immediately following it seem in succession. The limit of seven days given for nirodh may be due to its unique physiology. The meditator's heartbeat and normal metabolism, it is said, cease along with consciousness (or, more likely, continue below the threshold of perception). Metabolic processes continue at a residual level, and the meditator's body does not decay like a corpse. The meditator must set a predetermined length of time for his stay in this state before he enters. On emerging from it, he goes through the jhanas in reverse order to normal consciousness. At the eighth jhana, awareness resumes; at the third, normal bodily function; at the first, thoughts and sense perception.

At their highest extremes, the path of concentration through the jhanas and the path of insight to nirvana tend to meet. Even so, there remain extremely subtle but crucial differences between these rarefied states of consciousness. In the seventh jhana, "no-thing-ness," awareness is of objectless consciousness. In the eighth jhana, even no-thing-ness is not present; yet it remains as a latent function, and so no-thing-ness cannot be said *not* to exist: this is the supersubtle realm of "neither perception nor nonperception." In nirvana, consciousness is on the brink of extinction with the awareness of no consciousness at all. The cessation of awareness culminates in nirodh, in which there is no awareness whatsoever. Attaining even the highest jhanas does not lastingly alter the meditator's personality, while nirvana does so irrevocably.

These different paths mark two extremes in exploring and controlling the mind. A meditator who could marshal enough one-pointedness to attain the formless jhanas might easily enter the nirvanic state should he choose to turn his powerful concentration to watching his own mind. Conversely, a meditator who had entered the nirvanic state might well be so indifferent to hindrances and distractions that, should he choose to focus on a single object of awareness, he would readily enter and proceed through the jhanic levels. Those who traverse these distinctly different paths to their summits, then, may no longer belong solely to one but to both. With full mastery of either samadhi or insight, the other is readily attainable. At their end, the distinction between meditation avenues melts.

PART TWO

MEDITATION PATHS:
A SURVEY

EXPERIENCE IS the forerunner of all spiritual teachings, but the same experience can be expressed differently. In any given tradition, the map of meditative states set down is to some degree arbitrary. The map is not the terrain, and the territory traversed in meditation is nebulous to begin with. It is little wonder that maps of meditative states seem so different from one another. Lao Tzu recognizes this dilemma in the Tao Te Ching:

> The way that can be told
> Is not the constant way;
> The name that can be named
> Is not the constant name.

The Tibetans recognize two levels of religion: "the expedient teaching" and "the final teaching." The expedient teachings are the multitude of world religions, each shaped by and for the people who adhere to it. Part of the differences between meditation maps stem from this level. The survey of meditation maps in this chapter is aimed at the level of final teaching, in which doctrinal differences fall away. Here the unity of practice comes into focus. Religions may differ by virtue of accident of time and place, but the experiences that are precursors to beliefs are often the same. Some degree of unity in final teaching is inevitable: All human beings are alike in nervous system, and it is at this level that the laws governing final teaching operate.

The Visuddhimagga map undercuts seeming distinctions between spiritual paths in meditation techniques and states. These distinctions, in fact, stem from different ideologies. The Visuddhimagga road maps give us a typology for sorting out techniques in terms of their mechanics, cutting through the conceptual overlay of religions. This survey is meant to be seminal, not exhaustive. In most cases, I discuss only one illustrative technique of the many disciplines belonging to a given spiritual path. This comparison is one of parts, of specific practices and states, rather than a taxonomy of spiritual paths.

I based most of the summaries that follow on published sources rather than on my personal investigation. They may, therefore, seem incomplete or imprecise to a person on any of these paths. Each path is a living tradition that presents itself differently to each person according to his needs and circumstances.

The summaries are didactic, not definitive. My intent is to give those not involved in them an idea of what they are like. I discuss each path in enough detail to show its unique flavor, while demonstrating its points of similarity with other paths.

4. HINDU BHAKTI

Sri Ramakrishna, a Bengali saint at the turn of the century, once went to a theater performance of the life of Sri
Chaitanya, the seventeenth-century Bhakti saint known
for his songs and dances of love for Lord Krishna. At
several points during the play, on seeing portrayals of
Chaitanya's devotion to Krishna, Ramakrishna entered
samadhi, a deep meditative absorption.

Ramakrishna's samadhi marks him as a Bhakta par excellence. Bhakti, or devotion to a divine being, is the
most popular form of worship in contemporary world
religions. A Christian singing "Amazing Grace," a Has-
sidic Jew dancing and singing at the Wailing Wall, a Sufi
reciting "El Allah Hu," a Hindu chanting "Hare
Krishna," and a Japanese Buddhist repeating "Na-mu-a-
mi-da-bu-tsu, Na-mu-a-mi-da-bu-tsu" are all engaged in
more or less the same devotional process, though directed
toward different divine beings.

Bhakti is the strongest school of religious practice in
Hinduism; its roots are ancient. In the classic *Srimad
Bhagavatam*, remembering or constant chanting of
Krishna's name is recommended over all other practices
as the best path for this age. The *Kalisantaram Upanishad*
has Brahma extol to the bard Narada as the highest or
maha-mantra, "Hare Rama, Hare Krishna"—Hare,
Rama, and Krishna all being manifestations of Vishnu.
The essence of Bhakti is making the object of devotion
one's central thought. The devotee may choose any deity
or divine being as his devotional object, or *ishta*. The
thrust of his practice is to keep the thought of the ishta
foremost in his mind at all times. Besides *kirtan* (chanting
or singing), there are three levels of *japa*, repetition of the

name: spoken, silent verbalization, and mental. Some regard each succeeding form of japa as "ten times" more efficacious than the preceding one (Poddar, 1965).

Poddar suggests that the neophyte practice a minimum of six hours of japa per day. From the beginning, the devotee also strives to maintain japa in the midst of life's activities. The *mala*, or rosary, is a common technical aid to japa; with the telling of each bead, the devotee recites the name once. Other aids include gearing recitation to each breath or to every beat of the pulse. No matter what the mnemonic device, the principle is the same: The devotee returns his attention to the ishta at once whenever his mind ceases to be engaged elsewhere. The goal of this stage of practice is to make the habit of repetition stronger than all the devotee's other mental habits. Gradually, his mind will be occupied solely with the thought of the deity or centered on it as other thoughts come and go on the periphery of awareness. In this way, the devotee becomes one-pointed on his ishta.

Some advice to the devotee repeats the Visuddhimagga. Because the mental habit of constant worship through remembering is at first vulnerable to other pulls for attention, the devotee is urged to keep to *satsang*, the company of persons on the same path. Staying with satsang counters the pull of worldly attachments, as does *darshan*, the visiting of saints. The devotee is further urged to avoid talk of "women, wealth, unbelievers, and enemies." The devotee's success depends on virtue: Purity, says Vivekananda (1964), "is absolutely the basic work, the bedrock upon which the whole Bhakti-building rests." In giving advice to her own disciples, Ananda Mayee Ma, a contemporary Indian woman saint, echoes the Visuddhimagga's for Buddhist monks (1972: pp. 126–29):

Indolence and lust—these two are the greatest obstacles on the path . . . Choose carefully and abide
strictly by such occupations as awaken godly
thoughts and feelings . . . Engage in them even
when there is no desire so to do, as one takes medicine . . . Food, sleep, toilet, clothes, etc., should be
given only as much attention as is needed for the
maintenance of health . . . Anger, greed and the
like must be altogether abandoned. Neither should
you be swayed by praise or prestige.

The guru's help ranks in importance with purity for
the devotee's progress. Ananda Mayee Ma (1972) com-
pares the role of the guru to that of experts in any spe-
cialized field to whom one must turn in order to become
proficient. But the function of the guru transcends that of
the worldly expert. In addition to directing the disciple,
the guru is also the intermediary for divine grace needed
for the disciple's efforts to bear fruit. No matter how dili-
gent the devotee, without the guru's blessings his efforts
are useless.

Ramana Maharshi (1962) says of "Guru-kripa," surrender to a master whose grace descends on the devotee. "If
one's surrender is complete, all sense of self is lost."
When the devotee surrenders to the pure being of the
guru, his mind becomes purified. The purified mind easily stills, allowing the devotee to turn inward in meditation and find the self. This is the guru's "grace," which is
in fact immanent in the devotee. There is, says Ramana
Maharshi, no difference between God, guru, and self:
The external guru helps the devotee find the internal self
in meditation. The outer guide leads the devotee back
within himself.

As in all paths, virtue—in the beginning an act of

will—becomes a by-product of the practice itself. As the devotee's mind focuses on his devotional object, it withdraws from worldly objects. By love of God, says Vivekananda, love of the pleasures of the senses and of the intellect is all made dim. As his consciousness becomes more thoroughly imbued with the thought of his ishta, the devotee finds worldly delights repugnant. By this point, observes Poddar (1965), "compared to the joy of repeating the 'Rama nama' (i.e., mantra) all other enjoyments of the world are insipid."

Bhakti begins in duality, with the devotee separate from his ishta, as from any love object. The *Bhakti Sutras*, in fact, have a typology of Divine Love that includes loving the ishta as one's friend, as one's spouse, and as one's child. Prabhavananda and Isherwood (1969) suggest that "all human relationships may be sublimated through the practice of Bhakti yoga." Though this love may begin with the forms of, and energies invested in, interpersonal love, it ends in union with the state of love evoked by the love object. Here, says Vivekananda, "Love, the Lover, and the Beloved are One." With this union, Bhakti merges into the path of jhana. The fruit of japa is constant remembrance at every waking moment of the beloved. This yields a "love intoxication"; its signs are ecstasy and absorption. The feelings of bliss, rapture, and joy of this intoxication characterize access concentration. The love-intoxicated devotee's behavior, however, is sometimes as erratic as a madman's. The *Srimad Bhagavata* (XI, ii) describes this stage:

> . . . the devotee loses all sense of decorum and moves about in the world unattached . . . His heart melts through love as he habitually chants the Name of his beloved lord, and like one possessed, he now

bursts into peals of laughter, now weeps, now cries, now sings aloud and now begins to dance.

The enraptured devotee is on the threshold of samadhi, or jhana. His ecstasy indicates the access level; he verges on the first jhana. Should he concentrate with enough intensity on his ishta, he can enter samadhi. Once samadhi is reached, according to Swami Muktananda (1971), there is no further need for chanting or japa: They are a prelude to the deep meditation of samadhi. An accomplished bhakta can attain samadhi on the least stimulus, suggesting his devotion, as did Sri Ramakrishna.

The initial power of Bhakti is the element of interpersonal love felt by the devotee toward his deity. As he progresses on this path, that love changes from an interpersonal to a transcendental or transpersonal love. The devotee no longer depends on the object of devotion to bestow bliss. Rather, he finds that the transcendental states of which the bliss is one aspect exist within himself. He need no longer cling to the external form of his devotional object; the states once evoked by his beloved's form have come to be fixtures of his own consciousness. Sankaracharya, the founder of Advait Hinduism, noted that Bhakti ends in a quest for the self: What begins as an external evocation of love becomes in the end an internal absorption in which the devotee in samadhi delights uninterruptedly in "pure self."

The devotee brings his mind to one-pointedness through constant remembrance of the ishta and so finally reaches samadhi at the level of first jhana. But if he is to go beyond this level, he must transcend his own devotional object. Any thought of name and form, even that of a deity, binds the devotee to the first jhana. Sri Ramakrishna, for example, for many years an ardent devotee of the Divine Mother, had experienced many visions and states of bliss as Her devotee. Later, he took initiation from a naked ascetic (Swami Saradananda, 1963: p. 255):

> After initiating me . . . the Naked One asked me to make my mind free of function in all respects, and merge in the meditation of the Self. But, when I sat for meditation, I could by no means make my mind go beyond the bounds of name and form and cease functioning. The mind withdrew itself from all other things, but as soon as it did so, the intimately familiar form of the universal Mother appeared . . . But, at last, collecting all the strength of my will, I cut Mother's form to pieces with the sword of discrimination . . . There remained no function in the mind, which transcended quickly the realm of names and forms, making me merge in samadhi.

The Visuddhimagga says that on initial entry to a new plane of meditative consciousness the meditator must cut his ties to the preceding plane. Each plane has its special points of appeal, some exceedingly sublime. The prerequisite for gaining the next higher level is to become detached from the lower plane, as Ramakrishna did, lest awareness be pulled back to it. For the devotee, this means that his ishta's form must finally be abandoned in favor of becoming himself, in samadhi, that manifestation of pure being for which the ishta is himself worshiped.

Beyond the attainment of samadhi, there is a state in which a samadhilike awareness diffuses throughout all the devotee's activities. Japa, if developed to this point, repeats as if of itself virtually every moment, day and night. This state is *sahaj samadhi* and marks the end point in the devotee's spiritual evolution. In sahaj samadhi, there is no distinction between the devotee, the world, and the ishta; his perception of self and the world shifts radically. As Vivekananda (1964: p. 90) puts it, "When a person loves the Lord, the whole universe becomes dear to him . . . his whole nature is purified and completely changed." Renunciation becomes effortless, all attachments save to the beloved ishta having fallen away.

From this intense and all-absorbing love comes faith and self-surrender, the conviction that nothing that happens is against one: "Not my, but Thy will be done." This selflessness is evident in the words of Ananda Mayee Ma, speaking of herself (1972: p. 37): "Truly this body belongs to all; for this reason it behaves and speaks, as far as possible, so as to fulfill the needs of the people with whom it deals at any particular time." One at this ultimate point on the Bhakti path perceives the sacred within the secular; everything is sacred because it bespeaks the beloved. The devotee need no longer observe any special forms or symbols for worship. He worships in his heart, the world having become his altar. Kabir (1970: pp. 48–49) eloquently sums up his own experience of this state:

O Sadhu! the simple union is the best,
Since the day when I met with my Lord, there has
   been no end to the sport of our love.
I shut not my eyes, I close not my ears, I do not
   mortify my body;
I see with eyes open and smile, and behold His
   beauty everywhere;
I utter His Name, and whatever I see, it reminds me
   of Him; whatever I do, it becomes His worship.

The rising and setting are one to me; all contra-
dictions are solved.
Wherever I go, I move round Him,
All I achieve is His service:
When I lie down, I lie prostrate at His feet.
He is the only adorable one to me: I have none
other.
My tongue has left off impure words, it sings His
glory day and night:
Whether I rise or sit down, I can never forget Him;
for the rhythm of His music beats in my ears.
Kabir says, I am immersed in the one great bliss
which transcends all pleasure and pain.

5. JEWISH KABBALAH

"In every religion," writes the contemporary Kabbalist
Z'ev ben Shimon Halevi (1976), "there are always two
aspects, the seen and the hidden." The seen manifests as
rituals, scriptures, services; the hidden bears the light
that should illumine these forms. In Judaism, the hidden
teachings are called Kabbalah. These teachings, it is said,
originated with the angels, who were instructed by God.
Kabbalists identify the great figures of Biblical times—
Abraham, David, the Prophets—as well as the Essenes
and other mystical groups of Jewish history, as bearers of
this tradition. Halevi says Joshua ben Miriam, otherwise
known as Jesus, was a transmitter of Kabbalah. This hidden Jewish tradition first surfaced in Europe in the Middle Ages, and many lineages of its transmission continue
to the present day.

The cosmology of Kabbalah posits a multileveled reality, each level a complete world in itself. These planes are arranged hierarchically, the upper part of each corresponding to the lower aspect of the one above. The highest sphere is that of Metatron, the chief archangel, who teaches human beings. Each level embodies a state of consciousness, and most people exist at the lowest levels—mineral, vegetable, animal. In the Kabbalist view, normal man is incomplete, restricted as he is to these lower planes. He lives a mechanical life, bound by the rhythms of his body and by habitual reactions and perceptions; he blindly seeks pleasure and avoids pain. While he may have brief glimpses of higher possibilities, he has no desire to raise his level of awareness. Kabbalah seeks to awaken the student to his own limitations and to train him to enter a state of consciousness in which he becomes in tune with a higher awareness, no longer a slave of his body and conditioning. To become free, the aspirant must first become disillusioned with the mechanical games of life. He then builds a foundation for entry into a higher consciousness, the Paradise within. This, says Halevi, is the allegorical meaning of the bondage in Egypt: the slavery of the limited ego, the seeker's purification in the desert, and his entry into the land of milk and honey.

To achieve his task, the Kabbalist must observe the working of the *Yesod*, his ordinary mind or ego, so as to see through his own foibles and self-delusions and bring into awareness the unconscious forces that shape his thoughts and actions. To do this, he seeks to reach the level of awareness called *Tiferet*, a state of clarity that is witness or "watcher" of the Yesod. From this state of heightened self-awareness emanates what is sometimes seen as a guardian angel that guides one through difficult situations with ease and skill. Tiferet is beyond the ordinary mind dealing with everyday matters; here ego is transcended. It is the realm of the spirit, the bridge between man and the divine, the gate of Paradise. It is the soul. Thus, in a state of Yesod, the ego rules; when Tiferet is dominant, a higher state occurs in which one looks down on oneself. This state of awakened consciousness is typically glimpsed only briefly in the ordinary man's life. The Kabbalist seeks to gain permanent entry to this state and ascend to even higher levels still.

The specifics of the Kabbalist's training—his foundation for higher states—vary from school to school, though the basics are fairly constant. When the aspirant contacts a *Maggid*, or teacher, his training begins in earnest. The Maggid directs him in candid self-observation, using the stuff of the student's life as material for teaching. There are many systems that aid the seeker in knowing himself, such as an intricate numerology that transmutes Hebrew letters and words into a number code with mystical interpretations. One of the best-known Kabbalist systems is the Tree of Life, a map of the hierarchies and attributes of the many planes that interplay in the world and within man. The tree serves as a template through which the aspirant observes his own nature and a key to unlock the hidden dimensions guiding his life. But a mere intellectual understanding of the tree may be Yesodic, in the service of the ego. No matter how elegantly the seeker grasps the intricacies of the tree, his studies will be for naught if he neglects his spiritual development. The prerequisite is training of his will, his capacity for unwavering attention. For this the Kabbalist turns to meditation. Writes Halevi (1976: p. 126):

Preparation means to be able to receive and impart
. . . the degree of reception determines the quality
of Knowledge given. The exchange is precise, and is

paid for by the amount of conscious attention in a
complex situation. Where attention is, there is
power.

The instructions for meditation form part of the secret
teachings of Kabbalists and, apart from general rules, are
not made public. Each student learns from the mouth of
his Maggid. In general, meditation in Kabbalah is an
offshoot of the normal prayers of the devout Jew. Meditative concentration allows the Kabbalist to delve to the
depths of a particular subject—a word in a prayer or an
aspect of the tree—and also to arrest his thought so as to
remain one-pointed on the subject. This fine focus is *kavvanah*, cleaving of thought to a single subject. In one sort
of kavvanah, the meditator concentrates on each word of
regular prayer with his full attention, to the point at
which his mind transcends the simple meaning of the
words, and so uses them as a vehicle to a higher state.
Azriel of Gerona, a medieval Kabbalist, described the
process of kavvanah as when "thought expands and as-
cends to its origin, so that when it reaches it, it ends and
cannot ascend any further." As a result of this state, the
words of the prayer become transmuted, full of a divine
influx from this nothingness of thought.

According to Kabbalist lore, the entry into the inner
Paradise by one who has not properly prepared a foundation through self-purification can be dangerous. The Tal-
mud tells the story of four rabbis who entered Paradise:
one went mad, one died, and another lost faith; only one,
Rabbi Akiba, came back in peace. The influential writings of Abraham Abulafia, among the most detailed elab-
oration of Kabbalist meditation, were designed to teach a
safe approach to the inner Paradise. Abulafia's meditation
combines various letters of the Hebrew alphabet in a

meditation on the holy names of God. This method is distinct from prayer; the aspirant devoted himself to it in seclusion rather than in synagogue, at given hours and under guidance of his Maggid. Halevi describes the path traveled by one who practices such a meditation. As he repeats the name, he directs his attention upward from Yesod, the limited ordinary mind, into Tiferet, an awareness beyond ego. That is, he directs his thought away from all forms of this world, focusing on the name. If his efforts meet with God's grace, the self will suddenly rise up beyond Tiferet to an ecstatic state called *Daat*, or knowledge. Here his sense of separation from God dissolves, if only for a moment. He is filled with a great joy, and seized by a sweet rapture. When he emerges from this state, he will again become aware of the inner repetition of the name, which he had transcended for that instant in a state the Theravadans might call jhana.

The end of the Kabbalist's path is *devekut*, in which the seeker's soul cleaves to God. When the Kabbalist stabilizes his consciousness at this level, he is no longer an ordinary man but a supernatural man, a *Zaddik*, or saint, who has escaped the chains of his personal ego. The qualities of one who has attained this station include equanimity, indifference to praise or blame, a sense of being alone with God, and prophecy. The ego's will is submerged in the divine will so that one's acts serve God rather than a limited self. He need no longer study Torah, for he has *become* Torah. One classical commentator defines devekut as a state of mind in which (Scholem, 1974: p. 175):

You constantly remember God and his love, nor do you remove your thought from Him . . . to the

point when such a person speaks with someone else,
his heart is not with them at all but is still before
God. And indeed it may be true of those who attain
this rank, that their soul is granted immortal life
even in this lifetime, for they are themselves a dwelling place for the Holy Spirit.

6. CHRISTIAN HESYCHASM

The first Christian monks were hermits who lived during
the fourth century A.D. in the most remote parts of the
barren Egyptian desert. A record from that time (Waddell, 1957: p. 57) has it that "once a certain brother
brought a bunch of grapes to the holy Macarius," one of
the hermits. But the hermit

> who for love's sake thought not on his own things
> but on the things of others, carried it to another
> brother, who seemed more feeble. And the sick man
> gave thanks to God for the kindness of his brother,
> but he too thinking more of his neighbor than him-
> self, brought it to another, and he again to another,
> and so that same bunch of grapes was carried round
> all the cells scattered as they were far over the
> desert, and no one knowing who first had sent it, it
> was brought at last to the first giver.

The Desert Fathers, like present-day Indian yogis in
the high Himalayas, sought out the isolation of the
harshest desert to commune with God free of worldly

distractions. The meditation practices and rules for living of these earliest Christian monks bear strong similarity to those of their Hindu and Buddhist renunciate brethren several kingdoms to the east. While Jesus and his teachings were their inspiration, the meditative techniques they adopted for finding their God suggest either a borrowing from the East or a spontaneous rediscovery. The ways of the Desert Fathers influence Christian monasticism to this day; their selfless love remains a guiding example.

Constant remembrance of God—much as the Bhakti and the Kabbalist aim for—has been a mainstay of Christian worship from the beginning, though the present-day use of rosary beads is a dim remainder of more wholehearted remembrance. Thomas Merton (1960) observes that what is today practiced as "prayer" in Christian churches is but one—albeit the surviving one—of a range of more intensive contemplative practices. The Desert Fathers meditated with verbal or silent repetition of a single phrase from the Scriptures, a Christian equivalent of mantra. The most popular was the prayer of the Publican: "Lord Jesus Christ, Son of God, have mercy on me a sinner." In its short form, *Kyrie eleison*, it was repeated silently throughout the day "until it became as spontaneous and instinctive as breathing."

The Desert Fathers emphasized purity, and their ascetic acts are fabled; St. Simeon the Stylite, who lived thirty years atop a pillar, was one of the best known. As in the Visuddhimagga, purification was used to aid concentration; in the words of one of the fathers, "the soul, unless it be cleansed of alien thoughts, cannot pray to God in contemplation." A corollary maxim is that life in the world matters only insofar as it reflects an inner life of contemplative practice. The spirit of this tradition,

preserved in modern monastic orders such as the Benedictine Trappists, is summed up by St. Abba Dorotheus,
an early Desert Father, in giving directions on spiritual
training (Kadloubovsky and Palmer, 1969: p. 161):

> Over whatever you have to do, even if it be very
> urgent and demands great care, I would not have
> you argue or be agitated. For rest assured, every-
> thing you do, be it great or small, is but one-eighth
> of the problem, whereas to keep one's state undis-
> turbed even if thereby one should fail to accomplish
> the task, is the other seven-eighths. So if you are
> busy at some task and wish to do it perfectly, try to
> accomplish it—which, as I said would be one-eighth
> of the problem, and at the same time to preserve
> your state unharmed—which constitutes seven-
> eighths. If, however, in order to accomplish your
> task you would inevitably be carried away and harm
> yourself or another by arguing with him, you should
> not lose seven for the sake of preserving one-eighth.

One major tradition stemming from the practices of
the Desert Fathers, though virtually lost in Western
Christendom, has changed little in Eastern Orthodoxy
since the first millenium of Christianity. This is the practice of the Prayer of Jesus. Its repetition fulfills Paul's in-
junction to "pray always." The early fathers called it "the
art of arts and the science of sciences," which leads the
seeker toward the highest human perfection. This tradition is preserved in the collection of early Christian writings known as the *Philokalia* (Kadloubovsky and Palmer,
1971). Its translation from Greek to Russian at the turn
of the century came on the crest of a wave of revival of
the practice throughout Russia (French, 1970).

The practice of the Prayer develops strength of concentration. As in Hindu Bhakti, the prerequisites for success with the Prayer are "genuine humility, sincerity, endurance, purity." Hesychius of Jerusalem, a fifth-century teacher of the uses of the Jesus Prayer (known now in the West as Hesychasm), describes it as a spiritual art that releases one completely from passionate thoughts, words, and evil deeds, and gives a "sure knowledge of God the Incomprehensible." Practice of the Prayer brings purity of heart, which is the "same as guarding the mind, kept perfectly free of all fantasies" and all thoughts. The way to this purity is unceasingly calling upon Christ, with perfect attention, resisting all other thoughts. Hesychius describes thoughts as "enemies who are bodiless and invisible, malicious and clever at harming us, skillful, nimble and practised in warfare," who enter in through the five senses. A mind caught in the senses or in thought is distant from Jesus. To overcome sense consciousness and attain a silent mind is to be with Him.

Among the "Directions to Hesychasts" is the instruction to find a teacher who bears the spirit within him. Once found, the seeker devotes himself to his master, obeying all his commands. Other directions include seclusion in a quiet, dimly lit cell, eating only as much as one needs to keep alive, silence, full performance of church ritual, fasting, vigils, and most important, practice of the Prayer.

The *Philokalia* quotes St. Nilus: "He who wishes to see what his mind really is must free himself of all thoughts; then he will see it like a sapphire or the hue of heaven." His instructions for stilling the mind specify sitting on a low stool in the solitude of one's cell on first awakening and for an hour (or more, if one is able), "collect your mind from its customary circling and wandering outside, and quietly lead it into the heart by way of breathing, keeping this prayer: 'Lord Jesus Christ, Son of God, have mercy on me!' connected with the breath." When with practice it becomes possible to so pray with perfect one-pointedness, "then, abandoning the many and the varied, we shall unite with the One, the Single and the Unifying, directly in a union which transcends reason"— presumably, in jhana.

Prayer is not to be limited to specific sessions but practiced without distraction in the midst of every activity. The Prayer so performed brings purity to worldly activity. The monk who has mastered this ability has the stature of Christ because he enjoys perfect purity of heart. The goal of the Desert Fathers' efforts was what Merton calls a "nowhereness and no-mindness"—a condition known by the name *quies*, literally "rest"—the monk having lost all preoccupation with his limited self. Combined with ascetic life in the desert, these prayer practices, in the words of Merton, "enabled the old superficial self to be purged away and permitted the gradual emergence of the true, secret self in which the Believer and Christ were 'one spirit'." St. Isaac comments that one who has attained a state of effortless, constant prayer (Kadloubovsky and Palmer, 1971: p. 213):

. . . has reached the summit of all virtues, and has become the abode of the Holy Spirit . . . when the Holy Spirit comes to live in a man, he never ceases to pray, for then the Holy Spirit constantly prays in him . . . In eating or drinking, sleeping or doing something, even in deep sleep his heart sends forth without effort the incense and sighs of prayer.

The themes of acts of purification, deep meditation, and finally their fruition in spontaneous purity and constant remembrance of God are not unique to Eastern Orthodoxy's Hesychasts. These central threads are widespread in Catholic contemplative traditions. St. Augustine, for one, advocated these same basic practices. Furthermore, the similarity of entry into jhana and the union with the One of the Christian mystic is clear in St. Augustine's *Confessions*. Augustine advocated a long process of self-denial, self-conquest, and the practice of virtue as preparation for "the ascent to the contemplation of God." Only such ascetic self-discipline can bring about the readjustment of character prerequisite for entry into the higher stages of a spiritual life. Augustine is insistent that not until the monk has so become "cleansed and healed" can he begin the proper practice of what he calls "contemplation." Contemplation itself entails "recollection" and "introversion." Recollection is concentrating the mind, banishing all images, thoughts, and sense perceptions. Having emptied the mind of all distractions, introversion can begin. Introversion concentrates the mind on its own deepest part in what is seen as the final step before the soul finds God: "The mind abstracts itself from all the bodily senses, as interrupting and confounding it with their din, in order to see itself in itself." So seeing, the soul arrives at God "in and above itself." Augustine describes the physical side of the state induced by this experience in terms like the Visuddhimagga's for jhana (Butler, 1966: p. 50):

> When the attention of the mind is wholly turned away and withdrawn from the bodily senses, it is called an ecstasy. Then whatever bodies may be

present are not seen with the open eyes, nor any voices heard at all. It is a state midway between sleep and death: The soul is rapt in such wise as to be withdrawn from the bodily senses more than in sleep, but less than in death.

St. Benedict's still definitive *Rule for Monasteries* depicts this progression in terms of degrees of "humility" or purity. At the twelfth and highest degree, the monk not only seems by all appearances to be humble but also has a genuine internal humility. His humility stems from a constant thought very much like the Prayer of the Publican: "Lord I am a sinner and not worthy to lift up my eyes to heaven." At this point, formerly effortful self-discipline becomes effortless (Doyle, 1948: p. 28–29):

Having climbed all these steps of humility, therefore, the monk will presently come to that perfect love of God which casts out fear. And all those precepts which formerly he had not observed without fear, he will now begin to keep by reason of that love, without any effort, as though naturally and by habit. No longer will his motive be the fear of hell, but rather the love of Christ, good habit and delight in the virtues which the Lord will deign to show forth by the Holy Spirit in His servant now cleaned from vice and sin.

7. SUFISM

For the Sufi, the basic human weakness is being bound by the lower self. The saints have overcome their lower nature, and novices seek to escape it. Meditation is essential in the novice's efforts to purify his heart. "Meditation for one hour," said an early Sufi master, "is better than ritual worship for a whole year."

The main meditation among Sufis is *zikr*, which means "remembrance." The zikr par excellence is *La ilāha illā* 'llah: "There is no god but God." Bishi al-Hafi, an early Sufi of Baghdad, said, "The Sufi is he who keeps his Heart pure." The Sufi aims for a purity that is total and permanent. The way to this purity is constant remembrance of God. The Prophet Muhammed himself said, "There is a polish for everything that taketh away rust; and the polish of the Heart is the invocation of Allah." Remembrance of God through repeating his name purifies the seeker's mind and opens his heart to Him. A zikr, for example, always accompanies Sufi dancing; it enhances the dance's effect to maintain the remembrance of God throughout. "The dance opens a door in the soul to divine influences," wrote Sultan Walad, Rumi's son. "The dance is good when it arises from remembrance of the Beloved."

Zikr is also a solitary meditation. At first, it is an oral repetition, later a silent one; a fourteenth-century manuscript says, "When the heart begins to recite, the tongue should stop." The goal of zikr, as in all meditation systems, is to overcome the mind's natural state of carelessness and inattention. His mind mastered, the Sufi can become one-pointed on God. The Sufi comment on normal consciousness is that humans are "asleep in a night-

mare of unfulfilled desires," that with the transcendence
mental discipline brings, these desires fall away.

The normal state of attention—scattered and random,
thoughtless and heedless—is the mode of the profane.
Remembrance, which anchors the Sufi's mind on God,
focuses his attention and allows him to turn away from
the pulls of the world. A ninth-century Egyptian Sufi
commented on the special efforts the seeker makes: "The
repentance of the masses is from sins, whereas repentance of the elect is from distraction." After intensive
practice of meditation or group chanting, the following
relaxation of efforts may bring a floodtide of old habits of
mind. The degree of such a relapse serves as a gauge of
spiritual progress. No virtue is acquired if the conditioned habits and reactions take control as soon as the
seeker's intensity lessens.

There is an interplay between effort and grace on the
Sufi path. An eleventh-century itinerary of the Sufi path
by al-Qushari lists the spiritual stations (*maqam*) due to
one's own efforts. These purificatory acts prepare the
Sufi for achieving states (*hal*) that are independent of his
own effort. These effortless states are the gift of God.
The first station is that of "conversion," in which the
Sufi resolves to abandon worldly life and devote himself
to spiritual seeking. Then come a number of efforts at
self-purification. These include outright struggle against
his own carnal nature, helped by withdrawal into solitude for ridding himself of evil habits. At this stage, the
Sufi may minimize his involvement in worldly activities
and renounce even wholesome pleasures ordinarily permitted him. He may become a voluntary pauper, accept-
ing his tribulations as tests of purity and practicing con-
tentment with whatever comes his way. This last station

merges into the first God-given state, satisfaction with things as they are ordained by God.

The central premise supporting these renunciatory acts permeates Sufi thought: Abu Said of Mineh framed it as follows (Rice, 1964: p. 34): "When occupied with self, you are separated from God. The way to God is but one step; the step out of yourself." Al-Ghazali, a twelfth-century legalist turned Sufi, commented on the essence of the way of the Sufi (Nicholson, 1929: p. 39):

> . . . the gift of the doctrine lies in overcoming the appetites of the flesh and getting rid of its evil dispositions and vile qualities, so that the heart may be cleared of all but God; and the means of clearing it is dhikr Allah, commemoration of God and the concentration of every thought upon Him.

Along his way to desirelessness, the Sufi undergoes states typical of progress in many other kinds of meditation. *Qurb* is a sense of God's constant nearness induced by concentration on Him. In *mahabba*, the Sufi loses himself in awareness of his beloved. Among the fruits of mahabba are visions and the "station of unity," where zikr (the remembrance), *zakir* (the one who remembers), and *mazkur* (the one remembered) become one. A Theravadan Buddhist might see these experiences as entry into first jhana. Sufis recognize mastery at the point when the zakir's attention fixes on the zikr without effort, driving out other thoughts from his mind. Sufis see this state, called *fana*, as a pure gift of grace in which the zakir is "lost in Truth." Fana means "passing away in God." It is attained, notes Arberry (1972), when "self as well as the world has been cast aside." The cessation of both internal and external awareness in one-pointed focus on the zikr marks the Sufi's absorption of fana as comparable to the Buddhist's jhana.

Practice in the Sufi way extends to every waking moment, as is evident in directions for one technique of a proto-Sufi order (Bennett, 1973: p. 34): "Be present at every breath. Do not let your attention wander for the duration of a single breath. Remember yourself always and in all situations." The extension of practice to all situations culminates in *baqa*, abiding in some degree of fana consciousness while in the midst of ordinary activity. The tenth-century Sufi al-Junaid of Baghdad gives a classic definition of fana as "dying-to-self," which carries over as baqa, "life-in-Him." In this transition, the Sufi does not cease to function as an individual; rather, his nature becomes perfected. The Sufi Idries Shah (1971) speaks of this change in terms of an "extra dimension of being" operating parallel to ordinary cognition and calls it "objective consciousness." Others speak of an inner transformation wherein the Sufi acquires "reflexes that conform to spiritual reality."

Sufis insist that their teaching must never be fixedly dogmatic but flexible enough to fit the needs of specific persons, times, and places. As one modern teacher, Sufi Abdul-Hamid, puts it (Shah, 1972: p. 60): "The Work is carried out by the teacher in accordance with his perception of the situation in which he finds himself. This means that there is no textbook, no system, no method, other than that which belongs to the school of the moment." There have been many guidebooks prepared for the Sufi seeker in different times and places. One such is Abu al-Najib's (1975) twelfth-century *A Sufi Rule for Novices*, a classical manual of the Sufi path. Though this

Sufi rule may bear little resemblance to contemporary practice, it allows us useful glimpses into the specifics of Sufi method and instructive comparisons to other spiritual paths.

Ibn al-Najib (1097–1168 A.D.) set down his rules for conduct for beginners in the Suhrwardi order to which he belonged; its purpose is comparable to that of the Visuddhimagga. Though these rules pertain to a certain group in a specific time and place, they have been used throughout the Muslim world and are themselves the basis for later Sufi instructional works. These rules give one of many variations on Sufi training. Many rules resonate with advice to Buddhist, Hindu, Kabbalist, and early Christian seekers. Just as the Bhakti is told to keep to satsang, al-Muridan advises: "The Sufi should associate with people of his kind and those from whom he can benefit." The novice should attach himself to a qualified teacher, or *shayk*, constantly seeking his direction and obeying him fully. He is urged to render service to his shayk and his fellows. Service is exalted as the best calling for the aspirant; the servant is said to rank next to the shayk himself. As in the Visuddhimagga and Christ's Sermon on the Mount, the novice's rules dictate: "One should not be concerned about the provisions of livelihood nor should one be occupied in seeking, gathering and storing them." For the Prophet himself "did not store anything for the morrow." Coveting food, clothes, or shelter hinders the Sufi's purity, for God revealed: "Those hearts which were bound to their desires were screened from Him." Though celibacy is not required of Sufis, these twelfth-century rules adjure: "In our times it is better to avoid marriage and suppress desire by discipline, hunger, vigils, and traveling." Finally, the Sufi

must be a Moslem par excellence, observing all rules of
the faith to the letter, for "the more saintly the man, the
more strictly will he be judged."

Each Sufi master, order, and group has its own
methods or combination of teaching techniques. The
ways vary, but the goal is the same. Mahmud Shabastri,
a master and author of *The Secret Garden*, put it this way:

> That man attains to the secret of unity
> Who is not detained at the stages on the road.
> Your being is naught but thorns and weeds,
> Cast it all clean away from you.
> Go sweep out the chamber of your heart,
> Make it ready to be the dwelling place of the
> Beloved.
> When you depart out, He will enter in,
> In you, void of yourself, will He display
> His beauty.

Sufi doctrine holds men are bound by their conditioning—the thorns and weeds that keep them from God.
The ordinary man is trapped in suffering by his conditioning. Strong habits of thought, feeling, and perception
dictate human reactions to the world; man is a slave to his
habits. People are asleep but do not know it. To awaken
them to their condition—the first step in escaping it—
people need a shock. One function of Sufi teaching
stories, such as the tale of the blind men and the ele-
phant, is to provide such a shock. These tales have many
layers of meaning. Some are hidden to most hearers,
some obvious. Not everyone gets the same lessons from
the stories, for what the listener hears depends on his
stage along the Sufi path. The skillful teacher uses just

the right tale at the perfect moment to impart an understanding for which the student is ripe.

Such shocks and lessons all help the Sufi aspirant on
his way to inner purification. According to Sufi psychology, our habitual impulses are the stuff of the lower soul,
or *nafs*, which must be disciplined and watched continually lest it lead the seeker toward evil and away from
God. Al-Muridin recommends overcoming the influence
of nafs by detached observation of its workings. Nafs,
goes a saying, are like an idol; looking at it with sympa-
thy is idolatry; looking with scrutiny is worship.
Through detached scrutiny of his lower urges, impulses,
and desires, the Sufi can break their hold over his mind
and so replace his negative qualities with virtuous ones.

Al-Muridin comments in his rules that "the consum-
mate Sufi is in a position of stability, and he is immune
to the effects of the changeful states of mind or harsh circumstances." This equanimity allows the finished Sufi to
be in the world but not of it. A calm exterior, however,
may not reflect the inner ecstasy of a close communion
with God. One modern shayk describes the Sufi's supreme state as "being inwardly drunk and outwardly
sober."

One old master includes in his list of the finished Sufi's
attributes: a sense of being subject entirely to God rather
than one's own will; the desire to have no personal desire;
"grace"—that is, perfect performance of acts in God's
service; truthfulness in thought and deed; putting others'
interests before one's own; service with complete self-
disregard; constant remembrance of God; generosity,
fearlessness, and the ability to die nobly. But Sufis may
balk at such specific formulae for measuring spiritual
progress, or worse, at trying to gauge another's attain-
ments through such a checklist.

Those who would judge others should heed the advice in a Sufi tale retold by Idries Shah (1971: p. 75):

> Yaqub, the son of the Judge, said that one day he questioned Bahaudin Nawshband in this manner: When I was in companionship with the Murshid of Tabriz, he regularly made a sign that he was not to be spoken to, when he was in a condition of special reflection. But you are accessible to us at all times. Am I correct in concluding that this difference is due to your undoubtedly greater capacity of detachment, the capacity being under your dominion, rather than fugitive?
> Bahaudin told him:
> No, you are always seeking comparisons between people and between states. You are always seeking evidences and differences, when you are not you are seeking similarities. You do not really need so much explanation in matters which are outside such measurement. Different modes of behavior on the part of the wise are to be regarded as due to differences in individuality; not of quality.

8. TRANSCENDENTAL MEDITATION

Transcendental Meditation (TM) is the best-known meditation technique in the West and Maharishi Mahesh Yogi, its formulator, the most famous yogi. TM is a classic Hindu mantra meditation in a modern Western package. Maharishi has been artful in his avoidance of

Sanskrit terms and use of scientific findings to validate meditation in a skeptical culture so that normal Americans can feel comfortable joining in a practice developed by and for Hindus in India. He also downplays the orthodox nature of his beliefs. The theory behind TM— "Science of Creative Intelligence"—is an updated restatement of the basic teaching of Sankaracharya's eighth-century Advait school of Vedantic thought.

Sankaracharya wrote at a time when Buddhism dominated India. His highly successful religious crusade revived Hinduism, offering a final state of nonduality rather than nirvana to the seeker. The goal of Advait is union of the seeker's mind with the formless Brahma or infinite consciousness, a step beyond the Bhakti's goal of union with a form of God. The means to this formless union is samadhi. This is also the goal in TM, though Maharishi no longer describes it in these terms. TM traces its root back to Sankaracharya, though it is a reformulation of Advait thought tailored to Western ears.

Maharishi's technique of TM is in the mainstream of jhana practices, though it is often touted as unique. Like all Advait yogis, Maharishi sees that "duality is the fundamental cause of suffering." His technique for transcending duality begins with repetition of a mantra, a Sanskrit word or sound. Just as in the Visuddhimagga, in which different meditation subjects are given to people of different temperament, Maharishi claims that selection of the proper mantra for a particular individual is a vital factor in TM. And just as the Visuddhimagga depicts finer levels of one-pointedness as increasingly blissful and sublime, Maharishi describes the increasing "charm" as the mind is allowed to follow its natural tendency to go to "a field of greater happiness" by entering the subtler states of a thought—that is, the mantra.

There is a mystique about the specialness of each person's mantra, and teachers admonish newcomers never to reveal theirs to anyone or even speak it aloud. But as meditators are sometimes chagrined to learn, people who fall into general categories of age, education, and so on, are given the same mantra. The mantras themselves are by no means special to TM but come from standard Sanskrit sources used by many Hindus today. Like millions of modern Bhaktis in India, the TM meditator in Des Moines may be silently intoning "Shyam" (a name of Lord Krishna), or "Aing" (a sound sacred to the Divine Mother).

The beliefs that particular mantric sounds bestow certain boons or are appropriate to special types of persons is widespread in Hinduism. The ancient *Saiva Upanishads*, for example, contain a discourse on the fifty letters of the Sanskrit alphabet, treating each as a mantra in itself and describing its special virtures. The letter *umkara* (Ū) gives strength; *kumkara* (kā) is an antidote against poisons; *ghamkara* (gha) bestows prosperity; *phamkara* (pha) grants psychic powers.

In TM, meditators learn to avoid effortful concentration. The student is told to bring his mind gently back to the mantra as it wanders. In effect, this process is one of becoming one-pointed, though concentration is passive rather than forced. The following oft-quoted description by Maharishi (1969: p. 470) of the nature of TM well describes the focal narrowing of attention on a meditation object, and transcendence of the object, in ascending through access concentration to the second jhana. Transcendental meditation, he says, entails ". . . turning the attention inward towards the subtler levels of a thought until the mind transcends the experience of the subtlest state of the thought and arrives at the source of thought . . ."

As in the jhanas, bliss arises with the stillness of mind. The goal of mantra is what Maharishi calls "transcendental consciousness": when mind "arrives at the direct experience of bliss, it loses all contact with the outside and is contented in the state of transcendental bliss-consciousness." In the language of the Visuddhimagga, this is access concentration or jhana. The next phase in Maharishi's program is the infusion of jhana, or transcendental consciousness, into the waking, dreaming, and sleeping states by alternating normal activity with periods of meditation. The state thereby achieved he calls "cosmic consciousness" in which "no activity, however rigorous, can take one out of Being." Maharishi denies the need to impose renunciation on oneself. He sees purification as part of cosmic consciousness. It is an effect of transcendence, not a prerequisite. According to Maharishi, "Proficiency in the virtues can only be gained by repeated experience of samadhi."

Before the meditator gains cosmic consciousness, the effects of his daily meditation gradually wear off as time passes; in cosmic consciousness, these effects persist always. Maharishi elaborates the transition from transcendental to cosmic consciousness (1966: p. 53):

From this state of pure Being the mind comes back again to experience the thought in the relative world . . . With more and more practice, the ability of the mind to maintain its essential nature while experiencing objects through the senses increases. When this happens the mind and its essential nature, the state of transcendental Being, become one, and the mind is then capable of retaining its essential nature—Being—while engaged in thought, speech or action.

He sees cosmic consciousness as a state in which two distinct levels of organization in nervous system function. Usually, these levels inhibit each other, but here they operate side by side while they maintain their unique characteristics: Transcendental consciousness, for example, co-exists with the waking state. "Silence," says Maharishi, "is experienced with activity and yet is separate from it." The meditator in cosmic consciousness finds this inner peace persists in all circumstances as a "pure awareness" along with activity. Although the effects of transcendence during meditation can wear off after meditation is over, once mastered, cosmic consciousness is permanent. The person in cosmic consciousness has experienced in transcendence a jhanic state in which sense perception ceases. During waking, he remains relatively detached from sense perception, although he is more sensitive to both his own thought processes and external events.

As cosmic consciousness deepens, the meditator finds the bliss of transcendental consciousness persisting now in other states. As this bliss pervades other areas of his life, he finds that by comparison sensual pleasures are not so enchanting as before. While he still has desires, his actions are no longer driven by them. His state is one of equanimity: The turbulence and excitement of intense emotions—fear, grief, anger, depression, or craving—are softened by a permanent state of "restful alertness." Finally, they cease to arise. Equanimity also shows up in the meditator better resisting the fluctuating pull of life stress and daily tensions. He finds a new inner steadiness prevails, whereas once he would have wavered. Even-mindedness also manifests in the meditator loving others in equal share without undue fondness for specific people; his attachments weaken. He also finds he is more easily contented with whatever comes, more free from desires and dislikes. According to Maharishi, life in cosmic consciousness is tensionless. (1969: p. 287):

> . . . the enlightened man lives a life of fulfillment. His actions, being free from desire, serve only the need of the time. He has no personal interest to gain. He is engaged in fulfilling the cosmic purpose and therefore his actions are guided by nature. This is why he does not have to worry about his needs. His needs are the needs of nature, which takes care of their fulfillment, he being the instrument of the Divine.

A further step in the progression promised by Maharishi is God consciousness. This state is the result of devotion while in cosmic consciousness. In "God consciousness" the meditator perceives all things as sacred; "everything is naturally experienced in the awareness of God." At first, says Maharishi, this experience of unity in diversity can be overwhelming, and the meditator can become deeply lost in it. Gradually, however, God consciousness mixes with other activities, just as at an earlier stage transcendental consciousness merged with normal states to produce cosmic consciousness.

In God consciousness the meditator surrenders his individuality. This is "the most purified state" in which the meditator has overcome the least stain of impurity in thought or deed; he now dwells in perfect harmony with nature and the divine. Arriving at God consciousness, ac-

cording to Maharishi, entails a transformation, whereby
one is aware of God in all aspects of creation. Beyond
God consciousness the TM devotee may evolve into a
state called "unity." Here his consciousness is so refined
that he perceives all things free of any conceptual illu-
sion.

The means to these higher states in TM are advanced
techniques given to meditators over the course of several
years of practice and of service to the TM organization.
Though TM spokesmen may vaguely acknowledge these
more advanced methods, they never divulge their specifics. While the popular impression is that mantra meditation is the whole of TM, it seems that the meditator
must learn these secret, advanced practices in order to
reach the higher states described in the Science of Creative Intelligence.

9. PATANJALI'S
   ASHTANGA YOGA

The manual for meditators closest to the Visuddhimagga
in Hinduism is Patanjali's *Yoga Sutras*, still the most au-
thoritative source on yoga today (Prabhavananda and
Isherwood, 1969; Vivekananda, 1970.) Most every modern Indian meditation system, including TM, acknowledges the Yoga Sutras as one source of their own
method. There are numerous spiritual schools called
"yoga": Bhakti yoga is the path of devotion; karma yoga
uses selfless service; and gyana yoga takes the intellect as
its vehicle. The path outlined in the Yoga Sutras sub-
sumes them all.

Though their means may differ, all yogic paths seek to transcend duality in union. All these paths see the locus of duality as within the mind, in the separation between the mechanisms of awareness and their object. To transcend duality, the seeker must enter a state in which this gap is bridged, the experiencer and the object merging. This state is samadhi, in which the meditator's awareness merges with its contents.

The yoga aphorisms are a skeletal map to this state. The mind, it explains, is filled with thought waves that create the gulf that yoga seeks to bridge. By calming his thought waves, by stilling his mind, the yogi will find union. These thought waves are the source of strong emotions and blind habits that bind man to a false self. When his mind becomes clear and still, man can know himself as he really is. In this stillness, he can know God. In the process, his mistaken belief in himself as a separate, unique individual apart from God will be overcome. As his thought waves are subdued, the yogi's ego recedes. Finally, as a liberated man, he is able to don his ego or discard it like a suit of clothes. Donning the ego, he acts in the world; discarding it by stilling his mind, he unites with God.

But first he must undergo an arduous discipline of mind and body. This transformation begins with concentration, bringing his mind to one-pointedness. In Patanjali's system, one-pointedness is the main method around which all others turn. Some sources date the Aphorisms back more than fifteen hundred years, to about the same period as the Visuddhimagga. The spiritual *Zeitgeist* of that era is reflected in both; indeed, the paths they outline are in large part identical. The main difference between these two meditation manuals is Patanjali's insistence that samadhi rather than nirvana is the highway to liberation.

The royal, or *raja*, yoga outlined by Patanjali entails *ashtanga:* eight key practices or limbs. The first two, *yama* and *niyama*, are moral training for purity. The next two are *asana*, the development through physical exercises of a firm and erect posture, or "seat," and *pranayam*, exercises for controlling and stilling the breath. Both the third and fourth limbs have become intricately developed in their own right, so that some yogic schools use these practices as their main methods—and most Americans associate "yoga" exclusively with these two limbs.

Most textbooks of *hatha* and pranayam point out that these are helps to the attainment of samadhi, not ends in themselves. Some, however, focus solely on rigorous physical purifications as means to alter consciousness. Vyas Dev (1970), for example, details 250 *asana* postures, elaborates fifty different pranayam exercises and twenty-five *shat-karmas* and *mudras*—methods for cleansing internal organs. Before sitting in deep meditation for a long time, advises Vyas Dev, the yogi should clear his bowels completely by drawing in and expelling water through his anus, empty his bladder by drawing in water and then expelling it through a catheter, and purify his digestive system by swallowing and extracting about seventy feet of string made of fine yarn. He should also swallow two or three pints of lukewarm salt water to make himself vomit and swallow and extract a three-inch-wide strip of cloth seven yards long to finish the job. Then he is ready for serious meditation.

Patanjali's stipulation about these first four limbs, however, is that the yogi should do them simply to the point at which his body and mind are stilled. These are mere preliminaries for sitting in meditation, useful for overcoming the obstacles to concentration such as doubt, sloth, despair, and craving for sensual pleasures. Actual meditation begins with the second group of limbs. These are all steps in becoming one-pointed. In the fifth limb, *pratyahara*, the yogi withdraws his mind from sense objects, focusing his attention on the meditation object. In the sixth, *dharana*, he holds his mind on the object. The seventh, *dhyana*, involves "an unbroken flow of thought toward the object of concentration." The sixth and seventh limbs correspond to initial and sustained application of attention in the Visuddhimagga system. The final limb is samadhi.

The combination dharana, dhyana, and samadhi is a state called *samyama*. This highly concentrated state holds the key to supernormal powers such as clairvoyance and telepathy. The Sutras have a lengthy section on how to apply samyama to gain various powers. By focusing samyama on his memories, the yogi can retrieve knowledge of his past lives; samyama on the marks of another's body reveals his state of mind; samyama on the yogi's own throat stills his hunger and thirst. As in the Visuddhimagga, the Sutras see these powers as subtle snares for the seeker. The yogi is urged to give up these seductive traps as last temptations for the ego.

The aphorisms say that samyama on "single moments and their sequence" gives discriminative knowledge, or *prajna*, which "delivers from the bondage of ignorance." But this foray into the path of insight seems glossed over in most modern commentaries on Patanjali. It is samadhi that is taught as the heart of yoga; Vivekananda (1970) says, "samadhi is Yoga proper; that is the highest means." Patanjali lists many suitable objects for concentration: the syllable Om, or other mantra; the heart; a deity or "illumined soul"; or a divine symbol. The yogi, in merging consciousness with the primary object, will first achieve savichara samadhi—access concentration. In this level of samadhi, there is identity with the primary object "mixed with awareness of name, quality, and knowledge." After this comes *nirvichara* samadhi—first jhana, in which there is identity without other awareness. Once the nirvichara level is gained, the yogi is to wipe out even the thought of the primary object and so attain *nirvikalpa* samadhi (as in the example of Sri Ramakrishna), in which all sense of duality is obliterated.

Nirvikalpa is the deepest samadhi; in it, mind is at its stillest. Yogic lore has it that one in this state could remain for as long as three months in continuous deep meditation, his breath and other metabolic functions virtually suspended all that time. In this samadhi, says one commentator, "an avalanche of indescribable bliss sweeps away all relative ideas of pain and blame . . . All doubts and misgivings are quelled forever; the oscillations of mind are stopped; the momentum of past actions is exhausted." But one limit of nirvikalpa samadhi is that it can be enjoyed only while the yogi remains still, absorbed in deep meditation.

The final step in ashtanga yoga is extending the deep stillness of samadhi into the yogi's waking state. When samadhi spreads throughout other states so that no activity or inner stirring can dislodge its hold on the yogi's mind, this marks him as a *jivan-mukti*, a liberated man. In his introduction to Sri Ramakrishna's biography, the anonymous chronicler gives an eloquent account of the state enjoyed by that saint (M., 1928: p. 27). On emerging from nirvikalpa samadhi:

> he is devoid of ideas of "I" and "mine," he looks on the body as a mere shadow, an outer sheath encasing the soul. He does not dwell on the past, takes no thought for the future, and looks with indifference

on the present. He surveys everything in the world with an eye of equality; he is no longer touched by the infinite variety of phenomenon; he no longer reacts to pleasure and pain. He remains unmoved where he—that is to say, his body—is worshipped by the good or tormented by the wicked; for he realizes that it is the one Brahman that manifests itself through everything.

The Indian saint Ramana Maharshi (1962) proposed a simple operational definition for distinguishing between a yogi in nirvikalpa samadhi and one in sahaj samadhi: If there remains a difference between samadhi and the waking state, it is nirvikalpa samadhi at best; if no difference, the yogi has reached his goal of sahaj samadhi.

The yogi in sahaj partially resides in samadhi, no longer identifying with his thoughts or senses. His being is grounded in a consciousness transcending the sensory world, and so he remains detached from that world while operating in it. This "ideal of Yoga, the state of *jivan-mukti*," writes Eliade (1970), is life in an "eternal present" in which one "no longer possesses a personal consciousness—that is, a consciousness nourished on his own history—but a witness consciousness which is pure lucidity and spontaneity."

In sahaj samadhi, meditation is a self-sustained, spontaneous fact of the yogi's existence. He expresses his stillness of mind in his actions. He is free of all ego ties and interests; his actions are no longer bound by the deposits of the past. Meher Baba (1967) describes this as "a state of full wakefulness in which there is no ebb and flow, waxing or waning, but only the steadiness of true perception." The jivan-mukti has transcended his body consciousness along with the conceptual universe; he does not see the world as different from himself. For one who dwells in sahaj, there is no ego, and there are no "others."

10. INDIAN TANTRA AND KUNDALINI YOGA

The Tantric tradition native to India is, according to some sources, a refinement of ancient shamanistic practices that has found its way into both Hindu and Buddhist meditation systems (Eliade, 1970). Indian Tantra alters consciousness by arousing energies that are normally latent. Some meditation systems introduced to the West have their roots in "kundalini" yoga, a Tantric teaching. Kundalini, says Tantric physiology, is a huge reserve of spiritual energy located at the base of the spine. When aroused, kundalini travels up the spine through six centers, or "*chakras*," reaching the seventh at the top of the head. Kundalini has few specific correlates with Western notions of anatomy. Chakras refer to energy patterns, localized in certain physical centers.

When kundalini focuses in a chakra, it activates characteristic energies of these centers. Each chakra has an emblematic set of attitudes, motives, and mental states that dominate a person's mind when kundalini sparks it. The first chakra, located between the anus and the genitals, involves the struggle to survive. Territoriality, possessiveness, brute force, undue preoccupation with the body and health, and fear for one's safety all reflect the mental state of the first chakra. The second chakra embodies sexuality and sensuality. It is in the genitals. When this chakra is active, lust, greed, and craving for sensual delights are one's predominant states of mind. The urge to be powerful and influence others is tied to the third chakra, located near the navel. Persuasion or manipulation of others to serve one's own ends are third-chakra behavior.

Most people much of the time are motivated by mental states in which these first three chakras are active. Kundalini yoga aims to bring this energy up to the higher chakras, just as Kabbalah seeks to raise consciousness to higher planes. The fourth chakra, in the center of the chest by the heart, represents selfless love and caring for others. The pure love of a mother for her child is of the fourth chakra. But fourth-chakra love is not romantic; rather, it combines with a clear-sighted detachment to make for compassion. When kundalini activates the three topmost chakras, the yogi experiences transcendental states. These three centers are the fifth chakra at the throat, the sixth at the center of the forehead, and the seventh at the top of the head. The meditator seeks to free kundalini from his lower chakras, in which it ordinarily is trapped, and raise it to his higher ones. When it reaches his seventh chakra and stabilizes there, he feels a state of intense ecstasy and union with God. He is considered liberated, free of bondage to those habits and acts stemming from the lower chakras by which most men are bound.

The essence of Tantric practice is the use of the senses to transcend sense consciousness in samadhi. Though the senses are, of course, the means to transcendence in all techniques for one-pointedness, Tantrism is unique in the diversity of techniques it offers for transcending sense consciousness. Among them are the use of mantra;

yantra, objects for visualization exercises such as a mandala; concentration on *shabd*, supersubtle inner sounds; pranayam and asanas; concentration on the play of forces in the chakras; and *maithuna*, the arousal of *shakti*—kundalini energy—through controlled, ritual sexual intercourse.

Maithuna is the Tantric technique that most fascinates Westerners, who more often than not mistake it for an indulgence of sexual appetites rather than a means to their mastery. Ritual intercourse is a potent means to arouse kundalini energy, allowing the self-disciplined yogi to raise this energy to his higher chakras. Maithuna is one of five actions generally prohibited to Hindu yogis but used by Tantrics of the Bon Marg, or "left-handed path." The first four are imbibing fish, meat, liquor, and performing certain mudras, all of which the Tantric does in a strictly prescribed manner, as a prelude to maithuna. Throughout the ritual, he does silent japa of his own special mantra, given by his guru, and at points he recites certain other mantras. During maithuna itself, the yogi carries out carefully delineated ritual actions—including exactly where and how to touch his partner's body.

In maithuna, the male is passive, the female active; since the arousal of energy rather than climax is the goal, there is little movement. During intercourse, the Tantric mentally recites mantras such as "Om, thou goddess resplendent . . . into the fire of the self, using the mind as a sacrificial ladle, I, who am engaged in harnessing the sense organs, offer this oblation." At the moment of ejaculation, he is to repeat a mantra that consecrates his semen itself as a sacrificial offering (Bharati, 1970). The key to maithuna, as well as the goal of all Tantric practices, is the detachment borne of samadhi. This detachment converts the energy of desires into higher forms. Tantric texts frequently repeat (Eliade, 1970: p. 263): "By the same acts that cause some men to burn in hell for thousands of years, the Yogin gains his eternal salvation."

Tantric language is veiled and so is open to many levels of interpretation. Actions that from outside seem improper can have within Tantra a special, deeper meaning. An example of this double meaning in Tantra is a Tibetan *kapala*, a cup made of human skull mounted on a silver stand. Its description in a museum reads:

> The vessel holds the Amrit used for performing esoteric rituals. Those who have such dualistic concepts as the clean and the unclean cannot think of using a human skull. But the Tantrics, who have gained Transcendental Wisdom, have no superstition and to them golden cups and human skulls are the same. The skulls are used to symbolize this attitude of mind.

One modern version of kundalini yoga is *siddha-yoga*, taught by Swami Muktananda (Amma, 1969; Muktananda, 1969, 1970). This system begins with traditional practices such as asana, pranayam, chanting, and japa. He instructs the beginner to meditate with the mantra, "Guru Om," or with each breath, "so-ham." Muktananda emphasizes the guru-disciple relationships. The core of siddha-yoga training is the tradition in which the guru grants a direct, instantaneous transcendental experience to the devotee. This process, called *shaktipat diksha*, is an initiation by look, touch, or word. In this transmission the devotee who approaches the guru with love, devotion, and faith has his shakti—the energy of kundalini—aroused.

When this happens, all other practices can fall away. The inner action of kundalini produces spontaneous meditation, pranayam, asanas, and mudras without the devotee's prior training or volition. This process of purification through shaktipat is said to take three to twelve years. In this period it transforms the entire personality of the devotee, the "limited I" having been abandoned. The devotee attains a sense of "oneness with all-pervading Cosmic Intellect." The imagery and terminology with which Muktananda describes this process is that of kundalini (1970: p. 54):

> . . . . the Kundalini, which stays in the *Muladhara*, gradually travels upwards piercing the chakras on her way until she reaches *Sahasrara*, the thousand-petalled lotus in the crown of the head . . . and the spiritual endeavor of an aspirant gets fulfilled.

During shaktipat the meditator may experience a wide variety of involuntary reactions. These include powerful moods of joy, dullness, or agitation; strange bodily postures, gestures, tremors, or dancing poses; feelings of wonder or fright; a period of pain in all parts of the body; various internal stirrings, muscle throbbing or thrills; spontaneous deep meditation; visions of lights, deities, or celestial places accompanied by a great joy and bliss; and, finally, there is a "divine light of indescribable lustre" or a subtle inner sound during meditation (Muktananda, 1970).

These phenomena serve to purify the meditator so that he can sustain *turiya*—a state akin to jhana—while in the three ordinary states of waking, dreaming, and sleeping. He reaches the further state of *Turiyatita* when his kundalini has stabilized in the topmost chakra, the *sahasrara*.

A person in this advanced state has forgotten body consciousness, enjoys extraordinary bliss and profound tranquility, and has attained "the fruit of Yoga," remaining "ever absorbed in the Supreme State," whatever he does. He performs any and all acts with peace and equanimity. A disciple of Muktananda, Amma (1969: p. 11), says of one in this state, "He has nothing to do and nothing to achieve; still he does the activities of worldly life remaining a witness to them all." One in turiyatita has become a siddha, a name denoting the supernormal psychic powers he is said to possess, among which is the capability of raising kundalini in others.

Tantra yoga alone among traditional meditation systems sees the yogi's attainment of *siddhis*, or supernormal psychic powers, as marking the end of his path. Says one Tantric scripture, "For all sadhana ceases when it has borne its fruit in siddhi." Certain Tantric practices are devised to produce certain siddhis such as mind reading. One reason siddhis may signify liberation for some is the high states that the possession of powers betokens. But meditation is central to all Tantric practices; the raising of kundalini, the means; samadhi, the goal.

11. TIBETAN BUDDHISM

The techniques of Tibetan Mahayana are founded in the classical Buddhist tradition that the Visuddhimagga expresses. It also blends with the classical, purely Tibetan elements and Tantraism. In an outline of meditation theory and practice by the Dalai Lama (1965), the theory

presented is essentially that of the Theravadan Visuddhimagga—or as Mahayanists call Theravada, the "Hinayana" tradition, or "Lesser Vehicle," in contrast to their
"Greater Vehicle." A critical difference between these
two main Buddhist traditions is the Mahayana bodhisattva vow to gain enlightenment not just for oneself but
for the sake of the salvation of all sentient beings. This
difference in motive, says the Dalai Lama, is decisive; it
makes a difference in both path and goal. He sees the
hinayana nirvana as a prior stage to the Mahayana goal of
bodhisattvahood. Still, his conception of the nirvanic
state agrees with the Visuddhimagga: it is "liberation
from this bondage" of *samsara* by a cessation in which the
"roots of delusion are thoroughly extracted," the ego or
"I-thought" severed. But for Mahayanists the goal is
beyond nirvana, in returning to the world and helping
others toward salvation.

Motive makes the difference between where insight
into emptiness brings the meditator. If he developed insight solely to liberate himself, he will be what, as we
have seen earlier, the Visuddhimagga calls an "*arahant.*"
If he was motivated by the "Bodhi-chitta of love and
compassion," he gains the "superior release" of the bodhisattva, in which his state of consciousness makes him a
more perfect vehicle of compassion so he can lead others
toward liberation. In either case, says the Dalai Lama, a
bodhisattva has "cleansed his mind of all impurities and
has removed the motives and inclinations that lead to
them." He has severed ties to the normal world of name
and form, the locus of ordinary consciousness.

The Mahayana path begins with a close cousin of the
Visuddhimagga teaching. There are three "moral precepts," ways for the meditator to realize the "Triple Refuge"—Buddha, Dharma, and Sangha—as his internal

realities. The Tibetan Buddhist meditator's first precept is sila, vows of upright behavior. The second is samadhi (Tibetan: *shiney*), fixing the mind on one object to develop his one-pointedness. The recommended conditions in which to practice samadhi are as in the Visuddhimagga. The meditator should go into seclusion, sever his ties to worldly activities, and so on. The early meditation objects include those listed in the Visuddhimagga, such as mindfulness of the breath. Some, especially in later stages, resemble Indian Tantric deities. These more advanced subjects are the object of visualization. Such subjects come in innumerable aspects "so that they suit the physical, mental and sensuous attitudes of different individuals," and arouse strong faith and devotion. These visualization subjects embody different aspects of the mind. The meditator identifies with these mental states or qualities as he visualizes the figure. Chogyam Trungpa (1975: p. 47) describes one such figure:

On the disc of the autumn moon, clear and pure, you place a seed syllable. The cool blue rays of the seed syllable emanate immense cooling compassion that radiates beyond the limits of sky or space. It fulfills the needs and desires of sentient beings, bringing basic warmth so that confusions may be clarified. Then from the seed syllable you create a Mahavairocana Buddha, white in color, with the features of an aristocrat—an eight-year-old child with a beautiful, innocent, pure, powerful, royal gaze. He is dressed in the costume of a medieval king of India. He wears a glittering gold crown inlaid with wishfulfilling jewels. Part of his long black hair floats over his shoulders and back; the rest is made into a topknot surmounted by a glittering blue dia-

mond. He is seated crosslegged on the lunar disc
with his hands in the meditation mudra holding a
vajra carved from pure white crystal.

The Dalai Lama lists four steps in reaching samadhi.
There is an initial fixing of the meditator's mind on the
primary object while he tries to prolong his period of
concentration on it. In the next stage, his concentration is
intermittent. Distractions come and go in his mind, alternating with attention to the primary object. At this stage,
he may experience joy and ecstasy arising from his one-
pointedness; these feelings will strengthen his efforts at
concentration. This stage, like jhana access, culminates
when his mind finally overcomes all disturbances, ena-
bling him to concentrate on the object without any inter-
ruption whatsoever in the perfect one-pointedness of the
jhanas. The final stage is that of "mental quiescence," in
which his total concentration comes with minimal effort—that is, jhana mastery. The meditator can now concentrate on any object with effortless ease; psychic powers have become possible.

Jhana mastery matters in Mahayana not because of the
powers made possible but due to its usefulness in the
meditator's realizing "*Sunyata*," the essential emptiness of
the phenomenal world, including the world within the
meditator's own mind. The means for this breakthrough
is the meditator's third precept, the practice of vipassana
(Tibetan: *thagthong*). He uses the power of samadhi as a
steppingstone for meditation on Sunyata. The Dalai
Lama (1965) does not specify details of vipassana technique in Tibetan practice. But he does mention that the
flow of the meditator's undisciplined mind can be
stopped "and the wandering or projecting mind brought
to rest by concentration on the physical makeup of one's

body and the psychological makeup of one's mind"—two techniques of vipassana taught in the Visuddhimagga. By means of vipassana with Sunyata as focus, the meditator discards his ego beliefs, finally reaching "the goal that leads to the destruction of all moral and mental defilements."

This goal does not, however, represent the culmination of the meditator's spiritual development in Tibetan Buddhism but a stage along the way in his further practice and evolution. The control of mental processes he gains through concentration and insight prepare him for further training in techniques such as visualizations and the cultivation of qualities such as compassion. The many schools within Tibetan Buddhism each has its particular emphasis and unique program for advanced training. In all of them, the basic meditative skills of concentration and insight are prerequisites for more complex, advanced efforts in training the meditator's mind.

Chogyam Trungpa (1976), in summarizing the Tibetan Buddhist path, advises that before the meditator begins any advanced Tibetan techniques, he needs to develop "transcendental common sense, seeing things as they are." For this reason, vipassana meditation forms the meditator's foundation. With his seeing things clearly, the meditator relaxes his defenses in his daily living situation. This opens him to *shunyata*, "direct experience without any props." This, in turn, inspires the meditator to aim toward the bodhisattva ideal. But this is not the end of the path: Beyond the bodhisattva experience is that of the "yogi," beyond the yogi is the "siddha," and beyond the siddha lies the "Buddha." At each of these levels, the seeker has a unique sense of himself and the world—for example, the bodhisattva experiences shunyata. At a still higher level is the psychological space of *mahamudra.* Here, says Trungpa (Guenther and Trungpa, 1975: p. 36), "symbols do not exist as such; the sense of experience ceases to exist. Directly relating to the play of situations, energy develops through a movement of spontaneity that never becomes frivolous." This leads one to "destroy whatever needs to be destroyed, and foster whatever needs to be fostered." When one has arrived at mahamudra, there is no more struggling along the path.

It is difficult for someone to assess the true nature of any spiritual path without himself participating in its practices. This applies all the more to systems like Tibetan Buddhism in which the heart of instruction is esoteric. Vajrayana, the tantric segment of Tibetan Buddhism, is veiled in secrecy; the great legendary tantric Milarepa warns (Chang, 1970): "The teachings of Tantra should be practiced secretly; they will be lost if demonstrated in the marketplace." Even if told publicly, many Tibetan methods are "self-secret" so that one needs to practice them and experience their fruits truly to understand them. Translations like Evans-Wentz' (1968, 1969) give the reader a vivid taste of Tibetan teachings. But to follow this intricate path, one needs to find a lama as guru, for even now specific methods in Tibetan Buddhism are transmitted only from teacher to student in teaching lineages that date back centuries.

12. ZEN

The word "Zen" is a cognate of the Pali word *jhana*, and both derive from the Sanskrit dhyana (meditation). The cultural interchange that culminated in Japanese Zen links to the Visuddhimagga tradition through the Ch'an meditation school of China. The changes undergone in the voyage through time and space from India of the fifth century to Japan of the present day are more evident in doctrine than in the specifics of practice. Doctrinal differences—much like those between Theravada and Mahayana Buddhism—have emphasized these changes and obscured the similarities. Some versions of Zen meditation, or *zazen*, remain identical to mindfulness or insight. As with mindfulness, all varieties of zazen broaden their focus from sitting meditation to the meditator's whole range of life situations.

Zen's down-to-earth zazen matters, but extensive scriptural studies are discouraged. The early Soto master Dogen (1971: p. 62) stated:

No matter how well you say you know . . . the esoteric and exoteric doctrines, as long as you possess a mind that clings to the body, you will be vainly counting others' treasures, without gaining even half a cent for yourself.

Zazen begins, as does vipassana, with a firm grounding in concentration; a wide variety of concentration techniques are employed. Samadhi or jhana is, in Zen terminology, the "great fixation" or "a state of oneness" in which the differences between things dissolve so that they appear to the meditator in the aspect of sameness. This is an intermediate stage on the path toward Zen's final realization. Suzuki warns (1958: p. 135): "When this state of great fixation is held as final, there will be no upturning, no outburst of satori, no penetration, no insight into Reality, no severing the bonds of birth and death."

Deep absorptions are not enough. They are necessary but not sufficient steps toward enlightenment. The wisdom of insight follows after and flows from samadhi.

Among Zen techniques are some unique methods for achieving jhana. One such, the *koan* (used primarily by the Rinzai sect), is a puzzle utterly impervious to solution by reason. Its "solution" lies in transcending thought by liberating the meditator's mind from the snare of language (Miura and Sasaki, 1965). Assigned a koan such as "What was your face before you were born?" or "What is Mu?" the aspirant keeps the koan constantly in mind. No matter what he is doing, when other matters intrude on his mind, he immediately lets them go and returns to his koan. As he discovers that his rational mind is unable to solve the insoluble, he reaches a feverish pitch of concentration from which arises a supreme frustration. As this happens, what once was a fully stated koan reduces to an emblematic fragment, for example, simply "Mu." When his discursive faculty finally exhausts itself, the moment of "realization" comes to the meditator. His thought ceases and he enters the state of *daigi*, or "fixation." His koan "yields up all its secrets" as he attains samadhi. (Suzuki, 1958).

Yasutani, a modern roshi who came to teach in America, utilized the koan for his more advanced students. He assigned beginners concentration on breathing. He saw as the aim of zazen not rendering the mind inactive in jhana but "quieting and unifying it in the midst of activity." Consequently, his students practiced concentration techniques until they developed a modicum of *joriki*, mental strength arising from one-pointedness of mind. The fruits of joriki are equanimity, determination, and a potential ripeness in the student for *Kensho-godo*, the *satori* awakening of "seeing into your True-nature."

When the student uses a koan, for instance, his samadhi comes to fruition when there is "absolute unity with Mu, unthinking absorption in Mu—this is ripeness." At this point, "inside and outside merge into a single unity." With this samadhi experience, *Kensho-godo* can take place, where he will "see each thing just as it is." A given *kensho* experience may fall anywhere within a wide range of depth, degree, and clarity.

Joriki strengthens the meditator's satori. This helps him extend his awakening beyond the session of zazen per se. The joriki he develops in his zazen cultivates the satori effect until finally it shapes all the rest of his daily life. When the student gains some control over his mind via one-pointedness exercises like counting breath or has exhausted his rational mind with koan, Yasutani-roshi frequently set him to a more advanced method called *shikan-taza*, "just sitting." In this type of Zen meditation, the student marshals a heightened state of concentrated awareness with no primary object. He just sits, keenly aware of whatever goes on in and around him. He sits alert and mindful, free from points of view or discriminating thoughts, merely watching. This technique is quite similar to vipassana. A related practice is "mobile zazen," in which he enters fully into every action with total attention and clear awareness. This corresponds to "bare attention" as described in the Visuddhimagga. Kapleau (1967) has noted these close parallels and cites a key Pali Sutra on mindfulness as a "prescription" for zazen:

In what is seen there must be just the seen;
In what is sensed there must be just the sensed;
In what is thought there must be just the thought.

There are many kinds of "satori" in zazen practice, some of which may be experiences of jhana, some stages

in the path of insight. Yasutani warns his students, for
example, to ignore *makyo*, visions and intense sensations.
He says these may arise when the student's ability to
concentrate develops to a point within reach of kensho,
just as similar phenomena may arise when the meditator
approaches the access concentration level. Kapleau describes a "false satori" stage, sometimes called the "cave
of Satan," in which the meditator experiences deep se-
renity and believes he has reached his final realization.
Just as with the pseudo nirvana on the vipassana path,
this pseudoemancipation must be broken through. The
final drive toward enlightenment as described by Kapleau (1967: p. 13) also fits the stages just prior to nirvana
on the path of vipassana: The meditator's efforts are
"powered on the one hand by a painfully felt inner bondage—a frustration with life, a fear of death, or both—
and on the other by the conviction that through satori
one can gain liberation." Yasutani notes that satori
usually follows a period of samadhi. In an essay on his
own Zen training, D. T. Suzuki says of his first attainment of samadhi, on the koan Mu (1970: p. 10):

> But this samadhi is not enough. You must come out
> of that state, be awakened from it and that awaken-
> ing is prajna. That moment of coming out of sa-
> madhi and seeing it for what it is—that is satori.

Zen teachers stress the need to ripen an initial satori
through further meditation until it finally permeates the
meditator's whole life. Such full fruition means a state of
mind stilled beyond any need for further practice. Suzuki (1949) describes this final state of mind as one in
which the facts of one's daily experience are taken as they
come; all events come into the meditator's awareness and

are received with nonreaction. This nonreaction, clarifies Blofeld (1962), "does not mean trance-like dullness, but a brilliantly clear state of mind in which the details of every phenomenon are perceived, yet without evaluation or attachment."

Hui Hai, an old Zen master, put it, "When things happen, make no response: Keep your minds from dwelling on anything whatsoever." The fourteenth-century Zen master Bassui advised that zazen is "no more than looking into one's own mind, neither despising nor cherishing the thoughts that arise." This neutral stance is both means and end in Zen. It should extend beyond sitting in zazen into the rest of the meditator's day. Ruth Sasaki (*Miura and Sasaki*, 1965: p. xi) elaborates:

> The experienced practicer of zazen does not depend upon sitting in quietude on his cushion. States of consciousness at first attained only in the meditation hall gradually become continuous, regardless of what other activities he may be engaged in.

In the final Zen stage of "no mind," the spontaneous clarity of satori manifests in all one's acts. Here means and ends coalesce; the posture of mindfulness is built into the meditator's consciousness as a full awareness devoid of self-consciousness. Having experienced the impermanence of all things, that "life is pain, that all forms are *ku*, empty or voidness," he ceases clinging to the phenomenal world yet continues to act.

In recognition of the depth of this transformation of personality, there is little emphasis in Zen on moral precepts. Rather than merely imposing precepts from the outside, their observance emerges from within as a by-product of the change in consciousness zazen can bring.

Thomas Merton (1965) points out that Zen teachings inherit the spirit of the Taoist Chuang Tzu, who wrote these words (p. 112):

> No drives, no compulsions,
> No needs, no attractions:
> Then your affairs
> Are under control.
> You are a free man.

13. GURDJIEFF'S
FOURTH WAY

The spiritual system George I. Gurdjieff (1877–1948) brought to the West after extensive travel in Asia meeting "remarkable men" is, in the words of his pupil Orage, the religious teachings of the East disguised "in a terminology which would not alienate the factual minds of Western thinkers." Ouspensky (1971), another student of Gurdjieff, calls this system an "esoteric school," not suited to mass tastes, which tells *how* to do what popular religions teach *has* to be done, that is, transform one's consciousness. Gurdjieff himself called it "the Fourth Way": not the traditional path of the fakir, monk, or yogi but the way of the "sly man" who does not retreat from the world in solitary meditation but works on his consciousness in the mirror of his relationships with people, animals, property, and ideas. At an advanced stage, the Gurdjieff student must share his acquired knowledge with others in order to advance still further, so numerous second-, third-, and fourth-generation Gurdjieff groups have developed, each with its own style and idiosyncrasies. Since Gurdjieff's original school made use of a great range of techniques, any given latter-day group of his Fourth Way may or may not use the methods discussed here, which are primarily Ouspensky's.

Gurdjieff says most people are "asleep," living a life of automatic response to stimulus. "Contemporary man," writes Gurdjieff (1971), "has gradually deviated from the natural type he ought to have represented . . . the perceptions and manifestations of the modern man . . . represent only the results of automatic reflexes of one or another part of his general entirety." Like the Buddha, Gurdjieff understands man's normal state to be one of suffering. Human beings, because we are unable to see the situation as it really is, remain dominated by egoism, animal passions such as fear, excitement, and anger, and the pursuit of pleasure. Suffering, however, can give us an urge toward freedom. The way to liberation is not by conventional notions of virtuous living but by an intentional program for self-transformation. The remedy Gurdjieff offers begins with self-observation. Kenneth Walker (1969: p. 206), who studied with Ouspensky and Gurdjieff, puts it thus:

We are imprisoned within our own minds, and however far we extend them and however highly we decorate them we still remain within their walls. If we are ever to escape from our prisons, the first step must be that we should realize our true situation and at the same time see ourselves as we really are and not as we imagine ourselves to be. This can be done by holding ourselves in a state of passive awareness . . .

Walker here describes "self-remembering," a technique of deliberately dividing one's attention so as to direct a portion back on oneself. Within one's multiple, fluctuating selves, one establishes an awareness that only watches all the rest: the "observing I" or the "witness." At first there is great difficulty in coming to a stable observing I, the beginner constantly forgets to remember himself, and self-observation melts into his usual full identification with whichever "I" has reign over his mind at a given moment. But with persistence the beginner's self-remembering strengthens, for, in Ouspensky's words, "the more we appreciate our present psychological state of sleep, the more we appreciate the urgent need to change it." Self-remembering is like mindfulness. The psychological stance required in this method is self-directed detachment, as though one's own thoughts and acts were those of some other person with whom one is only slightly acquainted. Ouspensky (Walker, 1969: p. 40) instructs:

> Observe yourself very carefully and you will see that not *you* but *it* speaks within you, moves, feels, laughs, and cries in you, just as *it* rains, clears up and rains again outside you. Everything happens in you, and your first job is to observe and watch it happening.

When the student realizes there has been a lapse in his self-observation, he returns his wandering mind to the task of watching himself. Though various Gurdjieff circles use a range of techniques, these are most often subsidiary to self-remembering. The critical skill sought is the capacity to direct attention to self-observation. Ouspensky (1971) names both the samadhi trance state and the normal state of identifying that "imprisons man in some small part of himself" as antithetical to his goal. Just as with insight meditation, in self-remembering, the "distorting glasses of the personality" are abandoned in order to see oneself clearly. In self-remembering, like mindfulness and zazen, one acknowledges oneself in entirety without comment and without naming what is seen.

Another example of Gurdjieffian self-remembering exercises is to focus on one aspect of everyday behavior— for example, movements of the hands or facial gestures— witnessing it all day. Still another instruction for self-remembering is: "Wherever one is, whatever one does, remember one's own presence and notice always what one does." These instructions are parallel to those for mindfulness. The similarity between systems is possibly no accident. Both Gurdjieff and Ouspensky traveled in lands in which vipassana or similar techniques were taught precisely to learn such methods, and Gurdjieff was a great borrower, reshaper, and transmitter of Eastern teachings.

In the course of self-remembering, the student realizes (as on the path of insight) that his inner states are in constant flux and that there is no such thing as a permanent "I" within. He sees, instead, an internal cast of characters or "principal features." Each, in turn, dominates the stage and adds its idiosyncrasies to the shape of his personality. With self-observation, the multiplicity of these selves becomes apparent but then falls away. Through observing them, these selves lose their hold as the student ceases to identify with them. As he strengthens his observing I and remains detached from all the others, the student will "wake up." In waking up, he sacrifices his everyday selves. Walker describes this awakened state as "a sense of being present, of being there, of thinking, perceiving, feeling and moving with a certain degree of control and not just automatically." In this state, the witness crystallizes as a constant mental function. The student can see himself with full objectivity.

This order of self-knowledge is preliminary to the highest state, "objective consciousness." In this state, the student sees not only himself but everything else as well with full objectivity. Objective consciousness is the culmination of self-remembering. One's ordinary consciousness is not dislodged, but full objectivity is superimposed on it. This adds an "inner silence" and a liberating sense of distance from the continuing rumblings of the mind. One's experience of the world in objective consciousness is entirely altered; Walker (1969: pp. 47–48) describes this end state in Gurdjieff's training:

> The small limiting "self" of everyday life, the self which insists on its personal rights and separateness, is no longer there to isolate one from everything else, and in its absence one is received into a much wider order of existence . . . as the clamor of thought within dies down into the inner silence, an overwhelming sense of "being" takes its place . . . Such limiting concepts as "yours" or "mine," "his" or "hers" are meaningless . . . and even those old divisions of time into "before" and "after" have been drowned in the fathomless depth of an ever-present "now." So also has disappeared . . . the division between the subject and the object, the knower and the thing known.

Bennett (1973) gives seven levels of man in Gurdjieff's system, the last three of which are "liberated"; these final three are gradations of objective consciousness. As part of his transformation to objective consciousness, one attains liberation from arbitrary, irrational influences from internal and external sources, respectively. The liberated person at the sixth level, for example, is the same as "the bodhisattva of Mahayana Buddhism, or the great saints and *wadis* of Christianity and Islam. He is no longer concerned with his own personal welfare, but has committed himself to the salvation of all creatures."

14. KRISHNAMURTI'S CHOICELESS AWARENESS

J. Krishnamurti, born in South India in the 1890s, was educated in England under the guidance of theosophist Annie Besant. Krishnamurti's view of the human predicament is close to that of Buddhism. The mind and the world, says Krishnamurti, are in everlasting flux: "There is only one fact, impermanence." The human mind clings to a "me" in the face of the insecurity of this flux. But the "me" exists only through identification with what it imagines it has been and wants to be. The "me" is "a mass of contradictions, desires, pursuits, fulfillments and frustrations, with sorrow outweighing joy." One source of sorrow is the constant mental conflict between "what is" and "what should be." The conditioned mind, in Krishnamurti's analysis, flees from the facts of its impermanence, its emptiness, and its sorrow. It builds walls of habit and repetition, and pursued its dreams of the future or clings to that which has been. These defenses paralyze us. They keep us from living in the present moment.

Krishnamurti objects to methods of meditation, the solution so many others advocate. While the mind may try to escape from conditioning through meditation, Krishnamurti says, it simply creates in the very attempt another prison of methods to follow and goals to achieve. He opposes techniques of every kind and urges the putting aside of all authority and tradition: From them, one can only collect more knowledge, while understanding is needed instead. According to Krishnamurti, no technique can free the mind, for any effort by the mind only weaves another net. He, for example, emphatically opposes concentration methods (quoted in Coleman, 1971: p. 114):

> By repeating Amen or *Om* or Coca-Cola indefinitely you obviously have a certain experience because by repetition the mind becomes quiet . . . It is one of the favorite gambits of some teachers of meditation to insist on their pupils learning concentration, that is, fixing the mind on one thought and driving out all other thoughts. This is a most stupid, ugly thing, which any schoolboy can do because he is forced to.

The "meditation" Krishnamurti advocates has no system, least of all "repetition and imitation." He proposes as both means and end a "choiceless awareness," the "experiencing of what is without naming." This state is beyond thought; all thought, he says, belongs to the past, and meditation is always in the present. To be in the present, the mind must relinquish the habits acquired out of the urge to be secure; "its gods and virtues must be given back to the society which bred them." One must let go all thought and all imagining. Advises Krishnamurti (1962: pp. 8–10):

> Let the mind be empty, and not filled with the things of the mind. Then there is only meditation, and not a meditator who is meditating . . . the mind caught in imagination can only breed delusions. The mind must be clear, without movement, and in the light of that clarity the timeless is revealed.

Krishnamurti seems to advocate an end state only, a methodless method. But on closer scrutiny, he directly tells all who might hear the "how," while at the same time he insists that "there is no how; no method." He instructs us "just to be aware of all this . . . of your own habits, responses." His means is constantly watching one's own awareness. Krishnamurti's "nontechnique" is more clear from his instructions to a group of young Indian schoolchildren. He first told them to sit still with eyes closed and then to watch the progression of their thoughts. He urged them to continue this exercise at other times, including when walking or in bed at night:

> You have to watch, as you watch a lizard going by, walking across the wall, seeing all its four feet, how it sticks to the wall, you have to watch it, and as you watch, you see all the movements, the delicacy of its movements. So in the same way, watch your thinking, do not correct it, do not suppress it—do not say it is too hard—just watch it, now, this morning.

He calls this careful attention "self-knowledge." Its essence is "to perceive the ways of your own mind" so that

the mind is "free to be still." When the mind is still, one
understands. The key to understanding is "attention
without the word, the name." He instructs, "Look and
be simple": Where there is attention without reactive
thought, reality is.

The process Krishnamurti proposes for self-knowledge
duplicates mindfulness training. But Krishnamurti himself would most likely not condone this comparison because of the danger he sees inherent in seeking any goal
through a technique. The process he suggests for stilling
the mind springs spontaneously from the realization of
one's predicament, for to know "that you have been
asleep is already an awakened state." This truth, he insists, acts on the mind, setting it free. Krishnamurti
(1962: p. 60) assures us:

> When the mind realizes the totality of its own condi-
> tioning . . . then all its movements come to an end:
> It is completely still, without any desire, without
> any compulsion, without any motive . . .

This awakening is for Krishnamurti an automatic process. The mind discovers, rather, is caught up in, the
solution "through the very intensity of the question itself." This realization cannot be sought: "It comes unin-
vited." Should one somehow experience the realization of
which Krishnamurti speaks, he assures us that a new
state would emerge. In this state, one is freed from conditioned habits of perception and cognition, devoid of
self. To be in this state, says Krishnamurti, is to love:
"Where the self is, love is not." This state brings an
"aloneness beyond loneliness" in which there is no movement within the mind, rather a pure experiencing, "attention without motive." One is free from envy, ambi-

tion, and the desire for power, and loves with compassion. Here feeling is knowing, in a state of total attention with no watcher. Living in the eternal present, one ceases collecting impressions or experiences; the past dies for one at each moment. With this choiceless awareness, one is free to be simple; as Krishnamurti (Coleman, 1971: p. 95) puts it:

> Be far away, far away from the world of chaos and misery, live in it, untouched . . . The meditative mind is unrelated to the past and to the future and yet is sanely capable of living with clarity and reason.

PART THREE

MEDITATION PATHS:
THEIR ESSENTIAL UNITY

IN SOME respects, every method of meditation is like all others, like some others, and like no other. The first level is that of the most general commonalities, disregarding the idiosyncratic variations of technique, emphasis, or belief of any one system. At this most universal level, all meditation systems are variations on a single process for transforming consciousness. The core elements of this process are found in every system, and its specifics undercut ostensible differences among the various schools of meditation.

15. PREPARATION FOR MEDITATION

There is the least common ground among meditation systems on the preparatory groundwork the meditator requires. The systems surveyed here represent the full spectrum of attitudes toward the meditator's need to prepare himself through some kind of purification. They range from the emphatic insistence on purification as a prelude to meditation voiced in the Bhakti, Kabbalist, Christian, and Sufi traditions to the views of Gurdjieff and Krishnamurti that such efforts are pointless if they entail avoiding normal life situations. Finally, there is the notion among, for example, TM and Zen schools that genuine purity arises spontaneously as a by-product of meditation itself. Tantrics of the Bon Marg mark an extreme attitude toward purity in advocating the violation of sexual and other proprieties as part of spiritual practice.

Ideas about the best setting for meditation likewise cover a full spectrum. The Desert Fathers withdrew into the Egyptian wilderness to avoid the marketplace and worldly company; hermetic solitude was essential to their program of severe self-discipline. Modern Indian yogis seek out isolated mountains and jungle retreats for the same reasons. Westernized versions of Indian yoga such as TM, however, oppose any forced change in the meditator's living habits; instead, meditation is simply inserted into an otherwise normal daily agenda. Intensive Zen practice is done ideally in a monastic setting, but, like TM, it can be part of a meditator's normal daily round. Both Gurdjieff and Krishnamurti are emphatic that the settings of family, work, and the marketplace are the best context for inner discipline, providing the raw material for meditation.

In most classical meditation systems, however, a monastery or ashram is the optimal environment for meditation, monks or yogis the ideal companions, the role of the renunciate the highest calling, and scriptures the best reading. Modern systems such as TM direct the student to organizational ties and activities while he lives his ordinary life style without imposing any major change. Krishnamurti stands alone among spiritual spokesmen in not advocating that the aspirant seek out the company of others on the same path, just as he objects to the aspirant's looking for guidance from a teacher or master—essential elements in every other system.

In propagating no explicit doctrine, Krishnamurti is again unique. Though other schools such as Zen de-emphasize intellectual study, they all have both formal and informal teachings that students assimilate. In some traditions, formal study is a major emphasis: The Benedictine monk, for example, is to spend one-third of his day in study, the other two-thirds in prayer (or meditation) and manual labor.

16. ATTENTION

The strongest agreement among meditation schools is on the importance of retraining attention. All these systems can be broadly categorized in terms of the major strategies for retraining attention described in the Visuddhimagga: concentration or mindfulness. By using the Visuddhimagga map as an example, we can see similarities of technique obscured by the overlay of jargon and ideology.

The differing names used among meditation systems to describe one and the same way and destination are legion. Sometimes the same term is used in special but very different technical senses by various schools. What translates into the English word "void," for example, is used by Indian yogis to refer to jhana states and by Mahayana Buddhists to signify the realization of the essential emptiness of all phenomenon. The former usage denotes a mental state devoid of contents (e.g., the formless jhanas); the latter refers to the voidness of phenomenon. Another example: Phillip Kapleau (1967) distinguishes between zazen and meditation, saying that the two "are not to be confused"; Krishnamurti (1962) says only "choiceless awareness" is really meditation. The recognition that both zazen and choiceless awareness are insight techniques allows one to see that these seemingly unrelated remarks are actually emphasizing the same distinction: that between concentration and insight. By "meditation," Kapleau means concentration, while Krishnamurti denies that concentration practices are within the province of meditation at all.

Table 2 classifies techniques from each meditation system according to the Visuddhimagga typology. The criterion for classification is the mechanics of technique: (a) *concentration*, in which mind focuses on a fixed mental object; (b) *mindfulness*, in which mind observes itself; or (c) both operations present in *integrated* combination.

A second prerequisite for classification is internal consistency in descriptions. If it is a concentration technique, other characteristics of the jhana path are mentioned—for example, increasingly subtle bliss accompanying deepened concentration or loss of sense-consciousness. If it is an insight technique, other characteristics of insight practices, such as the realization of the impersonality of mental processes, must be present. If a combined technique, both concentration techniques as well as insight must be mixed and integrated, as in Theravadan vipassana.

TABLE 2
AN APPLIED ATTENTIONAL TYPOLOGY
OF MEDITATION TECHNIQUES

System	Technique	Type
Bhakti	Japa	Concentration
Kabbalah	Kavvanah	Concentration
Hesychasm	Prayer of the Heart	Concentration
Sufi	Zikr	Concentration
Raja Yoga	Samadhi	Concentration
Transcendental Meditation	Transcendental Meditation	Concentration
Kundalini yoga	Siddha yoga	Concentration
Tibetan Buddhism	Vipassana	Integrated
Zen	Zazen	Integrated
Gurdjieff	Self-remembering	Mindfulness
Krishnamurti	Self-knowledge	Mindfulness
Theravada	Vipassana	Integrated

In concentration, the meditator's attentional strategy is to fix his focus on a single percept, constantly bringing back his wandering mind to this object. Some instructions for doing so emphasize an active assertion of the meditator's will to stick with the target percept and resist any wandering. Others suggest a passive mode of simply regenerating the target percept when it is lost in the flow of awareness. Thus, an ancient Theravadan text exhorts the meditator to grit his teeth, clench his fists, and work up a sweat, struggling to keep his mind fixed on the movements of his respiration; a TM meditator, on the other hand, is told "easily start the mantra" each time he notices his mind has wandered. Though these approaches are opposite on a continuum of activity-passivity, they are equivalent means to constantly reorient to a *single object* of concentration and so develop one-pointedness. With mindfulness techniques—whether Gurdjieff's "self-remembering," Krishnamurti's "self-knowledge," or zazen's "shikan-taza"—the attentional fundamentals are identical: They all entail continuous, full watchfulness of each successive moment, a global vigilance to the meditator's chain of awareness.

There are perhaps few pure types among meditation schools, save for those systems centered around a single technique, for example, TM or Krishnamurti. Most schools are eclectic, using a variety of techniques from both approaches. They make allowances for individual needs, tailoring techniques to the student's progress. Sufis, for example, mainly use the zikr, a concentration practice, but also at times employ insight techniques like *Muragaba*, which is attention to the flow of one's own awareness. For simplicity, in the preceding sections a specific technique has been emphasized, generally the main one.

Different meditation systems may espouse wholly contradictory views from each other on the necessity for virtually every preparatory act, be it a specific environment, the need for a teacher, or prior knowledge of what to expect from meditation. But the need for the meditator to retrain his attention, whether through concentration or mindfulness, is the single invariant ingredient in the recipe for altering consciousness of every meditation system.

17. SEEING WHAT
YOU BELIEVE

The meditator's beliefs determine how he interprets and labels his meditation experiences. When a Sufi enters a state in which he is no longer aware of his senses, and his only thought is that of Allah, he knows this to be fana; when a yogi is no longer aware of his senses, and his mind is totally focused on his deity, then he will say he has entered samadhi. Many different names are used to describe one and the same experience: jhana, samyana or samadhi, fana, Daat, turiya, the great fixation, and transcendental consciousness. All seem to refer to a single state with identical characteristics. These many terms for a single state come from Theravadan Buddhism, raja yoga, Sufism, Kabbalah, kundalini yoga, Zen, and TM, respectively.

The history of religion is rife with instances of a transcendental experience interpreted in terms of assumptions specific to time, place, and belief. The Indian saint Ramana Maharshi saw his own transcendental states in terms of Advait philosophy. He conjectures that during Saul's great experience on the Damascus road, when he returned to normal consciousness, he interpreted what happened in terms of Christ and the Christians because at the time he was preoccupied with them (Chadwick, 1966). A person's reference group gives him a gloss on his inner realities; Berger and Luckmann (1967) point out that while "Saul may have become Paul in the aloneness of religious ecstasy . . . he could *remain* Paul only in the context of the Christian community that recognized him as such and confirmed the 'new being' in which he now located this identity."

The interaction among the meditator's beliefs, his internal state, and his self-definition is made clear by a recent example drawn from kundalini yoga. In this tradition, the guru is crucial to the meditator both in helping him achieve sought-after meditation states and in interpreting and confirming the significance of these same experiences.

Swami Rudrananda, a teacher of kundalini yoga, describes the incident that preceded his being awarded the rank of swami. While he was meditating, his master touched him on the shoulder, at which point (Rudi, 1973: p. 85):

> I immediately felt within me a surge of great spiritual force which hurled me against the stone walls and allowed a great electric shock to send a spasm of contortions through my body. Movements similar to those of an epileptic controlled my body for about an hour. Many strange visions appeared and I felt things opening within me that had never been opened before.

Rudrananda took his experience to confirm his worthiness of the title "swami," an advanced status. While a set of beliefs about altered states in meditation may render them safe, the meditator does not need specific foreknowledge of these states to experience them. In his autobiography (1972), for example, Swami Muktananda tells how his guru would assign him a meditation practice but give no further hints as to what to expect beyond the barest instructions. When Muktananda subsequently entered extraordinary states, he did so naively. Only after undergoing these states did he chance upon books that gave him an interpretive framework for understanding what had happened. Sri Aurobindo's biographer, Satprem (1970: p. 256), likewise describes the unusual states Aurobindo experienced in the course of his spiritual development but notes:

> . . . Sri Aurobindo was the first to be baffled by his own experience and . . . it took him some years to understand exactly what had happened. We have described the . . . experience . . . as though the stages had been linked very carefully, each with its explanatory label, but the explanations came long afterwards, at that moment he had no guiding landmarks.

18. ALTERED STATES
IN MEDITATION

In meditation, method is the seed of the goal: The contours of the state the meditator reaches depend on how he arrived. The concentrative path leads the meditator to merge with his meditation subject in jhana and then to transcend it. As he reaches deeper levels, the bliss becomes more compelling, yet more subtle. In the way of mindfulness, the meditator's mind witnesses its own workings, and he comes to perceive increasingly finer segments of his stream of thought. As his perception sharpens, he becomes increasingly detached from what he witnesses, finally turning away from all awareness in the nirvanic state. In this state, there is no experience whatever.

Every system that uses concentration describes the

same journey into jhana, though different schools cast the descriptions in differing terms. The key attributes of this state are always the same: loss of sense awareness, one-pointed attention to one object to the exclusion of all other thoughts, and sublimely rapturous feelings. Systems that use mindfulness describe the path of insight: increasingly finer perception of the meditator's mind, detachment from these events, and a compelling focus on the present moment. The nirvanic state, per se, is not necessarily cited as the end point of this progression.

These two altered states are the prototypical altered states in meditation. They do not, however, exhaust all the possible changes in consciousness that meditation brings. Attention is extremely flexible and can change awareness in many more ways than the two major ones described here. Attentional retraining can also be linked with exercises in other biosystems, for example, with movement in Sufi dancing. Additional practices such as controlled respiration, fasting, visualizations, or adopting strong beliefs all contribute to the final shape of the altered state, over and above the effects of the meditator's attentional exercises.

Attention is the key to meditative altered states, but the addition of other practices compounds the complexity of the calculus of the resulting changes in awareness. One example of a more complex altered state is that produced by the kundalini yoga technique of shaktipat-diksha. The seizurelike activity in this state may be due to breath-control exercises as well as to expectations arising from the intense guru-student relationship, and perhaps in part to modeling—all in addition to the basic effects of concentration. The more means used to alter consciousness, the more intricate the topography of the resulting state.

The literature of every meditation system describes an

altered state. Jhana is the prototype of one variety, in which the altered state is a neatly delimited enclave of awareness set off from other states. Jhanic states are mutually exclusive of the normal major states: waking, sleeping, and dreaming. Another type of altered state, however, merges with these major states. This merger appends new functions on the normal states, changing their character. This meets Tart's (1971) criterion for "higher states of consciousness": (1) all functions of "lower" states are available, that is, waking, sleeping, and dreaming; and (2) some new aspects, derivative of an altered state, are present in addition. This kind of transmutation of awareness is an altered *trait* of consciousness, an enduring change transforming the meditator's every moment. The "awakened" state is the ideal type of an altered trait of consciousness. Virtually every system of meditation recognizes the awakened state as the ultimate goal of meditation (Table 3).

In TM, for example, "transcendental consciousness" is the altered state that infuses normal states. The stages ensuing after "transcendental consciousness" from further evolution are "cosmic consciousness," "God consciousness," and finally, "unity." Each represents a deeper infusion of meditative awareness into normal states. Most systems agree that such altered traits occur gradually and to differing degrees. In the Visuddhimagga, for example, there is a similar gradient in the four levels of purification arising from increasingly deep penetration of the nirvanic state.

The goal of all meditation paths, whatever their ideology, source, or methods, is to transform the meditator's consciousness. In the process, the meditator dies to his past self and is reborn to a new level of experience.

TABLE 3

NAMES FOR THE AWAKENED STATE

System	Name of Awakened State
Bhakti	Sahaj samadhi
Kabbalah	Devekut
Hesychasm	Purity of heart
Sufi	Baqa
Raja Yoga	Sahaj samadhi; jivamukti
Transcendental Meditation	Cosmic consciousness; God-consciousness; unity
Kundalini Yoga	Turiyatita; Siddha
Tibetan Buddhism	Boddhisattva
Zen	Mujodo no taigeu ("no-mind")
Gurdjieff	Objective consciousness
Krishnamurti	Choiceless awareness
Theravadan Buddhism	Arahantship

Whether through concentration in jhana or through insight in nirvana, the altered states the meditator gains are dramatic in their discontinuity with his normal states. But the ultimate transformation for the meditator is a new state still: the awakened state, which mixes with and recreates his normal consciousness.

Each path labels this end state differently. But no matter how diverse the names, these paths all propose the same basic formula in an alchemy of the self: the diffusion of the effects of meditation into the meditator's waking, dreaming, and sleep states. At the outset, this diffusion requires the meditator's effort. As he pro-

gresses, it becomes easier for him to maintain prolonged
meditative awareness in the midst of his other activities.
As the states produced by his meditation meld with his
waking activity, the awakened state ripens. When it
reaches full maturity, it lastingly changes his consciousness, transforming his experience of himself and of his
universe.

Though sources like the Visuddhimagga draw distinctions according to the angle of entrance to this transformation (concentration or insight), it is likely that at this
point all paths merge. Or, more to the point, from our
perspective the similarities may far outweigh the differences. An awakened being transcends his own origins;
persons of any faith can recognize him as exceptional or
"perfect," or—if so inclined—revere him as a saint.

BIBLIOGRAPHY

ABU AL-NAJIB. *A Sufi Rule for Novices.* M. Milson (trans.). Cambridge, Mass.: Harvard University Press, 1975.

AMMA. *Dhyan-yoga and Kundalini Yoga.* Ganeshpuri, India: Shree Gurudev Ashram, 1969.

ANANDA MAYEE MA. *Matri Vani.* Gurupriya Devi (ed.). Varanasi, India: Shree Anandashram, 1972.

ARBERRY, A. J. *Sufism: An Account of the Mystics of Islam.* London: Allen & Unwin, 1972.

BENNETT, J. G. *Gurdjieff: Making a New World.* London: Turnstone Books, 1973.

BERGER, P. L. and T. LUCKMANN. *The Social Construction of Reality.* New York: Doubleday, 1967.

BHARATI, AGEHANANDA. *The Tantric Tradition.* Garden City, N.Y.: Anchor Books, Doubleday, 1970.

BHIKKU SOMA. *The Way of Mindfulness.* Colombo, Ceylon: Vajirama, 1949.

BLOFELD, J. *The Zen Teaching of Hui Hai.* London: Rider, 1962.

BUTLER, D. C. *Western Mysticism.* New York: Harper, 1966.

CHADWICK, A. W. *A Sadhu's Reminiscences of Ramana Maharshi.* Tiruvan-namalai, India: Sri Ramanasram, 1966.

CHANG, G. C. C. *The Hundred Thousand Songs of Milarepa.* New York: Harper Colophon Books, 1970.

CHOGYAM TRUNGPA. *Cutting Through Spiritual Materialism.* Berkeley: Shambala, 1975.

————. *The Myth of Freedom*. Berkeley: Shambala, 1976.

COLEMAN, J. E. *The Quiet Mind*. London: Rider & Co., 1971.

CONZE, F. *Buddhist Meditation*. London: Allen & Unwin, 1956.

DALAI LAMA, THE FOURTEENTH. *An Introduction to Buddhism*. New Delhi, India: Tibet House, 1965.

DOGEN. *A Primer of Soto Zen*. Honolulu: University of Hawaii Press, 1971.

DOYLE, L. J. (trans.). *St. Benedict's Rule for Monasteries*. Collegeville, Minnesota: The Liturgical Press, 1948.

ELIADE, M. *Yoga: Immortality and Freedom*. Princeton, N.J.: Princeton University Press, 1970.

EVANS-WENTZ, W. Y. *Tibetan Yoga and Secret Doctrines*. London: Oxford University Press, 1968.

————. *The Tibetan Book of the Great Liberation*. London: Oxford University Press, 1969.

FRENCH, R. M. (transl.). *The Way of the Pilgrim*. New York: Seabury Press, 1970.

GOVINDA, LAMA ANAGARIKA. *The Psychological Attitude of Early Buddhist Philosophy*. London: Rider, 1969.

GUENTHER, H. V., and CHOGYAM TRUNGPA. *The Dawn of Tantra*. Berkeley: Shambala, 1975.

GURDJIEFF, G. I. *The Herald of Coming Good*. New York: Samuel Weiser, 1971.

HALEVI, Z'EV BEN SHIMON. *The Way of Kabbalah*. New York: Samuel Weiser, 1976.

KABIR (R. Tagore, transl.). *Poems of Kabir*. Calcutta: Macmillan, 1970.

KADLOUBOVSKY, E., and PALMER, G. E. H. *Early Fathers from the Philokalia*. London: Faber & Faber, 1969.

————. *Writings from the Philokalia on Prayer of the Heart*. London: Faber & Faber, 1971.

KALU RIMPOCHE. *The Foundation of Buddhist Meditation*. Dharamsala, India: Library of Tibetan Works and Archives, 1974.

KAPLEAU, P. *The Three Pillars of Zen*. Boston: Beacon Press, 1967.

KASHYAP, J. *The Abhidamma Philosophy*. Vol. I. Nalanda, India: Buddha Vihara, 1954.

KRISHNAMURTI, J. (D. Rajagopal, ed.). *Commentaries on Living*. Third series. London: Victor Gollancz, 1962.

LAO TZU. *Tao Te Ching*. D. C. Lau (trans.) Baltimore: Penguin, 1963.

LEDI SAYADAW. *The Manuals of Buddhism*. Rangoon, Burma: Union Buddha Sasana Council, 1965.

————. *Gospel of Sri Ramakrishna*. Mylapore, India: Sri Ramakrishna Math, 1928.

MAHARISHI MAHESH YOGI. *On the Bhagavad Gita*. Baltimore, Md.: Penguin Books, 1969.

————. *The Science of Being and the Art of Living*. Los Angeles: SRM Publications, 1966.

MAHASI SAYADAW (Nyanaponika Thera, transl.). *The Process of Insight*. Kandy, Ceylon: The Forest Hermitage, 1965.

————. *Buddhist Meditation and Its Forty Subjects*. Buddha-gaya, India: International Meditation Center, 1970.

MAHATHERA, P. V. *Buddhist Meditation in Theory and Practice*. Colombo, Ceylon: Gunaseca, 1962.

MARMION, REV. D. COLUMBA. *Christ the Ideal of the Monk*. St. Louis: Herder, 1926.

MEHER BABA. *Discourses I, II, III*. San Francisco: Sufism Reoriented, 1967.

MERTON, T. *The Wisdom of the Desert*. New York: New Directions, 1960.

————. *The Way of Chuang Tzu*. London: Allen & Unwin, 1965.

MIURA, I. and SASAKI, R. F. *The Zen Koan*. New York: Harcourt, Brace & World, 1965.

MUKTANANDA PARAMAHANSA, SWAMI. *Soham-japa*. New Delhi: Siddha Yoga Dham, 1969.

————. *Gurukripa*. Ganeshpuri, India: Shree Gurudev Ashram, 1970.

————. *Guruvani Magazine*. Ganeshpuri, India: Shree Gurudev Ashram, 1971.

————. *Guru*. New York: Harper & Row, 1972.

NANAMOLI THERA. *Mindfulness of Breathing*. Kandy, Ceylon: Buddhist Publication Society, 1964.

————. *Visuddhimagga: The Path of Purification*. Berkeley: Shambala, 1976.

NARADA THERA. *A Manual of Abhidhamma, I & II*. Colombo, Ceylon: Vajirarama, 1956.

NICHOLSON, R. A. *Studies in Islamic Mysticism*. Cambridge: Cambridge University Press, 1929.

NYANAPONIKA THERA. *Abhidhamma Studies*. Colombo, Ceylon: Frewin, 1949.

————. *The Heart of Buddhist Meditation*. London: Rider, 1962.

————. *The Power of Mindfulness*. Kandy, Ceylon: Buddhist Publication Society, 1968.

NYANATILOKA MAHATHERA. *The Word of the Buddha.* Colombo, Ceylon: Buddha Publishing Committee, 1952 (a).

———. *Path to Deliverance.* Colombo, Ceylon: Buddha Sahitya Sabha, 1952 (b).

———. *Buddhist Dictionary: Manual of Buddhist Terms and Doctrines.* Colombo, Ceylon: Frewin & Co., 1972.

OUSPENSKY, P. D. *The Fourth Way.* New York: Vintage, 1971.

PODDAR, H. P. *The Divine Name and Its Practice.* Gorakhpur, India: Gita Press, 1965.

PRABHAVANANDA, SWAMI, and ISHERWOOD, C. *How to Know God: Yoga Aphorisms of Patanjali.* New York: Signet, 1969.

RAMANA MAHARSHI. *Maharshi's Gospel, I & II.* Tiruvannamalai, India: Sri Ramanasram, 1962.

RICE, C. *The Persian Sufis.* London: Allen & Unwin, 1964.

RUDI, *Spiritual Cannibalism.* New York: Quick Fox, 1973.

SARADANANDA, SWAMI. *Ramakrishna the Great Master.* Mylapore, India: Sri Ramakrishna Math, 1963.

SATPREM (Tehmi, transl.). *Sri Aurobindo: The Adventure of Consciousness.* Pondicherry, India: Sri Aurobindo Society, 1970.

SCHOLEM, G. *Kabbalah.* New York: Quadrangle/The New York Times Book Co., 1974.

SHAH, I. *Wisdom of the Idiots.* New York: Dutton, 1971.

———. *The Sufis.* New York: Doubleday, 1972.

Srimad Bhagavatam. Gorakhpur, India: Gita Press, 1969.

SUZUKI, D. T. *The Zen Doctrine of No-Mind.* London: Rider, 1949.

———. *Essays in Zen Buddhism (second series).* London: Rider, 1958.

———. *The Field of Zen.* New York: Harper & Row, 1970.

TART, C. "Scientific Foundations for the Study of Altered States of Consciousness." *Journal of Transpersonal Psychology 3:* 93–124, 1971.

VIVEKANANDA, SWAMI. *Bhakti-yoga.* Calcutta: Advaita Ashrama, 1964.

———. *Raja-yoga.* Calcutta: Advaita Ashrama, 1970.

VYAS DEV, SWAMI. *First Steps to Higher Yoga.* Gangotri, India: Yoga Niketan Trust, 1970.

WADDELL. *The Desert Fathers.* Ann Arbor, Michigan: University of Michigan Press, 1957.

WALKER, K. *A Study of Gurdjieff's Teaching.* London: Jonathan Cape, 1969.

WEI WU WEI. *Posthumous Pieces.* Hong Kong: Hong Kong University Press, 1968.

INDEX

ABOUT THE AUTHOR

DANIEL GOLEMAN is associate editor of *Psychology Today* and has his Ph.D. in personality and clinical psychology from Harvard. He spent two years in India and Ceylon as a Harvard pre-doctoral fellow and post-costoral fellow from the Social Science Research Council. While there he studied meditation and Asian psychologies with yogis, lamas, monks, and other spiritual teachers. This book grew out of that experience.

DUTTON PAPERBACKS OF RELATED INTERESTS